A GLASS AND A HALF OF FRANCE

WINE SOAKED TALES FROM THE PICARDY TRIANGLE

JULIAN MAXWELL PAIGE

Published by Particular Media

Front cover illustration by Chez Bonne Idée

Book cover design by Bookconsilio

www.bookconsilio.com

Proofread by Bridget Gevaux www.abcproofreading.co.uk

T.S Eliot quote from Little Giddings, the last of The Four Quartets appears with the kind permission of Faber and Faber Limited.

Back cover photo by Jordana Theriault

This book is dedicated to my mother, Colleen, and my father, Lee. Mum, thanks for showing me how to open a bottle of wine, and Dad, merci for giving me a love of France.

I'd like to give a special thank you to Dionysus, a.k.a Bacchus (by the Romans), the ancient Greek god of the grape harvest, winemaking, fertility, festivity, insanity, and ritual madness. And a shout-out goes to all the soaks, sponges, and winos, without you, this book would not have been possible.

FOREWORD

When I began reading *A Glass and a Half of France* I knew that
it was based on Julian Maxwell Paige's experiences moving to
the Picardy region of France and I think I was expecting something in the vein of Peter Mayle's *A Year in Provence*. Certainly
he grapples with the challenges of restoring a house while
rubbing shoulders with his Gallic neighbours but what
delighted and surprised me is the way the author does not just
observe provincial French life, he embeds himself in it. What is
more the people he sets his sights on are the kind that most
people, even if they did spend time with them, would never for a
moment consider capturing in such exquisite detail. These are
people existing on life's margins, marooned in a somewhat
forgotten corner of France, for whom a drink or two - or three -
is not an addendum to life but the very stuff and purpose of it.
Yet for the writer of *A Glass and a Half of France* they are worth
listening to, worth observing and worth befriending.

I love the stories that follow because, by some strange
alchemy, the author has managed to pin down these unforget-
table characters so that they live and breathe on the page. But
my admiration really soars when I consider that spending time

with them required him to match them drink for drink. That the author could still recall detail and infuse it with poetry and wit is a remarkable achievement. But ultimately it is the quality of the writing that carries these delightful stores above the realm of light humour and into that great tradition of alcohol-soaked literature, as practiced by such luminaries as Charles Bukowski and John Steinbeck.

And all, of course, with a very French twist...

Enjoy!

Adam Preston (Editor)

THE WINE CRITICS

The ancient alarm clock hammered and clanged intensely next to my head for a good twenty seconds before I reached across and moved the lever to block it.

Silence.

It was early – too early. Six o'clock was not my usual time to wake up and I almost never used the archaic alarm clock – but today was special.

It was the third Thursday in November – Beaujolais Nouveau Day. The new vintage had been released to the world six hours earlier as the clock struck midnight. Over sixty million bottles of the fruity, light-bodied, and extremely easy-to-drink, Gamay grapes from the Beaujolais area of Bourgogne (Burgundy) were on their way to be distributed to the waiting masses.

The owner of the local café, L'Escale bar, had arranged a Beaujolais Nouveau breakfast extravaganza. He'd recently taken over the place and wanted to impress his punters and attract a new clientele. He had been planning the event for a couple of weeks and I said I would go along.

I stuck my head out from under multiple layers of sheets

and blankets, braving the cold. The last log in the wood-burning stove had burnt through hours before, transforming the ambient room temperature from a toasty twenty degrees Celsius to a fresh ten with underlying dampness.

"One, two, three..." I pushed back the covers and jumped onto the cold, wooden floor. I staggered around the bed and glided my foot an inch above the floor to locate my flip flops. Everything was covered in a thin film of dust and sand, part of the daily challenge of living in a house that's being renovated.

I had moved the bed into the living room next to the wood burner, as it was the only room in the house capable of retaining heat. I had also nailed two old blankets to the wooden door frame and stuffed expanding tape into the gaps around the old windows, but nothing seemed to keep out the draught. As I breathed, a thin mist emerged from my mouth. I shivered and my teeth began to chatter. If this was the warmest room, what was waiting beyond those blankets?

I hadn't yet experienced winter in the house, which was one of the oldest buildings in the village, and the nights were starting to get colder. Winter was closing in quickly and all the other residents were prepared, their piles of wood neatly stacked in regimental fashion and covered by corrugated iron or plastic sheets, with large stones placed on top to hold the sheets down in the wind.

I had watched the truck deliver a load of cut wood to the house opposite. The whole family spent an afternoon stacking it along the stone wall that ran along their property. They piled the wood on old pallets and covered it with a blue tarpaulin. I had a small stack of wood that had come with the house, piled up in one of the outhouses. It was going down quickly.

The house had been built around the time of the French Revolution and had not been touched since electricity was installed in the 1950s. There was no inside toilet, just a small, brick outbuilding in the garden. Night-time visits were lit by a candle and accompanied by spiders. A large plastic barrel captured rain from the little roof. To flush, you used a ladle that hung on a nail, scooping water from the barrel and flinging it down the hole. After the first frost, I found a thick crust of ice on the top.

The kitchen was at the centre of the house, with two large windows and two interior doors opening onto two small rooms, which the previous owners had used as bedrooms. The exterior doors were opposite each other – one opened onto the road, the other onto the courtyard. The courtyard was gated off from the little road, Rue d'Église, which led to the church, *Mairie* (Mayor's office), school, a farm, and a huge derelict château with a large moat around it.

I grabbed my towel from the back of a chair in front of the fireplace and shuffled to the doorway. I'd nailed the blankets down with wooden slats and I had to push my arm through the tight gap, squeezing my body through until my head finally popped through into the kitchen.

I thought the living room was cold, but this was something else. I'd forgotten to close the shutters that opened onto the courtyard. A white mesh of heavy frost covered the glass and I could just make out a blanket of frost covering the ground and the outhouse opposite.

I shivered again and pulled the towel around my shoulders. I looked over at what the estate agent had called '*Ze Barzroom*' – a tiny cabin in the corner of the kitchen. A garden hose was attached to the smallest gas heater ever made. The water had to pass from the tap of the sink, situated on the courtyard side of the kitchen, up into the loft (*grenier*) and along the bare floorboards, where it was covered with hay for insulation.

The faded orange pipe peeked out of a hole drilled in the wooden floorboards above the Ferrari-red shower tray. A too-short rigid plastic shower curtain did little to stop water from splashing onto the floor. By the time the lukewarm water arrived, it dribbled on my head just enough to dampen a *gants de toilette*, a glove-like flannel, to wash your bits and pieces as quickly as possible.

I had to connect the end of the garden hose to the tap above the sink, switch the cold water tap on, then light the gas-powered heater.

I turned the tap and it made a sound like it was clearing its throat, but no water came out. It was frozen. I raced back into the living room and dressed myself as quickly as possible before I turned into a statue.

"Whhhhhhat thhhhhhhe fuuuuuuuuuck ammmmmmm I dooooooooooing heeeere...?" I asked myself through chattering teeth.

The old *fermette* was typical of the local architecture, an elongated house with an attached barn, small courtyard and a garden with a cherry tree, a pear tree and two apple trees on a third of an acre of land. The dilapidated outhouses, once used for livestock, were still standing by the grace of God, though most of the terracotta roof tiles had been displaced by wind, and the rain had drenched the beams and they were now all rotten.

The house hadn't been lived in for over ten years when I bought it. The original owner had died and the family who inherited it only came up from Paris once a year in the summer months for a short holiday.

After the sale, they filled their small car with a few mementos, the rest they left behind: the tables and chairs, farming tools, engine parts and an old TV aerial.

As they were ready to leave, the mother turned to me and said in good English, "Good luck. The house is very damp and very cold at night. There's also a weird ambiance. We never liked coming back here – *bonne chance!*" We shook hands and they got in their car and drove away.

I dressed as quickly as was physically possible while shivering like a leaf on a windy day. I went back into the kitchen and reheated the coffee from last night's meal in a small pan.

The kitchen was still as I bought it. They had left not just the furniture, but plates, glasses, and all the utensils. They had planned to take everything to the local tip, but I told them not to bother. I wouldn't be throwing any dinner parties too soon, but there was enough for me to eat and drink with.

The cooking apparatus was a small, two-ringed gas hob placed on two building bricks. I drank my coffee and prepared to face the elements outside.

I put on my coat and turned the large key in the door. It clunked into position and I pushed down on the handle. You had to be careful, as the door was split in two and you could get a crack on the side of your head if the two halves were not bolted together. I pulled and, sure enough, the top part hit me with a dull thud.

Glacier-cold air hit my face as I stood on the doorstep outside. I turned around and slipped the old key in the lock. The metal gate was covered in a thick coat of frost. I pulled my arm into the sleeve of my jacket and used the end to grab the metal bar and slide it backwards. I gave it a heavy yank and it clanked loudly as it hit the stopper. The gate swung open and I stepped into the road, closing the gate behind me.

The windows of my old Alfa Romeo Sprint had a thick film of frost. I turned the key in the ignition; the engine murmured and began to turn over. I pumped on the accelerator and the engine died. I turned the key and tried again and the car croaked into life. I pumped on the accelerator and the engine started to warm up. I pulled out the choke to keep the revs up and turned the heating up full to defrost the windscreen. I pushed on the button for the back window defroster and grabbed an empty cassette box.

I got out and closed the door to keep the hot air inside and scratched at the frost as best I could. My fingers quickly froze and I could barely hold on to the box. I rubbed my hands on my trousers to try and warm them. I managed to scrape enough of the frost away so that I could see to drive, the heater would do the rest. I jumped back into the driver's seat and rubbed my hands together and blew on them. I made a mental note to buy a hat and a pair of gloves. Bad weather alerts had been issued for the area and it was the main topic of conversation in the café.

I drove past the school and the *Mairie* and turned onto an unpaved track with tall poplar trees running down either side. It led away from the church and the ornate gates of the old château. The gates were nearly four metres high, the metal bars decorated with flowers and the initials of the original owner who had built the place in 1687. Jesus on the large cross in front of the church looked down on me as I passed by.

I manoeuvred around the potholes with care – one false move and I would rip off the exhaust. The heater started to do its work, and a small frost-free arch had appeared on the windscreen. By stooping and peering through the steering wheel, I saw enough to navigate off the track and onto the narrow country road.

The tyres spun on the frozen surface and the car twitched as it struggled to keep its grip, then accelerated away towards the great metropolis of Rue. The two small lakes were beautifully decorated by the frost and a white sheet spread over the flat countryside. I was soon out on the open plain, where the road cut across two immense fields. I drove past the quarry with its old rusty machinery. Metal towers housing a conveyor belt stretched over the road from the large disused red brick warehouses. I passed another abandoned château and then, for a while, the road ran parallel to the railway line.

At the level crossing, the barrier was raised and the car rattled as it crossed the tracks. I slowed down in front of the Lion d'Or Hotel and looked either way at the crossroad. Give way to the car coming from the right, but when? It was never clear in town.

I passed the small petrol station with its tiny slip road. The old pumps dated from the 1960s, with a glass bowl that showed the colour of the petrol. The owner still filled your tank himself, with a cigarette in his mouth. His prices were nearly twenty centimes more per litre than the new supermarket petrol station on the outskirts of town. He had seen the good old days, but now he couldn't compete. They called it progress, but all the small shops were losing business and many had closed.

I was early. Fred, the landlord of the L'Escale bar, had told me to be there promptly at seven. 'Le Beaujolais Breakfast' had been planned for nearly a month and he had reminded me about it more than a million times.

I parked in front the Credit Agricole bank. The doors of the café where still closed and I could see Fred frantically running around inside, moving back and forth between the bar and the kitchen in the back.

A few people were already gathered in front of the café. I could see the mist coming from their mouths, as well as the heavy cigarette smoke that hovered above them in the glacial air. I stayed in the car with the motor running. It was too cold out there.

More people started to appear. Sunlight was starting to break up the shadows as the local clan of *piliers de bar* (barflies) arrived in front of the café. They were coming from the direction of the 421 café that opened at five in the morning to accommodate the local alcoholics.

The herd of early-rising wine tasters bunched together like cows in a field, some shaking while drawing on their cigarettes as others stomped their feet or shouted at the owner to open the doors.

Fred had bought the café when he retired from the army. He was clean, well organised, and he ran it like clockwork. He opened at seven o'clock in the morning, not a minute before or a minute after. When it came to closing time, he was more flexible. It all depended on his consummation of Martini or the number of women in the café. He was a lady's man and pruned himself like a peacock. He constantly sprayed himself with aftershave, which wafted throughout the café. He wore Lacoste polo shirts in bright colours and he would roll his shoulders as he pulled up the collars. The shirts were worn with freshly pressed Levi 501 jeans, polished shoes, a large gold-plated Rolex, two gold chains around his neck, and a chunky gold bracelet on his right wrist. His glasses had stylish frames specially ordered at the opticians a couple of doors down from the café.

I switched off the engine as the clock in the car clicked to seven, zero, zero. I got out and approached the crowd, greeting everyone with a general, *"Bonjour."* We huddled together, battling the biting cold.

"Ah... ch'vent du Nord, ti, that northern wind mate, it's so cold," said Didier, the station master, in his heavy Picard accent. I could smell alcohol on his breath and just about make out what he was saying.

"We tasted the Beaujolais Nouveau at Chez Sam and it tastes like bananas mixed with blackcurrants this year," he continued, "but I think he bought some cheap stuff, like he does every year. The only thing you can do with it is cook. Hopefully, Fred has something different." He chatted on as I smiled and nodded.

"Brrrrrrrrrrr," he went and I used one of my limited phrases, saying *"Oui, il fait froid."* I stomped my feet on the ground to keep the circulation going.

Inside the café, Fred reached up and slid the bolts down. He turned the key in the first lock and then the second at the bottom of the door.

The café was now officially open.

We piled into the warm bar. The bright neon lights and dazzling green Formica counter top pierced my eyeballs. The place hadn't been renovated since the mid 1970s. The temperature was an ambient twenty degrees, twenty degrees warmer than outside, and Didier's glasses steamed up. I started to thaw out and pulled myself onto a stool in front of the bar. Signs and banners proclaiming *'Le Beaujolais est arrivé'* hung behind the bar and on the walls.

Jérôme walked into the café. He was small in stature, with a swollen liver and a face showing the ill effects of his constant slurping. He elbowed his way to the bar to be served first. The night before, in a drunken stupor, he had endlessly repeated his only joke, based around the name of the bar *'L'Escalier'* (staircase).

"Ear iz l'escale, ze sturway to ze eeevurn," he'd said over and over again, breathing his halitosis into my face. He was wasted and owed the bar over two hundred Francs. Eventually, Fred had refused him any more credit.

"He is ze Satan and ear iz ze hell," he ranted.

He had got up early to be back in hell. I scratched the stubble on my chin and turned my head away so he wouldn't try to speak to me. He had the memory of a goldfish and would likely start breathing his one joke back into my face again.

The café had become my university of choice as I tried to decipher people spewing their broken English, while I tried my French. It got easier after a few drinks. I attended lessons daily.

The various pâtés, saucissons and baguettes were neatly laid out on the tables. The straight lines of shiny wine glasses stood like soldiers. A number of bottles were already open and turned to show the labels. Fred pulled a cork and it made a loud 'pop'.

"*Il est arrivé!*" shouted Fred, pouring out the wine.

Everybody cheered. Fred passed the bottle to me so I could continue pouring. He picked up another bottle and began pouring wine into the waiting glasses. The full glasses were passed out to the eagerly waiting crowd.

The bar quickly packed out. There were about thirty blurry-eyed men and women stuffed into the place. Fred tapped on the counter top with a corkscrew and the café went quiet. He lifted his glass and everybody followed his action and cried out in unison:

"*Santé!*"

I lifted the glass to my lips and took the first sip of the first glass of fruity nectar. The deep red berry flavours exploded around my mouth, then hit the back of my throat. It was crisp and full of vibrant, in-your-face fruit.

I looked at the different faces people made as they tasted this year's offering. Some nodded agreeably, others scrunched up their faces in disgust. Maybe it was too early to be drinking wine, but everybody was suddenly a serious wine taster, a '*Critique*'.

"It's fresh and fruity as a Nouveau should be," said Fanny in my ear. She was studying English and wanted to be an English teacher. "This one has a rich red-cherry flavour to it, with a touch of blackcurrant, *c'est très bon*," she affirmed with authority, smiling. She was pretty and slim with long black hair, but she had a boyfriend.

"*Oui, c'est bon, yum, yum, encore!*" I said laughing, smiling back at her.

"The bouquet of the wine is best revealed by gently swirling the wine in the glass," Fanny continued. "This will help to expose it to more oxygen and release the beautiful perfume to your nose." As she spoke, she swirled her glass in front of me, nearly hitting my nose. I turned around and looked at the label on the bottle. Fred saw me looking at the bottle.

"Georges Duboeuf," he said. "He's the King of Beaujolais Nouveau. For over thirty years, he's been the leading Beaujolais producer. He always has the best Nouveau. I only buy what he makes. The others are no good. You can always rely on his quality every year. For a wine meant to be consumed now, this is almost too tannic. It has the necessary bright fruit, but it's too dry."

"*C'est bon, merci*," I said.

He filled my glass, poured wine into two more glasses, and passed them to recently arrived customers. Then he came back to me and continued,

"Fruity tannins, with a nice flavour, I like this one. Normally, I don't like Beaujolais, it's too young and I think the whole process is just a big marketing scam to get people to drink undrinkable wine."

"But hey, when it's free, it tastes great," I said and we laughed. He moved down the bar and started talking to the couple next to me.

I worked hard to understand the slurred and garbled northern French slang. People were trumpeting their opinion, analysing the messages their taste buds were sending to their brains. I didn't understand a lot of it, but onomatopoeic sounds and arm and hand gestures helped.

"Ohhhhhhhhh, black berry, bambalam," Kiki shouted in my ear. He was in his early forties, skinny, his face showing the first signs of serious alcohol addiction.

"No, Black Betty," I said. "The song is called Black Betty."

"No zat is black betty skin. Chuck Berry is black, so black

berry is good." His words dribbled out of his wine-stained lips. His teeth had a red tinge to them.

"Yeah, whatever man." I didn't want to talk with him. I turned my head and he moved away from me. He'd already been on the juice up the road and was now launched into his second session of free Beaujolais. He intended to get as many down his neck before he either fell over or got thrown out. Kiki always left in style. I'd seen him hauled outside and propped up on the bench opposite the café at closing time. Today, he was a wine critic, but his career was likely to be short lived. The way he was going, he wasn't going to make it to 9 am.

Fred refilled my glass regularly and I was bombarded with wine jargon.

"This one has the exuberance of fruity, jammy plums, strawberries, red currants, and peaches. It's definitely meant to be enjoyed young," said Gérard from behind me. I hadn't seen him enter the café. He was a long-distance lorry driver and told me stories of when he went to England. He loved a full English breakfast, but today he was happy with a liquid one. He spoke with authority and swirled the wine round in his glass, spilling most of it on his shoes.

"Just say what the wine is saying to you," he said, gulping down the rest of his glass and turning to find another bottle. "It's not necessary to know everything about wines to enjoy them, but the more you taste the better your knowledge." He was starting to slur his words. "However, a little bit every day and you gradually expand your knowledge, *voilà*, simple."

"Ah, the enjoyment of drinking Beaujolais on Beaujolais Nouveau Day, *salut*," said David, the plumber. We shook hands.

"*Salut*, David," I said.

"Everybody is in a jovial mood this morning," he said looking at the pack of red-faced connoisseurs. "Wine for breakfast on an empty stomach usually makes people too jovial and their tongues wag too much." He sipped on his glass.

"The wine critics are in full cry," I said.

"Full, ripe and fruity, this is true *merveille* (marvel)," proclaimed Patrick, like he'd just struck oil. He was a flyweight with a pot belly, his skinny frame barely holding his jacket on his tiny shoulders.

"It is delicious and juicy," I replied.

"It has a real character, you can taste the crisp cherry flavour, truly formidable." Patrick twirled his glass in front of his nose and glared momentarily at the wine swirling around the glass. We chinked our glasses together and he swigged the last mouthful. He grabbed a full bottle from the counter. Wow, this guy was going to go to work today?

Eight o'clock came around quickly and Fred looked at his watch. The 7 to 8 am liquid breakfast-bonanza was over and it was time for people to leave. Fred started to clean away the empty plates from the tables and arrange his café as normal.

"*Voilà, c'est fini, d'être merci venu*, thanks for coming," he said waving to the people leaving. "It's time to go. Everybody has a job to go to, whether drunk or sober. The second half is tonight, in eleven hours' time, at seven this evening, OK?" He was collecting up the empty glasses and placing them on the counter near the sink and glass-washing machine.

"*Merci*, Fred, see you tonight," I said pulling on the heavy door.

"See you later."

I walked out of the café and the chilly, biting wind hit my wine-warmed face. I adjusted the collar of my jacket and tightened my scarf to combat the savage north wind. The fresh air shot up my nostrils and a numbing pain hit me between the eyes. I pinched the bridge of my nose to ease the pain.

I fumbled for the car keys in my pocket. I turned the stiff

lock of the car door and the black plastic knob popped up. I opened it and got in.

I'd managed to eat a few lumps of meat and pâté that Fred had placed on the bar before the vultures dived in and devoured all the free grub. I stopped the car opposite the boulangerie and bought two *croissants* and two *pain au chocolats* to mop up the wine. I stuffed them into my mouth as I drove through the winding lanes in the direction of Le Crotoy on the coast. The sun eventually broke through the clouds and started to heat up the frozen surface of the road and lift the mist. On a frozen pond, the ducks were slipping about on the icy surface.

I had a heavy diary of appointments. There was another breakfast meeting at the builders' merchants at eleven o'clock. I had been invited by Jean-Paul to taste their own labelled Beaujolais, printed in the distinctive blood orange colour of their Point P logo. After that, I had an important lunch appointment at The Casino bar and restaurant. The owner, Monique, liked to take care of her customers and arranged a special menu to go with the Beaujolais Nouveau. I had reserved a VIP ticket.

I recognised Freddy walking along the side of the road and I touched on the brakes. He lived in Fort Mahon, just around the bay, and was the barman at a bistro called Le Globe, in Saint Valery-sur-Somme. His mop of jet black hair blew in the wind. He was wearing blue jeans and a large green anorak he had kept from his military service. He had his arm extended out, thumbing a lift. I pulled the car up next to him.

"*Bonjour,* Freddy, do you want a lift?" I said, stretching over to open the passenger door.

"*Bonjour, oui merci*, my car broke down up the road just after Quend village," he said climbing into the car.

"What happened?"

"It started to overheat, the red warning came on, then steam poured from the radiator. I left it on the side of road with a note on it. I was lucky and got a lift with a truck going to Le Crotoy. He dropped me at the roundabout. I only walked about a hundred metres before you stopped." He warmed his hands on the heater outlet on the side of the dashboard.

"*Quelle chance*, because it's cold this morning," I said, changing gear. I told him about my morning and the free Beaujolais at the L'Escale bar.

We drove around the bay on the elevated road towards Saint Valery-sur-Somme. Freddy looked out of the window at the misty bay and the fluffy clouds floating above the shooting huts.

"You know you can't drink or sell it before the stroke of midnight on the third Thursday of November," he said. "Only then, at one second past, can they start to transport it. They have to ship it all over the world. Like, how quickly can they get it to Japan or California in America? It's on the other side of the world. It's nearly the next day in Australia when it's the morning in France. Anyway, the Japs put Coca-Cola in the wine, so I don't see any reason to rush it to them at all. They drink that Sake rubbish made with rice. They eat rice, they drink rice. They probably shit rice. Think about it!" He was flabbergasted.

Freddy was on form this morning. He always had something to say. He was a dedicated fan of Saint Etienne football club and wore the team shirt on match days.

"Think about it," he said again, then he thought for a couple of seconds. "Right, it's what time in Australia when it's midnight in France? It's just impossible to drink Beaujolais Nouveau on the third Thursday. How long is a flight to Australia? You have to ship it up to Paris, then fly it to Australia. Imagine that, around the world. It's a bloody national treasure; it's when France erupts into a massive celebration in honour of wine, and only French wine can be Beaujolais! It's like Christmas but in November!

"Any excuse for a piss-up," I said.

"It's a good excuse to have a drink for all those who died in the World Wars, *oui!* Beaujolais Nouveau Day is always a couple of days after the eleventh of November," he said seriously.

"If I keep up the pace I was drinking at the L'Escale bar, I'll end up having a glass for every fallen soldier!" I said.

I concentrated on the road. Some of the corners were still icy where they were shaded by poplar trees. I took the road into the little port of Saint Valery-sur-Somme and drove along the harbour front, past the sailing club and along the quay. I parked up on the lower bay-side road.

We squeezed through one of the very narrow alleyways that gave access to the sea for the fishermen – enabling them carry their nets to their boats without having to walk to the end of the long high street.

Freddy was still expounding on Beaujolais Nouveau as we walked. "I read they did a wine tasting in America. They got the people to taste wines labelled 'France', 'California', and 'Texas'. They have vines in Texas – can you imagine? Anyway, most of them said the French wine was the best, but in fact all three were the same Texan wine." He threw his hands in the air and looked up to the grey sky as if he was looking to God for answers. "People don't know what they are drinking!" I followed him up a slight incline and we popped out on Rue de la Ferté.

Our fate was decided for us. Roberto, with his arms of steel and saucer-sized hands, grabbed me by the arm as we passed Le Culvert café on the narrow pavement. He dragged me inside and that was it. I was kidnapped.

Roberto and Thierry were brothers by birth and roofers by trade. They had patched up my roof and I would see them regularly in the cafés of the village.

"*Boire un coup Anglais*," he ordered me and poured a glass from the bottle on the counter. His big, round tomato face beamed as he passed me the small glass in his giant hands.

"It has a heavy banana scent, with a bitter cherry taste to it," he said.

"It's for the children!" Thierry added.

"This is a classic, a fun Nouveau, it's bold and fruity. *Salut Anglais*," chipped in Jacky, the barman and owner. He reached out his little arm to shake my hand.

"Experience the *Ch'ti* way of celebrating Beaujolais Nouveau Day, you'll see, *ti*," said Roberto.

Freddy started to rant about wine critics.

"What do they know?" he said. "They hold too much power. They can make or break a wine even before it comes on the market. The ratings of these few critics have a huge effect on the prices of wines. The chosen few dictate to the rest of us. It makes me so mad."

"Critics, my ass," Roberto barked.

"It's a scam," Freddy said loudly and angrily. "All the critics are on kickbacks for writing nice articles about certain wines." Whether they liked it or not, everybody in the café was going to have to listen to Freddy's speech. "The likes of that American, Parker, Robert Parker Junior. Him and the others, they are either British, Americans or Canadians, *merde alors!*" Freddy was really pissed off about the wine industry.

"Not one of them is French, how can that be?" Roberto asked, recharging his glass. "Imagine, an American decides what wines are drinkable!" He was horrified.

"*Impossible!*" shouted the landlord.

"The world is going to the dogs," Thierry said.

Alain was not part of the clan and was seated on a stool at the other end of the bar. He was trying to listen in to the conversation, and I saw his eyeballs expand and his eyebrows rise up on his forehead in surprise.

"Ray Parker Junior is the most influential wine critic in the world?" he said loudly. "Ray Parker Junior, the black guy that sung the Ghostbusters song?" He broke into song. "When there's something strange in the neighbourhood... Who ya gonna call?" We all shouted out in reply, "Ghostbusters!" and broke into laughter.

"His nose and palate are insured for a million dollars," I said, bringing the subject back to the correct 'Parker Junior' and remembering something I had read. "It's the reason for his nickname, "the million-dollar nose.""

"It just really annoys me, that's all. An American decides what is good or bad wine." Freddy made one more horrified face, then broke into a wry smile. "I have to go to work now and prepare for lunchtime. Thanks for the lift and thanks for the drink. See you all later." He walked out of the café, crossed the road diagonally and walked the short distance to Le Globe.

The next rendezvous was just down the road at the builders' merchants. I drove through the open gates; white Renault Express vans and flatbed trucks littered the yard. Every builder, roofer, plumber, electrician, and plasterer from the surrounding area was parked up. People were milling around, some were loading their trucks with materials, but the majority of them were hanging out, waiting for something to happen, smoking cigarettes, leaning up against their vans talking.

I parked and walked over to the front door. Inside, the newly renovated shop was all lit up and decorated with vibrant-coloured banners, balloons and streamers hanging from the shelves.

On a long table there were bowls of pâté the size of motorcycle helmets, slices of cooked meats in huge piles and enough baguettes to feed a starving rabble. A dozen bottles of wine stretched out in front of me.

Jean-Paul swaggered over to me in his heavy branded and matching jacket and trousers. His heavy twill trousers emitted a sound like sandpaper being rubbed together. Jean-Paul was the neighbour of Freddy's parents and was married to Freddy's late mother's second cousin, who was married to the cousin of his wife's sister, who was married to his brother-in-law's brother, whose sister was living with his nephew, something like that. They were all family.

Whenever I went to the builders' merchants, Jean-Paul would add an extra scoop of sand, and not charge me for the twisted timber or the split bags of plaster. In turn, Freddy and I would help him bring in the massive pile of wood outside his garage door. We were always rewarded with a glass of his 'Extra, super-over-proof calvados moonshine' that he made himself from the apples in his garden. We shook hands.

"*Ça va*, OK?" he enquired.

"*Ça va* bien, merci."

He took a plastic beaker, poured out the wine, and thrust it into my hand. We knocked our two containers together and Jean-Paul knocked the wine back in one large gulp, then wiped the side of his mouth with the back of his hand.

"*Excusez-moi, je dois faire le tour*, I have to do the rounds," he said as he turned and scooted off to serve other people.

I bumped into people I knew. Everybody and his dog were gathered for a free drink and they were all commenting on the new decor. I had never seen so many people in there at the same time. The yard was blocked with vehicles and, through the windows of the office at the end of the shop, I could see cars and trucks parked on the verge of the track that led up to the gates.

Antoine walked over to me and we shook hands. His lumberjack shirt, craggy, weather-beaten face, and bad back spoke of the years he had spent chopping down trees with an axe. He comically swilled the wine around in the plastic cup like a connoisseur admiring a prestige vintage.

"The serving temperature that the wine is served at can greatly affect the way it tastes and smells," he said in a snobby aristocratic voice. He lifted the plastic goblet to his nose.

"Not exactly the most refined way to taste wine," I said.

"It's the annual Point P picnic," he said. "Smell *le bouquet, mec,* ze nose. Warmer temperatures help increase the aromatics and open the wine up."

Beber, the captain of a big fishing boat, walked into the shop rubbing his large hands together. He moved both of his arms around in a circle like a human windmill, and his deep voice boomed out as he roared a greeting at everyone in the shop.

"*Bonjour!*"

Jean-Paul thrust a goblet into Beber's huge hand and filled it to the top. He carried on serving the other customers, enjoying a swig from his own glass as he went.

"Hey, *les gars,* we'll have a little drink tonight, OK?" Beber said with excitement, his beaming smile stretched across his face.

"*Oui, bien sûr,*" I said.

I turned around and took a plastic plate and a knife. I had to eat something to soak up some of the alcohol. I gorged on bread, pâté and saucisson. Jean-Paul charged our glasses constantly until midday came around. It was now lunchtime and time to leave. People finished their drinks and started to filter out into the car park, making their way back to their vans and cars.

I finished my cup of purple juice and headed for the door.

"*Merci* Jean-Paul," I said pushing the door open, "*à bientôt.*"

"*Attends*, wait, I have a present for you, follow me," Jean-Paul said as he raced in front of me and scampered over to the shed opposite. My car was parked alongside a stack of bags of cement and plaster.

Jean-Paul pulled back the corner of a large tarpaulin and picked up a white cardboard box hidden underneath. It was a case of wine and he thrust it into my hands. He quickly turned on his heals while making a waving gesture with his arm.

"Hurry up, go, *bon appétit*," he said and raced back to the shop.

I placed the wine in the back of the car, blocking it with two bags of plaster so it wouldn't slide around and break. I drove slowly back to the village and parked the car in the free car park.

Thankfully, the walk to the restaurant was all downhill. The view of the Bay of the Somme from the top of the hill was spectacular. I stopped and took it in. The damp pan-tiled and slated rooftops shimmered in the bright light, as smoke bellowed from the chimney stacks. Seagulls hovered over my head, screeching. The tide was coming in quickly. The ripple of the small tidal wave caressed the banks as fifty million litres of seawater flowed in and recaptured the coastline. The water tower in Le Crotoy, the small fishing port in the distance, gleamed in the sunshine.

A small, cobbled staircase led down to the narrow street, one of the little rat runs that divided the compact fishermen's cottages. The telephone and electrical cables intertwined like spaghetti and dangled from post to post above the street. I walked past the Place de la Fontaine and turned onto the road on the bay front.

I pushed the heavy doors of The Casino, the stiff springs creaking as I entered the café. The dining area's windows looked out over the bay and bright sunlight lit up the bar.

I stepped into the next round. Seconds out...

"*Il est arrivé*," shouted Bruno as I entered.

Yves was standing at the bar. He was known in the village

as 'Special agent Yves'. Agent double-dose more like, for he drank his Pastis 51 by the double (or a '102', as the singer Serge Gainsbourg famously put it). He would always complain that his free-poured calvados or brandy measure wasn't a full measure and demand a top up. He was a self-styled Humphrey Bogart meets Columbo, a mystery man with a nebulous past. Friendly and verbose, his dishevelled attire consisted of a rumpled beige trench coat, worn in all weathers over a suit, even in the height of summer. The look was rounded off with yellow-tinted teardrop Ray-Bans and a small café-crème cigar.

He would tell you half a story, then stop as if there were 'people' listening in. He'd apparently worked on a petrol plat-form in the North Sea for years, and told amazing stories about his endeavours around the world. The more he drank, the more elaborate and dynamic his stories became, fit for a James Bond script. He kept in character until the alcohol finally got to him, then he would end up a crumpled mess on the floor of the urinals or laying across a bench in the square.

Yves shuffled across the tiles and slowly lifted himself up onto a bar stool. His suit was all ripped down one side, as though a big cat had run its claws down him. A lion, maybe? You never knew with Yves. There were holes in the knees of his trousers and grit and blood was stuck to the material. He made excuses not to shake hands, as a large area of skin had been grazed from the palm of his right hand. He looked in a right state.

"What happened to you, Yves?" I asked.

The side of his face was also grazed, with small pebbles and stones stuck to the wound. He swayed on the stool.

"What happened, did you fall over?" I asked again, concerned.

He stared at me with glazed eyes. After about thirty seconds, he replied through swollen lips.

"I was attacked by loads of them, there must have ten – maybe twelve."

"Who was it?" I enquired.

"Did you see any of their faces?" Bruno asked. "Did you get a look at them? What did you do? Were you all alone?"

"I put up a good fight, but they outnumbered me," Yves said. He slid down from the bar stool and shuffled to his feet, swaying back and forth. He gained his balance and started to show us his Kung Fu moves. He crossed his arms and spread his legs apart in a karate stance. He bent forward, bowing, then he started waving his arms around, wildly chopping the air.

"I was like *zis*," he said in English, "zen, *comme ça*."

He plunged forward, losing his balance as his body lurched in my direction. I stepped to the side as he launched himself along the bar with his arm extended and his fist clenched. He tried to regain his balance, but his feet ran before him. He grabbed hold of a chair to stop his forward motion, but he jack-knifed at ninety degrees and was projected between two tables. He crashed into the partition window, headbutting the wooden panel, just missing the glass. He collapsed onto the floor.

"Then they stole my car," he said, turning his head to look up at me as he lay splayed out on the ground. He tried to get up, but he stood on the tails of his overcoat. I gave him my arm and pulled him to his feet.

"Are you sure you're OK?" I asked.

"*Oui, oui, ça va*," he confirmed. He wiped himself down. "*Il est arrivé, ce n'est pas grave c'est le Beaujolais qui est là.* That's all that counts on the third Thursday of November. Come on, let's have a drink."

He wobbled slowly back to his place at the bar like nothing had happened.

"You look in a bad way," I said. "You should go home and get changed, have a shower, clean yourself up."

"They left me on the ground for dead." He lifted his elbow onto the counter to steady himself. "I'm just going to have a little drink and something to eat, then I'm going to the police station to report it," he said, slurring his words through his badly swollen lips. "I'm going to show them how they left me. They can take photos of my suit and my injuries. I'm going to press charges, the insurance company will pay for a new car, you'll see." Yves knew how the system worked.

"Can I get some service over here? I want to order," he growled at Bruno. He ordered a bottle of Beaujolais Nouveau. The bottle and three glasses were placed in front of us. Bruno popped the cork with a 'plop', a sound that was becoming all too familiar. He poured the red liquid into the glasses.

"*Santé.*" We raised our glasses and clinked them together.

I sipped the wine and analysed its taste.

"It's got spicy fruity tones, with upfront juicy cherry and banana flavours," I said. It really did taste like bananas.

Yves took off his sunglasses and replaced them with his reading glasses. His black eye still had stones and gravel congealed into the wound.

"You should clean that up, Yves," I told him again. He read the label of the bottle.

"Most people are unable to distinguish expensive wines from inexpensive ones," he said. "They have no idea whatsoever. They just judge it on the price they pay and the region. They cannot tell the difference between Bordeaux or Bourgognes. I prefer a Gamay that has aged a little. I particularly like the *crus* from *Moulin-à-Vent* and a *Fleurie, j'adore!*"

He hadn't heard what I said, or was avoiding the question.

"This is a wine with baby tannins," he confirmed, looking me straight in the eyes. He was giving me some inside knowledge.

"Baby tannins – the wine is going to have children?" I enquired sarcastically.

It was hard to understand him. The way he was mushing his words sounded like he had concussion. He shuffled off to the toilet.

"He's been in the café since nine o'clock this morning, when we opened up," said Bruno. "He was sitting on the bench outside. He looks a right state. He told me his car was stolen." Bruno leant over the bar to get as close as possible to my ear. "He's already drunk a bottle of Beaujolais. He's on his second bottle with you."

"What really happened to him?" I asked.

Bruno lifted his pale eyebrows and pushed his hands outwards, his palms upwards.

"I found him once on one of the benches between the café and where he lives in the old *Gendarmerie*. He was so drunk he couldn't walk. It took me over an hour to get him home. I put him on the sofa and left. His courtyard has been recently gravelled with shiny white stones, like the ones on his face, hands, and knees. He's fallen face first into the gravel, it's the same gravel. Have a look."

Yves came out of the toilet and moved slowly across the bar.

"Car-jacking, *monsieur*," he said, raising his voice as he wiped his hands on his trench coat. Car-jacking was the new 'in' word in the French vocabulary.

Yves bored me again with the story of how he was attacked, car-jacked and had all his keys stolen. The restaurant was busy and Marie ran about the dining area with generous plates of food. Rolland, a retired fisherman, stopped off with his dog for his daily aperitif, before heading back to his house to catch the local news. He shook my hand and ordered a Beaujolais Nouveau.

Didier walked in from the other end of the bar. His huge

frame and broad shoulders barely passed through the door. His muscly arms hung out about a foot from his hips in a gorilla-like stance. His eyebrows touched in the middle of his forehead. He looked half asleep, but he gave me a toothless smile as we shook hands.

"You're drinking that crap," he said. "I tasted it up the road, it's shit this year. They've got *Bière de Noël* here, it's better than that rubbish." He took off his heavy jacket and hung it on a hook. He always sat at the same place at the end of the long, wooden bar. Didier, or *Ch'gros*, 'The Big' as everybody called him. He perched on his stool with his arms crossed over his chest, leaning back against the wall.

Didier stared at Yves' war wounds with a smirk on the side of his face.

"Today is Beaujolais day," I said to Yves with real concern, "but you should get a Perrier or something. You really shouldn't drink anymore."

"I'm drinking Beaujolais, don't worry about a thing," he slurred. "There are four stages to wine tasting," he said, adjusting his bent sunglasses. He held his glass up in the air and observed it. "Appearance." He looked at the wine as it lapped the edge of the glass in his shaking hand. "Zen, in ze glass, ze aroma of ze wine…" He sniffed the top of the glass under his nose. "And zen, ze mouzz, quelle sensation!" He took a large gulp from his glass and placed it on the counter. "Nice finish, very good, ze flavour comes after, very good, is good," he said proudly.

"In English it is known as the five S's." I said to Yves. "First you 'see', you look at the wine, then 'swirl'," as I turned the glass in my hand.

"Then 'sniff'," and I stuck my large nose over the rim of the glass and breathed in heavily. Didier turned from the jukebox and bumped my elbow, causing the glass to judder. I tried to absorb the shock, but to no avail. My nose plunged into the red liquid as I breathed in. The wine shot up my nostrils and into my mouth. I pulled my head backwards and the wine that I hadn't inhaled splashed down the front of my shirt.

"I'm glad I wore black today," I said, wiping the end of my nose with the back of my hand. The wet shirt stuck to my chest.

"*Désolé Anglais,*" Didier said.

I walked to the toilet to wash my face and shirt – and to rinse my nostrils.

I returned to my spot at the bar. I never got to explain the last of the S's.

"This year, it is definitely drinkable. It has a well-balanced bouquet, it's fruity," Yves, the agent-connoisseur, said.

"Funky," I added.

Yves slurred his way through another express version of the preceding evening's events.

"So, you are going to go to the police station to get France's CIA or FBI involved in the case?" said Bruno. "To find the people who beat you up and stole your car, that mysteriously turned up in the parking lot opposite the café. How come the thieves stole it and parked it over there?" He pointed to the car park. Then he produced Yves' keys, dangling them in front of him.

"I found them on the ground, by your car door, last night when I walked home after locking up. Your car is on the other side of the car park. You didn't see it there?"

The whole café roared with laughter. Yves looked perplexed and mystified. He went to look out of the front door window to see where his car was.

"You really don't need to have another drink, Yves," said Bruno. "And I won't give you the keys, because you should not drive in the state you're in. I'll only give them back to you if you promise not to drive, promise before all of us," he added, teasing Yves with his keys.

"OK, but give me my keys," said Yves. "I need to have a shower now that I can get into my house." He held out his hand and Bruno dropped the keys into his open palm.

"*Promis*," Bruno persisted.

"*Oui, oui, promis*," Yves said sheepishly.

I could smell the aroma of cooking coming from the kitchen. The smell was mouthwatering. All this wine tasting was hungry work.

"*Le coq au vin* smells so good," I said to Monique as she poked her head through the small hatch, where the plates were passed from the kitchen into the restaurant.

"I drowned them in Beaujolais since this morning. They've been swimming in it for the last three hours on a low flame," she said smiling. "You'll see, you'll enjoy it. I tasted the sauce and it's delicious." Monique knew how to cook – she'd run a café and restaurant for the past forty years.

Yves slid out of the bar and crept towards his car; he opened the door, climbed in, and promptly fell asleep.

I sat down at the table and looked out at the full bay. It was now high tide and water lapped against the quay. I took my time eating and finished off the bottle Yves had left on the counter. The meal was delicious and I finished it off with a *crème brûlée* and a coffee.

I headed back to my car. As I walked along the main high street, Dominique, the tall skinny barber, sprinted out of his shop, his wiry greying curly hair dishevelled as always. He skidded along the pavement in his leather-soled shoes like a ballerina and stopped by the front door of the café next to his shop. He didn't wait for Beaujolais day to drink a glass of wine for breakfast. He did that every day to steady his hands. He would leave his clients waiting in the chair as he dashed next door to '*changer la monnaie*' by having a swift *balon,* which he would neck in one shot.

"A quick one," he said, shaking my hand.

"OK," I said.

"You know I've got a client waiting," he chuckled and opened the door.

"*Deux Beaujolais Nouveau, s'il vous plait,*" I ordered in my best French.

"Uh?" The old lady behind the bar turned around and looked at me. She never understood, or wanted to understand, what I said. She took the prize for being the rudest bar person in the world.

"*Deux Beaujolais Nouveau,* please," I repeated in my extra precise French. She flexed her face and made a grunting noise. She placed the glasses on the counter top and grabbed the open bottle from the counter behind her. She poured out the wine up to the white line. We picked up our glasses and raise them for a toast.

"*Santé,*" said Dominique. We touched our glasses together and they chimed. I took a sip.

"This year's vintage is ripe and fruity, unlike her," Dominique said pointing to the landlady.

The door pinged open and Beber the fisherman walked into the café. His giant frame took up the whole space of the door and blocked the light.

"*Bonjour,*" his megaphone-voice filled the airwaves of the café. Everybody knew Beber and nobody messed with him. His brothers and cousins were renowned for their fishing skills, but more so for their fighting antics.

"You have to let it breathe for a few minutes before drinking it, stupid," he said as he grabbed the glass out of my hand and glugged it back in one gulp.

"Give us a bottle, madame, please," he commanded the

woman. He winked and stuck out his cherry red tongue at me. "And make it snappy," he insisted, smiling.

Dominique placed his glass down on the counter with force. He shook my hand and turned on his heels in rapid speed.

"Stay and have a drink with us," Beber growled at Dominique.

"*Non merci*, I have a client waiting in the chair," he said slamming the door behind him. The woman put the bottle in front of Beber with clean glasses. He lifted the bottle and poured the ruby red juice. The woman returned to her corner to observe everyone with her arms firmly wrapped across her chest, leaning back on the counter behind her. Beber passed me a full glass. He lifted his glass in the air and shouted out.

"I now declare the Beauj-olympics open, may the best man win."

ICE

It had all begun when I parked the car on the seafront of the small seaside resort of Le Crotoy. The town is perched on the north side of the Bay of the Somme, where the mouth of the river Somme flows into the English Channel.

As I got out, I heard ducks quacking and I lifted my head up to the grey skies as a covey flew over. I watched as they turned towards the port.

I looked out at the magnificent estuary. I could clearly see Saint Valery-sur-Somme, with its city ramparts, and the point of Le Hourdel in the distance on the other side of the bay. The tide was out and people were walking over the sandbanks.

I walked through the narrow streets lined with fishermen's cottages, the shutters painted in an array of colours and secured by little metal figurines, standing to attention.

A sign above an estate agent's door flashed in the sunlight. I crossed the road and stepped onto the narrow pavement. There were two large windows full of pictures and house descriptions. One grabbed my attention. It was so cheap I assumed there must be a mistake.

I pushed open the door and walked into the triangular

office. A short, chubby, bearded man jumped up from behind his desk and shook my hand.

"*Bonjour Monsieur, j'ai vu une maison...*" I stopped to gather my French vocabulary that was hidden somewhere in my brain.

"*Bonjour Monsieur*. My name's Yves, as you can hear I speak fluent English," he continued. There wasn't even the trace of an accent.

"That will make things easier," I said.

"How can I help you?"

"One of the houses caught my eye, the small one near Saint Riquier. It looks like it needs some work, but it's in my price range."

He passed me a large red ring binder.

"Have a look through this. It has all the properties we have for sale." I took the heavy folder from him.

"Make a note of any houses that interest you," he added. I placed the folder on a table and began flipping through the pages.

After a while, I closed the file.

"See anything else you like?"

"I've seen six houses that caught my eye."

"Very good." He came over and took the file from me.

"I'll make you some copies of the property details for you. It's nearly lunchtime. What are your plans?" He turned and stepped towards the photocopying machine.

"There's a little family-run place nearby. The mussels and chips are very good," he said. "The mussels and cockles come from the bay. All the fish is locally sourced. They also serve the famous *ficelle picarde*, a crêpe stuffed with ham, mushrooms, and shallots cooked in a cream and cheese sauce."

He picked up his little leather bag and pushed it under his arm, like a sergeant major with his baton.

"This is France," he said, "everything stops for lunch here."

We walked the short distance to the restaurant. The endless sandy beach, and the huge bay with its open water stretching into the far distance, exploded before us. We climbed the steps and arrived on a large, raised terrace. The owner greeted Yves with kisses and showed us to our table.

We washed down our fish with two litres of crisp, white wine as the tide rolled in.

After lunch, we returned to Yves's estate agency. He collected the keys and spoke to his secretary, Anne, as I smoked a cigarette and looked at the other properties for sale in the window.

"*A toute à l'heure, ma chérie*," Yves cooed as he closed the door, giving Anne a camp little wave.

"Let's go," he said to me, moving to the other side of a car parked in front of the door of the agency. "We'll take my car. I'll drop you back here afterwards, OK?"

We drove slowly through the narrow high street with its shops selling seaside paraphernalia. Yves beeped the horn and waved to people. Once out of the village, he turned towards Abbeville and we followed the elevated road that hugs the extremities of the bay.

The car crossed peaceful meadows and gently rolling dark green hills. Grey sky, sprinkled with delicate light-blue wispy clouds, floated above the flat landscape, the road following the natural contours of the terrain. It was a mixture of straggly hedges, tree-clad knolls, and farmyards. There were big, lush fields full of fat cows, and huge modern tractors worked the land.

I stared out of the window as the stone houses and churches and other buildings made of wattle and daub flashed past. Crumbling barns were in various states of collapse, while modern villas with neat flowerbeds huddled on the edges of the villages.

"There are plenty of little picturesque villages with hidden treasures out here, it's a question of finding them," said Yves. "The area is very rich in history. Some of the most famous battles were fought here – Crécy, and of course the Battle of the Somme. The house you want to see is just after Saint Riquier. First, we will go through Nouvion and you'll see a bit of the Forest of Crécy."

He gave me a short lecture on the area – how it was a prosperous agricultural region, but the young were all moving to Paris.

"The local people of the region are called Picards. They speak a patois, *le Ch'ti*. You just replace *Le* and *La* with C-H, and say 'Shh' before every word. Simple French for simple people. Education was optional around here back in the day. They had to get them working on the land or down a mine as soon as they could hold a shovel or a hammer."

Yves spent three full days driving me around the countryside. I looked at different houses scattered over the undulating fields and valleys around the Bay of the Somme. His routes were planned around his old drinking holes and restaurants. We stopped at nearly every bar and café in the surrounding labyrinth of country roads as we criss-crossed the open potato and sugar beet fields under dark-grey skies.

After visiting over twenty properties, I found the house of my dreams.

It was a two hundred and fifty-year-old cow shed attached to a four-roomed house in the small village of Villers-sur-Authie, near the town of Rue. Yves arranged everything and accompanied me to the notary's office to translate the contract for me. Before signing it, the notary informed me that I would become the 139th member of the community. I signed the *Compromis de Vente* and arranged the official key exchange and big signing transaction date in four months, the time it took to arrange all the paperwork.

Yves and I walked out of the office and we both lit cigarettes.

"Happy? You're on your way to owning a château in France," he joked.

"Thanks for your help," I said.

"Let's have a drink and celebrate," said Yves. "I have to go back to the office and check the messages, it'll just take five minutes. Then we can go and get a drink, maybe something to eat. Let me see what Adam's doing. I'll call him from the office. Follow me back to Le Crotoy." He walked towards his car.

"I think I know the way now," I said.

"Good, you don't want to get lost around here. It all looks the same."

I followed Yves back to the agency. The sun was setting across the bay. He was already in the office when I parked behind his Peugeot. I could see him inside the office through the large window, scampering around looking at the faxes and letters on his desk. He plucked yellow Post-it Notes off his telephone like a chicken pecking the ground.

I walked into the agency.

"She only works part time. I could do with her doing more," Yves said, frantically looking at his messages. He lifted the handwritten notes up to his nose and squinted as he read them. The telephone burst into action. Yves picked it up.

"*Bonjour, Agence du Littoral*," he said. "Oh, hello, how are you?"

A loud voice was yelling down the telephone. I could only make out two words: 'fuck' and 'fucking'. Yves flipped the palm of his hand up in the air, shrugged his shoulders, and dipped his hips to the right. He smiled at me.

"Listen, OK, OK... OK, OK, OK, I'm coming home now.

OK, OK, I'm coming... Yes, straight away." He slammed down the phone.

"If Adam asks you where we got the ice from, say the supermarket, OK?" he said. "Not at the fisherman's, OK? He thinks their ice smells of fish. It's in sealed plastic bags in the freezer, which is cleaned every day! When do they clean the insides of freezers in supermarkets?" Yves looked up to the sky as if looking for the answer.

"Good question," I said. I was catching up fast. We were going back to his home, and I was going to meet Adam.

"So, if he asks, say we drove all the way back to Rue. It takes about twenty minutes to get there, then you wait in the queue. Then drive all the way back here again. He's bonkers. Really, when I can just go up the road and turn right. There's a garage there. I go into the freezer, load up a couple of bags and leave. I'll pay later if I don't see them there. They're fishermen, they get through tons of the bloody stuff. Plus, it's not even a third of the price of the supermarket. If there is not any ice in the house, it's the Third World War, so you understand? We'll get a drink at home, we have everything there."

I nodded. This Adam dude sounded bizarre to me. I'd heard he was from South Africa. I put the smelly ice phobia down to being stuck in the bush without any ice for his gin and tonics. Yves had mentioned Adam to me a few times, but not in any detail. Our relationship had been professional and Yves had been very competent and assuring with his perfect English.

"Yes, don't worry, I won't say a word," I said. "What's the name of the supermarket? Just so I can have an answer if he interrogates me."

"In Rue? It's *Champion*. Ice is fucking twenty-five Francs there – for a bag of frozen water!" he exclaimed. "God knows how big these other bags are, but they're at least twice the size. He only charges me ten Francs a bag, a bargain."

We were ready to get going. Yves could see that I was wondering about Adam. He smiled comfortingly. "Adam is one of South Africa's greatest exports," he said. "He is ripe for exploitation. He's exploited the rest of the world, me included, but I didn't say 'no', did I?"

I got into my car and waited for Yves to lock the door of the agency.

I followed him through the narrow streets and we stopped by a garage door. Yves opened it and we walked over to an industrial freezer. We took two large bags of ice and walked back to his car and placed them in the boot.

"OK, follow me," he said. "You'll see the signs for the restaurant, La Clé des Champs. We're just near there. It's owned by friends of ours. If you lose me, you turn right after the duck pond and follow the little track to the end. We're the last gates on the left."

"La Clé des Champs?" I asked.

"Yes, you can't miss it. The duck pond is opposite the restaurant. There's a parking area in the middle of a three-road intersection, just follow me." He climbed into his car and started the engine.

We exited Le Crotoy as darkness descended. A light fog thickened as we headed into the marshy meadows. Large ditches full of wetland plants ran along the side of the narrow, elevated roads that crossed the flat fields.

After fifteen minutes, we arrived at the junction in front of the restaurant. Yves braked and I took in the scene. The small duck pond was surrounded on one side by a hedgerow, on the other by gently sloping land. The pond was in full cry, with quacking ducks and croaking frogs. More ducks flew in and landed, gliding to a halt on the murky water.

A street lamp attached to a telegraph pole flickered. Yves turned right. I accelerated and the back wheels span momentarily on the manure-covered road, the rear of the car drifting off to the left. A second street lamp flickered like the first, illuminating the hedgerow and trees towering over the road. It looked like the entrance to a secluded night club.

I passed a row of small, tightly packed cottages and followed his car down a narrow track riddled with water-filled potholes. I slowly rounded a sharp corner, but I couldn't see the tail lights of Yves' car and the tarmac suddenly stopped. I braked hard. The car's headlights lit up a grass track, leading to fields.

As I reversed, I spotted Yves standing about two hundred metres down the track frantically waving and pointing.

"Park over there behind mine," he shouted. "It's easier to turn around to get out."

I parked and got out.

"You can't see the gates from the corner," I said.

"Yes, I know, that's why we bought it," replied Yves. "Can you put the ice in the freezer, then fill up one of the plastic shopping bags with the scooper?"

Yves opened the boot of the car. I picked up the first bag and carried it over to a huge, rusty freezer. Yves tugged the heavy lid upwards and, as it woofed open, the cold air sprung out and hit my face. I dropped the sack into the freezer and scurried back for the second one. I lifted the cold sack with two hands and backed away from the car. Yves slammed the boot down. I took a better grip on the bag and walked back to the freezer. At the bottom of the freezer was an encrusted mass of frozen plastic bags of different colours, entrapped in frozen sludge.

"Can you grab some ice to take to the house?" Yves asked me. "Please fill two sacks while you're there. You can never have too much ice. We've got plenty of room in the freezer in the house. This is just the old one where I store the big bags that I get from the fisherman so he doesn't see them. I fill those smaller bags. That way, he sees *Champion* on the side of the bags, and thinks it's from the supermarket and he's happy."

I tugged on two shopping bags with '*Champion*' printed on the side from a large pile. A small, metal ice shovel hung on a rope hooked to an old rusty nail next to the freezer. I wiped the shovel with my jumper to clean off the dust. I made a hole in the sack with my fingers and pulled it open, wide enough to get the shovel in. I scooped the ice and filled the two sacks while Yves waited at the door.

"I need to double up these bags, they're too heavy," I said. "I think they will split before we make it to the house."

I reached over and pulled two more bags and wrapped them around the full sacks, then I pushed the door of the freezer closed. Yves' finger hovered over an old maroon Bakelite switch fixed to a wooden beam. I saw a long car hidden under a dust-covered tarpaulin.

"What's under the tarpaulin?" I asked, walking past him and stepping onto the gravel driveway. He flipped the switch and closed the tall, wooden barn door, locking it with a large key.

"It's a Rolls Royce Corniche," he said. "We've had it for years. We'll go out in it one day. The car was delivered in April 1971. It only had one owner before I purchased it. The previous owner had bought it as a present for his wife, but she never drove the thing. They had it for over ten years and only used it for Sunday drives, going out to dinner or family gatherings. It was garaged up when I bought it."

I followed Yves as we crossed a large courtyard in front of the house, our feet crunching on the gravel. I could hear thumping music and I recognised the song. The two shopping bags full of ice dangled down past my knees and swayed with my footsteps. Yves looked at me over his shoulder.

"He's heard the cars," he whispered. The light above the

door came on and lit up the courtyard. The door flew open and the music became much louder. Adam stood silhouetted in the doorway.

"*I'm too sexy, I'm too sexy for my shuuuuuurt!*" he sang. "That's why I'm not wearing one. *Ach* man did you get the ice?" he shouted.

The music boomed from the house and resounded round the courtyard.

"Yes, I did," replied Yves. "What do you think's in those bags Max is carrying?" He nodded in my direction. "Don't you say hello? This is Max, I told you all about him. He just signed the *Compromis* for a great little *fermette* in Villers-sur-Authie this afternoon."

"Hello, Max, nice to meet you," said Adam. "Come in, come in, it's too cold out there."

Adam was wearing a pink dressing gown, which he adjusted, tightening the knot on the cord.

"Thank God for that, coz I can't live without ice, you know that," he added. "That's too much of a fucking nightmare." He looked at me and smiled as I followed Yves up the steps and into the hallway. Adam slammed the door behind us. There were two passageways heading off in different directions. The walls were covered in paintings and we entered a large living room with French doors on the opposite side.

"Christ, it fucking smells like someone's gaffed," said Adam, launching into a tirade. "That bloody smell from the farm next door, or should I say that fucking temple of cow turds. The smell of the countryside, fuck that! It stinks all year long. Every fucking mosquito in the fucking world has to visit it, too. And while flying past our house, they all have to stop off and bite me, fucking things!" He turned his head to the side and started to move his hips to the music.

His movements became more accentuated and he started to

dance. His fluffy pink dressing gown fanned out around his legs as he twisted from side to side. He lifted his arms up in the air and twirled them around, like a belly dancer in rhythm to the music. He smiled at me as I looked on bemused.

"Ooo, I'm toooo sexy for my body, too sexy..." he sang along. "I love this song, it's number one at the moment. It's fabulous. I love it, *oooo!*"

His dressing gown splayed out as he spun on his tiptoes like a grey-haired Sufi dancer. He held his arms out to the side as he sped up, then he lost his balance. He stumbled and fell backwards, but he was still turning. He just managed to push his arms out in front of him before he slammed into the wall. He slid down it and came to a stop on the tiled floor.

He turned around slowly and sat with his legs spread out in front of him, his dressing gown wide open. Grabbing hold of the wall, he pulled himself to his feet. He regained his balance and combed his hair with his hand. He tilted his head and lifted his eyebrows; his piercing blue eyes met mine.

"Are you OK?" I enquired.

"You had more than an eyeful there," he joked. "Not everybody gets to see the Crown Jewels at the first meeting! Oh, Christ man!" he coughed. "Christ man, that was lucky. I'm going to get a bath, a quick ploof! Wash my bits and I'll join you afterwards. Everything is ready, the scented candles are lit and I've already taken my drink down there. Yves will show you how to get a drink upstairs, in what we call the den."

"OK, you sure you're alright?" I asked.

"Don't worry about me *boykie* (a young, cool white male in Afrikaans)," he replied. "It takes a lot more than that to sink my ship! Anyway, upstairs is where all the bottles are and it's the warmest fucking room in the house. We live up there during the winter months. The downstairs just can't be warmed up, the fucking ceilings are so high. Lovely in summer with the doors open. But winter, even with the radiators on and all the fireplaces going, you can't warm the fucking place up. Plus, it's such a fucking pain in the arse to get the wood. Carry it in, poke it, sit down, stand up, poke it again! Imagine you spend all your life just poking, poking, and fucking poking. God forbid." He held his hand up to his mouth as he coughed again. "I was just about to have a bath when I heard the car on the gravel," he said mincing past me, his slippers sliding across the tiled surface. He made his way down the passageway slowly.

"We're nearly out of ice upstairs, Yves!" he shouted from halfway down the corridor.

The windows in the passageway looked out onto the courtyard. Adam pushed the bathroom door open, walked in and shut it behind him.

I chuckled to myself. I had stumbled into *La Cage aux Folles*.

"Come through here," Yves hollered to me.

I walked into the kitchen. He opened the door of the upright fridge-freezer and grabbed a Champagne bucket from next to the sink, and he placed it on the counter top.

"Put one of the bags in there and as much ice as you can in the bucket. We'll take that upstairs. That should last us a bit," he said.

I stuffed the bag of ice into the freezer and rammed it home.

"Grab the bucket and come upstairs," Yves said.

I followed him out of the kitchen into the living room and climbed up the wooden staircase. The long room was dimly lit. The large, wooden beams were stained a rich dark brown.

"This is the bar," said Yves. "What do you want? I think we have over fifty types of whisky, there's vodka, Pastis, Martini, red and white. What do you need?"

"I'll have a vodka and tonic, please."

Yves poured a large dose of vodka over the ice, leaving hardly any room for the tonic. He passed me the glass.

"Cheers," he said, and we chinked our glasses together.

"Cheers." I took a large gulp, pure vodka with a light splash of tonic.

"Sit down over there. That one's his seat," he said. I sat down on the sofa.

Yves and I drank a couple of drinks and he gave me some insights into living in France. About half an hour passed, when Yves heard a noise coming from downstairs.

"He's coming," he said quietly.

I could smell Adam before I could see him, as a pungent aftershave wafted up the stairs. He slowly clambered up, pulling himself up with each step. Finally, he floated into the long room and walked over to his chair. He was dressed in white trousers and white loafers with no socks. His bright pink shirt was open past his chest and fitted his torso tightly. It was topped off with a pink cashmere jumper draped over thin shoulders. He sat down in the chair surrounded by two tables, with a reading lamp, five ash trays and a collection of lighters and packets of cigarettes, all within the radius of his outstretched arm.

"I'm here now. I told you I wouldn't be long," Adam said proudly. "I kept my word, like a good boy. I'm chuffed with myself! I don't think I've spent such a short time in the bath in my whole life!" He laughed and Yves chuckled.

"Someone's used up a bottle of aftershave to make themselves smell nice," Yves said sarcastically.

"I adore vintage l'eau de Cologne," Adam replied, his tone serious. "I love the romance. I love how they tell a story and evoke memories. I love how they develop and unfold on my skin. Only a handful of modern perfumes can make me feel the way this one does. It all boils down to one's personal taste, of course."

He sighed contentedly.

"I'm in normal wear now," he added with pride, "and all clean, all over, I'll have you know."

He leant towards me, dipping his hand in an effeminate gesture, like he was bouncing a basketball to me. He pulled his trousers upwards and fell back into his chair, his little carcass enveloped by lush cushions.

"Right man, let's have a little drinkies!" he said. Turning to me he asked, "Now, what about this house you are going to buy. Do I know it, Yves?"

"Yes," replied Yves, "it's the house on the corner diagonally across from your favourite little café in Villers."

"I love that little café, and the little shop next to it," replied Adam. "They sell cigarettes, too. What else do you need in life, for fuck's sake?"

"There's also a campsite in the village," said Yves. "Adam, remember when you drove into the campsite, literally!" Yves turned towards the bar and filled a glass with ice. He fixed Adam's drink and handed it to him.

"They used to have a restaurant and we used to go there a lot," continued Yves. "They had a great barbecue, big steaks, sausages, as much as you could eat, and as much wine as you could drink for a ridiculous fixed price. Anyway, he gets the hump for some reason, snatches the car keys, and storms off to the car park. He was going to leave me there." He looked over to Adam.

"He must have said something to piss me off," said Adam.

"Probably, it's always my fault," said Yves. "So he goes out to the car, it's an automatic. He starts the car and it shoots forward and smashes into the restaurant. Thankfully, he drove into the tables and chairs that weren't being used. It was the end of the evening, and the restaurant had cleared out. The car smashed through the thin wooden cladding."

"You should shut up next time," heckled Adam.

"I had to pay to have it all rebuilt," Yves added.

They were a double act. Yves was the reasonable, serious, deadpan one – the stooge. Adam was the funny man. A dry-witted trilingual comic with a fondness for unorthodox language.

"Lovely house you have. How many bedrooms?" I asked.

"We've got six bedrooms, four with en suite bathrooms and two toilets," said Adam. "The French people that come here think we're crazy with all the bathrooms and toilets as there's only the two of us. That's because they didn't even think of putting in a fucking toilet in the Palace of Versailles, dirty fukkas! Not even a bathroom, for Gaaaawd's sake, only the French! They really are peasants. We visited Versailles not too long ago," he went on. "The last time we went to Paaaaaaaaaarissssssssss," turning a five-letter word into a twenty-letter one.

"Get me another drink, Yves," Adam ordered. "I'm in the mood tonight. I think it's going to be a late one."

POSTMAN JACQUES

The heat gun, also known as a builder's hairdryer, bubbled the heavy lead-based paint as I peeled it away from the wooden frame with a scraper.

The framing housed two doors that led to small, damp rooms with rotten wooden floors. The doorpost divided the wall in half. I was transforming one room into a bathroom with an inside toilet and the other into a storage room, as there weren't any cupboards or storage space in the kitchen.

The table and four chairs stood in the middle of the room and took up most of it. I had kept everything in the same place ever since I'd bought the house and moved in. The table and chairs were made of wood of a certain age. When you sat down on the weaved raffia seats, the frames creaked and told a story of many years of use.

I had also inherited a small selection of oddly shaped glasses, some in forms and shapes I had never seen before, shot glasses advertising drinks that no longer existed. They had all belonged to the old man who lived in the house before. He died and left it all to his family. The only thing they took with them was the large, wooden stove with an oven, and a reservoir to heat water. The space where it once stood in the fireplace was now empty.

I heard the unmistakable sound of the metal gate. It was better than a doorbell. The rusty metal bar had to be yanked with a firm pull, which resulted in a loud 'clunk' that resonated through the hollow tubing.

The old square letterbox had served as a bird box. The first time I opened it, I found an angry starling shouting at me to shut the door. I waited for them to move on before I cleaned it out and gave it a fresh coat of black paint. I sanded and painted the gates at the same time.

"Hello, hello, *bonjour*," called a voice. "Hello, hello, is there somebody about?"

I could hear someone crunching on the small, white stones of gravel in the courtyard, the second 'doorbell'. I put down the scraper and the heat gun on the stepladder. The smell of the burnt paint was repugnant. I jumped from the step onto the ground and pulled my safety goggles up on to my forehead.

The front door split in two, like a stable door. The top half was open and bottom part closed. A chubby round face, with a large hat perched on top, was peering above the lower door. It was *Monsieur Le Facteur*.

"The postman always says 'hello' twice," I said. "*Bonjour Ferdinand, comment ça va, la forme?*" We shook hands. His jacket was so tight he couldn't move his arms higher than forty-five degrees.

"*Ça va?*" he replied. "*La Poste est toujours là, depuis 1477. The Post Office is always here, since 1477, monsieur.* Invented by King Louis XI to transport royal messages, it was only in 1576 we were allowed to carry the mail of private citizens," he said proudly.

"I knew it was old, but I didn't know it was that old," I said.

"I always imagined it was founded at the time of the revolution, but what do I know."

"A rural service was set up in 1829. Army officers operated the collection and delivery of the mail back then." Ferdinand gathered his breath. "Fifty years later, in 1879, two administrations, the Post and the Telegraph, were merged to form the Post Office and Telegraph and Telephone, the PTT. There were twenty-three thousand two hundred and twenty-nine rural and local postmen in France on the eve of the First World War." He beamed a proud smile. He was a tiny, quick-talking, Post Office encyclopaedia.

Ferdinand was short and as round as a globe, with a cherry red balloon of a face; a mixture of Danny Devito and Postman Pat. He was always impeccably dressed in his regulation blue uniform and donned his oversized hat that made him feel taller. His blue jacket was too tight and the material stretched over his inflated waistline. His matching blue trousers hung nearly two inches above his ankles, and at the end of his tiny legs sprouted freshly polished black boots. His light blue shirt had a dark blue tie tightly tied and squeezed under his third chin, all topped off with puffy, purple cheeks.

He was a kind, friendly and admirable country postman who served Villers-sur-Authie, and the surrounding villages, in the heart of the Picard countryside.

During one of our chitchats, Ferdinand told me he had the honour of being the third generation of his family to be a postman. If I was at home, he delivered my letters directly into my hand. He was always punctual, come rain or shine, six days a week.

He told me he started his career doing his rounds in the village on foot. The van would stop and he would be kicked out with the bundles of mail at the limit of the village by the gates of a large château. The château is hidden from the road, behind a large mound called Rabbit Hill.

After a while, they gave him a clunky bicycle, which made life easier. Then he was promoted, and presented with a motorbike, but he skidded on black ice and broke his arm. Recently, he had traded it in for a flashy new yellow Citroën van. He was now driving around the countryside in pure luxury. It was a lot quicker and, during the winter months, the heater warmed his feet.

He carried his satchel around his neck at all times. It contained stamps, money, and registered letters. He did not even take it off to drive. The ordinary letters and parcels stayed in the van. He always made sure to lock it before coming into the house. Not that there was any danger of anybody stealing it, as there was nobody around.

The length of his round didn't depend on how many letters there were to be delivered, but how many people would offer him a little drink. Most of the elderly people didn't get to see many people and the postman was a ray of sunlight through the dark grey Picard skies. It was all part of his personalised service.

I grabbed a cigarette from the box on the table and stuck it in my mouth.

"I have something for you, a registered letter, you have to sign for it," he said, beckoning me over to him. I sensed he was waiting for an invitation to come in.

"Come in, come in," I said, looking at the mess on the kitchen table. Ferdinand pushed down on the door handle and kicked the lower door with his foot.

"I know how to open that door, the old technique," he said and stepped into the room. The door had swelled over the years and stuck on the floor tiles. It needed sanding down, yet another thing on the to-do list, which was getting longer by the day. I pushed the pile of tools to one side and, with my arm, I swept the dry paint that had landed on the table onto the floor. I raced over to the sink and placed in it the plate and glass from last night's meal. With a wet cloth, I wiped down the cleared half of the table.

"Excuse the mess," I said sheepishly.

"Don't worry about it," Ferdinand said smiling, his cheeks puffed out on his jovial face. He opened his leather satchel. The strap had stretch marks from the constant use and the leather was worn by the movement of him opening the flap. He pulled out the letter and a pen.

"Sign here," he said, turning it over, "and here," holding the top copy down. I signed in both boxes and he tore his copy off and put it in the satchel. I turned the letter over and saw it was from France Télécom. They were chasing me for payment of last month's bill. I filed the letter with the pile of scrapers, pliers, screwdrivers, and hammers.

"Would you like a coffee?" I enquired naively. He looked at me with an expression as if I had insulted his entire family.

"*Café, non, non, non.* It's too late for a coffee. I have one at the house before I leave home. I start work at six o'clock. I have another one at the Post Office when we sort the letters out for delivery. It's now nearer the time for an aperitif," he affirmed. He cheekily grinned at me and continued, "Have you got something else?"

It was only ten fifteen in the morning. I thought about what I had to drink and went over to the fridge. The fridge had been left by the sellers. The large metal box, a 1960s Frigidaire, had a solid metal lever that you pulled on to open. The glass above the white plastic salad tray at the bottom reflected the green bottles piled inside it. At least they were the same colour as a lettuce! There wasn't much else in the fridge. One bottle of rosé wine, some salted butter from Brittany, horseradish sauce, a jar of Chivers Olde English marmalade, HP sauce, Heinz ketchup, mint sauce, jars of Patak's cook-in curry sauces, some whole grain mustard, a carton of milk, and a bottle of cooking wine that had been in the fridge for the past two weeks, ever since I had used it in a sauce. A Camembert had started to turn and I backed away to avoid the pungent smell.

"Beer?" I asked him.

"*Non, du vin, as-tu du vin?*" he asked.

"I have some rosé. It's chilled." I turned my head in his direction with my hand propped against the top of the fridge.

"*Parfait, un rosé, allez,*" he grinned.

I pulled the bottle from the fridge and placed it on the table. I moved to the sink and took two glasses from the draining board. I turned on the tap and rinsed them under the water to remove the thin film of dust that covered everything. I flicked off the excess water and returned to the table. The corkscrew was in its usual place on the table.

I pulled the cork from bottle.

"Ah, I love that sound," said the postman with a wry smile.

I poured the wine into the two glasses and passed him one.

"These are the same glasses Éric, the old man who lived here before you, used to use for drinking his wine," said Ferdinand. "That's funny you should use them, too."

"They're not matching glasses, but they are the ideal size," I said. "I love them. I'll treat them with care."

"*Santé,*" we said in unison and raised our glasses; they met with a chiming 'ping'. We swigged our drinks.

"Nicely chilled, *c'est bon ça,*" said the postman. "Where's it come from?" He turned the bottle round to look at the label. "A Côtes du Roussillon, from the region near Perpignan. I like it down there, I actually went on holiday there last year. My wife and I visited the Cathar castles in the Corbières region. We also went to Carcassonne, *c'est fantastique*. The medieval castle is still standing. It's never been attacked, so it's still as it was since in the fourteenth century. We ate fresh anchovies in Collioure with a delightful rosé from Banyuls. The vines are perched above the village on steep hills. I don't know how they manage to pick those grapes. You have to watch your step or you'll slide down the hill into the sea." He was not short of words.

"I've never been there," I replied. "I follow what the Perpignan Rugby team does, though. They play in the same colours as Lens football team, my friend told me," I added, not without pride.

"*Oui, Les Sang et Or* (Blood and Gold), that's my team. I go regularly when they're playing at home." Ferdinand stopped and took another large gulp, nearly finishing his glass. "You should go there and see a game. It's the closest ambiance you will find to any British football match. The fans sing and shout loudly, no other club in France is like it."

I saw that his glass was nearly empty.

"Another?" I asked, stretching for the bottle.

"*Oui, allez*, then I have to finish my round before I'm too..." He moved his hand up to the end of his nose and clenched his fingers shut, then turned his hand making the sound a cappuccino machine makes as it froths the milk. "*Quassshhhhh.*"

I sat back down. We again raised our glasses and delicately brought them together.

"You know," said Ferdinand, "those people, the workers in the coal mines in the north? They are brave, honourable people. It's sad, but most of the mines are now closed or are being shut down. That means there's a lot of unemployment in the area." He looked at me and hunched his shoulders up to his ears. "*C'est la vie,*" he said with a glum look.

He took another sip from his freshly charged glass and looked about at the work I was doing.

"Me, too," he continued. "I'm building a house, from start to the finish. I'm doing everything myself, building the walls, the roof, adding the tiles. I've spent over ten years so far and it's far from finished. I only get the weekends and I like to go away on holiday in the summer, and visit my beautiful country. I'm not Ferdinand Cheval, but that's why they call me 'Ferdinand'. My real name is Jacques, Jacques Leconte, *parce que mon compte est bon*, (because my account is good). I have been doing this round for the last fifteen years. I have never missed a day, only when it's been impossible to drive the car, either too icy or too much snow. We're not prepared for that here. But that's not my fault, that's the fault of the DDE. They have to make sure that the roads are passable. They have to grit the roads, otherwise we're not allowed to go out and deliver our letters." He lifted his glass, I reached for mine and we raised them in the air for a toast.

"To Ferdinand," he said loudly.

"Who is Ferdinand?" I asked. "Why do they all call you Ferdinand?" Everybody in the village referred to him as 'Ferdinand the postman'. I had assumed his name was Ferdinand.

"You have never heard of Ferdinand Cheval?" he asked. I shook my head.

"He was born in 1836," he said. "He was a postman, like me, similar, but he wasn't so..." Ferdinand tapped his large, plump belly. "Big boned." He laughed and I laughed with him. "The great Ferdinand is a national treasure, the greatest postman France ever had. He spent thirty-three years of his life building *Le Palais Idéal* (The Ideal Palace) in Hauterives, in the Drôme department. Can you imagine that? Thirty-three years of his life." He looked at me sternly.

"I hope it doesn't take me thirty-three years to finish this place," I said.

"It will if you spend all day drinking wine," Ferdinand said, lifting his glass to his lips. "It is incredible, really. The Palace is regarded as an extraordinary example of naïve architecture. He also made sculptures, statues, gargoyles; it's like a Hindu temple. I went to see it, we took our summer holiday down there three, maybe four years ago. We like to visit the area when we go somewhere," he said brazenly.

"I've never heard of him," I replied. I felt ignorant. I knew about Charles de Gaulle and Napoleon, but of France's number one builder-come-postman, I knew nothing.

"Ferdinand Cheval was born in a small village called Charmes-sur-l'Herbasse, not far from Valence," explained Ferdinand. "He grew up in Châteauneuf-de-Galaure, a bigger town about fifteen kilometres away. He left school at the age of thirteen to become a baker's apprentice, but he left and became a postman." He delivered his tale in meticulous detail.

"Why did he start to build it in the first place?" I asked.

"He got the idea when he was out walking, probably on his round. Of course, no bikes and cars back then." I grabbed another cigarette and lit it as I listened to Ferdinand. "He was running along a track when he snagged his foot, or twisted his ankle on a stone that was sticking out of the ground, and he fell. I personally think he must have bumped his head when he fell," he laughed. "He thought about things and wanted to know what was the cause of him falling over or tripping. He wanted to know why things happen to us. He was like a sort of philosopher.

"Then, one night he had a dream about building a palace, or a castle. Apparently, so the story goes, he didn't tell anyone about the dream for fear of being ridiculed by people and being taken for a *fou* (madman)." Ferdinand lifted his arm and brought his hand up to the side of his head. He opened and closed his fingers in a half arch in quick succession.

He leant forward and grabbed hold of the bottle of wine. "*Puis-je*, can I?"

He had already poured the wine into the glass and filled it to the top before I could reply, "*Oui, bien sûr.*"

"About, fifteen or so years later," continued Ferdinand, "when he had almost forgotten about his dream, his foot started to hurt and that jogged his memory, and reminded him of the dream. He went back and found the unusually shaped stone that he had tripped on. He put it in his pocket. The next day, he got up and went back to the same place and found more weird-shaped stones, even more beautiful than the first one. He started going back every day and gathering more stones. He began building in April 1879." Ferdinand paused to take a sip of his wine. "Later, he bought a wheelbarrow so he could work quicker. Old Ferdinand worked his balls off." He smirked. "He really worked hard, every day, back and forth with his wheelbarrow, shovelling stones, wheeling stones, pouring stones... he was a rolling stone, literally," he chuckled.

"Just him on his own?" I enquired.

"Yes, just him alone. He often worked into the night, using an oil lamp. It's a truly crazy building, like I said. I think he banged his head really hard when he fell over."

"What type of architecture is it? What does it look like?" I moved my boot onto the wooden crossbar of the chair.

"Ah, it's a mish-mash of many types and styles of architecture," said Ferdinand. "He did whatever came into his head. I don't think he had any plans. He just built bits and kept adding to it. He got his ideas and inspirations from Christianity, Hinduism. I'm sure Gaudi inspired him, too, with some Gothic emblems thrown in for good measure. He stuck the stones together with lime mortar and cement. He did a good job, because it's still standing today. He wanted to be buried in it, but that is illegal in France," he said seriously.

"Where is he buried then?" I asked.

"When he was told he couldn't be buried in it, he spent the next eight years building a mausoleum for himself in the village cemetery in Hauterives. He died on the nineteenth of August

1924, about a year after he'd finished building it. He's buried there, *et voila!*"

Ferdinand looked at his watch without really looking at it. He knew what time it was. He was more regulated than time itself. He knew every second of the time it took him to do his round. He pushed his chair back and stood up.

"I have to get going," he said.

I looked at the bottle on the table. There was enough for two glasses left inside.

"Let's finish it, it's bad luck to leave it," I said.

"*Non, non, non,*" he hesitated, then corrected himself. "OK, *allez,* quickly," he said.

I poured the last of the wine equally into the two glasses. Ferdinand tilted his head backwards to a nearly horizontal position as he lifted the glass to his mouth with precision, and the wine slid down his throat in one large swig. He placed the glass delicately on the table.

"Just before he died, Ferdinand began to receive some recognition from people like André Breton and Pablo Picasso," he added. "In 1969, André Malraux, the Minister of Culture, declared the Palace a cultural landmark. It's officially protected, which is good. Then, in 1986, we, the Post Office, put him on a stamp, *fantastique non?* What an honour for a postman, to have your face on a stamp. Maybe they'll put me on one, one day." He laughed and his whole body vibrated.

"They should, you would look great on a stamp. Stamps with your local postman's face on them, what a great idea," I said.

"You know Picasso was short, some of the greatest people on earth have not been tall as we imagine them to be. You'd be surprised how many short people have left their mark on world history." Ferdinand had done his research on vertically challenged superheroes. "Picasso, for example, he's probably the most popular painter of all time. He was just five feet four inches tall. That's the same height as me."

I looked at Ferdinand; his strawberry red face glowed like the sun.

"His paintings and sculptures are masterpieces and sell for millions of dollars. Napoleon Bonaparte was only five feet six inches, so was Joseph Stalin. Genghis Khan, who consolidated the largest empire in history, was only just five feet one inch tall – a midget. That didn't stop him from being one of the best commanders and also a ferocious warrior, scared of nothing." Ferdinand lifted his arm in the air to express his excitement.

My general knowledge just expanded to include the heights of the world's smallest dictators.

"Yuri Gagarin, the famous Russian astronaut, the first person to travel into space and orbit the earth, was only five feet two inches tall. Mahatma Gandhi," he said suddenly, beaming a broad smile.

Suddenly, I could see Ben Kingsley standing before me in my kitchen, dressed in only a sheet with his little round John Lennon glasses.

"He's known as the founding Father of the Indian Nation," Ferdinand went on. "He fought and won independence from your country, those British colonisers. He was just five feet three inches. Francois-Marie Arouet, the famous French writer and philosopher, otherwise known as Voltaire – his witty and humorous works are classics – he was smaller than me," he declared. "He was only five feet three inches. Small in stature but big in ideology, the advocate for civil liberties, he opened up people's way of thinking."

Ferdinand stood at the door and stepped through it, and down onto the cement step.

"Merci, for the history lesson, Ferdinand. Take some gravel

for your house," I suggested as he crunched his way to the barrier.

I turned back into the house and grabbed the two glasses from the table and placed them in the sink. My head was full of images of what I imagined the famous postman's palace looked like. I thought about what a crazy guy he must have been. There was a loud tap on the shutter. I turned around.

"It's me again," said Ferdinand standing at the door.

"I've only got beer if you need another drink," I said.

"I wanted to tell you something. I've wanted to tell you for a long time, but I've never had time, or it was never the moment." He was excited and agitated at the same time. He walked back into the kitchen and stood by the wooden door frames that had been half stripped of paint.

"You see this mark here on the wood," he said pointing with his chubby sausage-like finger. "Here, in the middle."

I noticed a horizontal groove on the architrave between the two doors.

"I was the first person to find him. He was sitting on his chair, balancing against the wall. The same one you were sitting on when we had a drink," Ferdinand said. "I always stopped off to *boire un coup* (have a drink) with him. Every day I would say hello, even if I didn't have any mail for him." He moved his arms around, almost flapping them like he was preparing to launch himself. "I found him in his favourite position, he always sat like this. His head against the wall, sitting up straight, perfectly balanced." He stopped and composed himself. "He was always pleased to see me." His memories were flooding back to him and tears welled up in his eyes. "I found him on that chair," he repeated. "I was the first person to find him, like this." He took hold of the chair and turned it upside down to show me the bottom of the legs. "You see, it's worn away at the bottom, you see – at an angle?"

"Yes," I said. The two rear legs of the chair were worn down. He put the chair into position and grabbed my arm and manoeuvred me onto the chair. I sat down and pushed back with my feet; the chair moved backwards and came to a stop against the wall. The chair balanced perfectly, the top of the chair nestled in its groove like a hand in a glove.

"He always balanced in that chair, in that exact position," Ferdinand continued, slightly choked up with emotion. "He was a nice man, he won't come back to haunt you, don't worry about that. I just wanted to tell you. *Bonne chance, au revoir.*"

He turned on his heels and retraced his footsteps towards the door and then onwards to the gate. He closed it behind him.

I started to sing.

"*Stop, oh yeh, wait a minute Mr Postman, wait, wait Mr Postman...*" I hummed the rest of the song and waved to Ferdinand as he climbed into the driver's seat of his canary-yellow van. I watched him drive off down the road to give his next history lesson and sip another glass of grape juice.

I opened the fridge door, took out one of the cold green bottles and twisted the cap.

PICCARDEE TENNESSEE

"Hi, it's Jeremy," said the voice on the phone. "I'm stuck in Dover, at the port. We're all waiting to get on the next bloody boat to Boulogne, but as you probably know the French are at it again. Their national sport of striking is fucking everything up for everyone."

"Yeah, I heard about it on the radio this morning," I said.

"No boats are getting into any of the French ports. I'm thinking of trying to go to Zeebrugge in Belgium then driving down, but I really have no idea what to do. Listen, I told you about my good friend from America, Frank? Can you do me a favour? He landed in Paris yesterday and is catching the train. He arrives around four o'clock this afternoon. I can't remember exactly what time, maybe fifteen or twenty minutes before. Could you pick him up and let him stay at your place tonight, or until I can get there?"

"Yeah, sure, no problem. What station is he getting off at? Noyelles-sur-Mer or Rue?" I asked.

"Ru..." and the phone cut off.

I put down the receiver and looked at the old clock above the fireplace in the kitchen. It was now quarter past two. The only way to find out the times of the trains was to go down to the station and ask.

I was covered in dust from sanding the old beams in the living room. Standing on a ladder, having lead-based paint fall and stick to my face, was the norm in my new life.

I took a shower and put on clean clothes.

I parked in the empty station car park, directly in front of the ticket office. I walked towards the old building and looked up at the date on the façade of the building: 1847. Nearly a hundred and fifty years of service. The large minute hand clicked forward, making it three thirty-four. I pushed on the heavy wooden doors and stepped into the foyer.

Didier shot out of the little door to the side of the ticket booth and scampered across the polished tiles. Skidding to a stop, he grabbed hold of the metal door handles and pulled the door open. He burst through the door and ran down the platform with a square table tennis bat in his hand. His tie flew in the air over his shoulder as he ran along the platform.

I could feel the building tremble as a large locomotive rumbled past the station. It slowed and eventually stopped. The compressed air from the brakes made a sound as if it was a dragon breathing fire from its nostrils. I walked onto the platform and watched vigilantly as people slowly got down from the train and meandered towards the open gate on the platform. It led directly to the parking area. Cars drove up in succession, stopped for a second, and passengers climbed in, all with the speed and precision of a Formula One pit crew.

I looked at the notice board and saw that it was the train from Amiens, not the direct train from Paris. I didn't bother looking at the rest of the people on the platform. Didier looked down the long platform and blew his whistle. He waved his ping-pong bat in the air from side to side frantically. He blew another loud whistle and the train slowly rolled forward, the wheels gripping the damp tracks. He waved to the ticket inspector on the train as the carriage clattered down the platform in the direction of Rang-du-Fliers, Le Touquet, Boulogne – terminating at Calais in the north.

Didier walked nimbly towards me, and smiled a broad, drunken grin. He was a professional, and took his drinking seriously. He'd invited me into his office on a few occasions while I was waiting for a train. There, he had proudly shown me his mini bar. The small fridge was full of little green bottles of beer, and a bottle of Pastis was hidden in the draw of his desk.

He took off his hat and we shook hands. I could see in his eyes that he had been 'hard at work' in between the infrequent trains.

"*Ça va?*" he asked. "Are you waiting for someone?"

"Yes, I am," I replied. "When does the direct train from Paris arrive, the next one?" He walked off towards his office and I followed.

"At 19.39 tonight," Didier said as we walked. "That was the 14.47 from Amiens, the next train stopping here from Amiens is in three hours, 18.35." He knew his train times.

Another three hours to wait. Jeremy had said the direct train was at three forty-fiveish!

Didier stopped suddenly.

"Wah, check that out. It's Bruce Willis, *regarde le, là-bas,*" Didier insisted, tapping my arm with his hand. "John McClane, *c'est lui,* it's him, look!" Didier pointed with his hand enthusiastically.

I could only see the silhouette of a large, bald-headed man wearing a rucksack on his back. A long, military-style duffle bag lay by his feet. He definitely wasn't from around here.

Jeremy had shown me pictures of Frank. All the photos were scenes of him camping, sipping moonshine around campfires, with either a fishing rod, or a gun in his hand. I had heard wild stories of their crazy exploits in the savage wilderness of the Georgia-Tennessee border country in the Appalachian Mountains

I approached the man who was standing at the little gate, looking out onto the car park, getting his bearings.

"Frank? Hi," I said, hesitantly, although I was sure it was him.

"Yes, sir," he replied with a deep southern drawl. We shook hands.

"I'm Max. Jeremy is stuck in Dover, they are striking and all the boats are blocked from entering the ports in France. He's going to try and get here via Belgium, but it sounds like a nightmare. So, he asked me to pick you up, show you around and give you a bed. How was the trip?" I asked. "Can I help you with that bag?"

"Hi, Max. No man, I'm all good. OK, he's stuck there, damn."

Didier was hovering by my side. I could smell the vapours of alcohol as he moved his head closer to me. He put his oversized SNCF hat on his head, placed his ping-pong bat under his left arm and held it tightly down by his side. He saluted Frank with his right hand.

"Welcome to Rue, *Monsieur*," he said. Both Frank and I looked at each other, surprised. I lifted my eyebrows. This wasn't planned. Frank stood up straight and saluted him back.

"You look like John McClane. Bruce Willis, are you, er, is it you?" Didier asked Frank.

"That foul-mouthed, wisecracking, no-nonsense, itchy trigger finger, never-say-die maverick-spirited, yippee-ki-yay motherfucker! Yeh, I can handle that, thanks man." Frank smiled and tipped his head. "Fantastic man, I get the official SNCF VIP treatment! Thanks again, man," Frank added, tapping Didier on the arm.

"*C'est vrai*, wow. I'm going to tell everybody Bruce Willis came to Rue, merci," Didier said.

Frank bent down and picked up his bag.

"Well, I don't need to wait for the next train. Bye, Didier, see you soon," I said.

"See you in the café some time," he said and walked towards his office.

Frank and I walked towards the car.

"Great timing, thanks a lot," said Frank. "I arrived in Paris yesterday morning a bit jet lagged. When I saw everybody revved up for the day, that got me going. I had a coffee and a croissant and caught *Ze Metro* to the centre of Paris. I found my way to the Eiffel Tower, checked that out, then I had lunch in a little restaurant. I walked around a bit more and then I started to get tired. I saw a taxi rank, jumped in one and went back to the hotel and chilled out. I hung out near the hotel last night. In the morning, I walked around a bit more, but got a taxi over to the Gare du Nord earlier than I planned. I wanted to make sure I got the train, as Jeremy told me there are not too many trains a day. The taxi dropped me off outside. I strolled in through those big ol' doors and bought a ticket. The woman even spoke English with me. I showed her the name of the town, but hey, Rue is about the height of my vocabulary, so even I couldn't get that wrong. Boom, with the ticket in my hand she told me to run to platform five. I ran as fast as I could with my big bag, jumped on the train. The doors clunked shut and the dude blew his whistle, and the train pulled away. I changed in Amiens. Amazing, I looked out the window and checked out the countryside. Plenty of duck ponds, good fishing rivers and shooting round here, I can see."

We reached the car.

"Hop in," I said.

"Cool, what's this Euro-jet on wheels?" Frank looked at the white car, intrigued.

"An Alfa Romeo Sprint, Milan's finest. It's a front-wheel drive, modern-day Roman chariot – just don't look at the rust patches," I said.

The motor growled into life and we put on our seat belts. The engine purred as it turned over. I revved the engine.

"Can I?" Frank enquired, holding a packet of Dunhill International cigarettes in his hand.

"Sure can," I said. Checking for cars, I pushed the gear stick into first gear. The tyres gripped the wet surface and squealed as the car pulled forward to the exit. I slowed down for the slight bump of the kerb and the car roared down the road. Frank lit his cigarette.

"Do you want one?" he asked.

"Sure." He passed me a cigarette from the box. I put it in my mouth and pushed on the cigar lighter in the middle console. It clicked out of its slot and I lit up.

"Thanks for coming to pick me up," Frank said.

"No problem."

We drove through the countryside.

"I'm only going to hang here for a couple of days, if that's OK with you," said Frank. "I'm joining up with my girlfriend in Lyon. She's just started a job down there, moved over here about six weeks ago."

"That's fine with me," I said. "Hopefully, Jeremy will make it back in time to see you. I heard you're a cowboy?"

"Yes sir, but that's not really a job unless you're in Hollywood, the circus, or a rodeo," Frank replied. "I use horses to get around my cattle as I don't want to use a tractor. The weight of the machinery compacts the top soil, then the grass can't grow properly. The water can't seep into the soil, then it cracks and fucks up," he continued. "Grass-fed beef. It's not rocket science, that's what beef eat. Not steroids and all that crap they put in the feed these days. I've got chariots, too, chicken chariots that I drag behind the cattle. After a couple of days drying out, the chickens scratch and pick at the turds and break them down, looking for all the fly larvae inside. I give them water and have an electric fence to keep out the critters at night. We get a lot of foxes, coyotes, and raccoons round my way."

"Coyotes?" I said surprised. "They live near people – coyotes? The animal from the ACME trading company that always tried to catch Road Runner!"

"We get plenty of 'em round our way," Frank said assertively.

"Wow, cool."

"I was going duck hunting the other morning, and I bumped into this old guy who had served during the war. I told him I was going to France. He said, 'France! Have they rebuilt that place?' He told me this story about when he got sent over for the D-Day landings. He was just eighteen year's old when they called him up. They sent him to Chattanooga."

"On a choo-choo?"

"Funny you should say that, he did!" laughed Frank. "Caught the train from Knoxville, where he's from. They cut all his hair off and gave him an anti-lice scrubdown, a uniform and pair of boots. They asked what he did. He said he worked on the land and helped out at his uncle's gas station. Said he knew about mechanics, so they gave him a tank! They dropped him off on the beach in Normandy and he said they just destroyed everything in front of them in more a less a straight line all the way to Berlin. Then, about a month after the war was over, he was shipped back to the US. He was disbanded not long after that and returned to doing what he did before. Never been back since!"

"Are you from Knoxville?" I asked.

"I'm a Sparta man, due east of Knoxville and north of Chattanooga. I'm from the town named after the Ancient Greeks and learned scholars. It's a small hick town in 'Tennesseeeeeee'. America at its best, that's what we say there. It's the slogan for the State, we have it on the car licence plates."

"So, you're what's called a true hillbilly?"

"Not exactly. I got out. I lived in Atlanta. I've seen the lights, man. Lester Flatt of Flatt and Scruggs came from Sparta. His band The Foggy Mountain Boys played all the music and wrote the theme tune for the TV show, The Beverly Hill Billies. Sparta was way cooler in the music business back in the day, man. Lester Flatt, the Elvis of Bluegrass. Benny Martin, the Bluegrass musician who invented the eight-string fiddle. That instrument became the sound of all the great Bluegrass tunes. It's the forefather of every country tune ever made!"

I was interested. "Carry on, man," I said.

"Benny Martin was a member of The Grand Ole Opry and had his own show, The Benny Martin Show. Over the years, he performed and recorded with many different artists. He hired Colonel Tom Parker as his manager and worked as the opening act for some of the early Elvis Presley concerts. He's from Sparta," Frank continued. "It's right on the Calfkiller River, established in 1809 as a county seat for White County, which had been created way back in 1806. That's not old in Euro years, but we only got started in 1776. Sparta nearly became the capital of the state of Tennessee. They had a vote between Sparta and Nashville. Sparta only lost to Nashville by one vote coz a dude sold his vote for some moonshine. Imagine – it could have been the centre of the universe!"

"Where is Sparta from Nashville?" I asked.

"About an hour and a half's drive west from downtown Nashvegas."

"Nashvegas?" I asked, naively. "Is that near Nashville?"

"No man, that's what we call Nashville! What happens in Nashvegas stays in Nashvegas. Did you know that Tennessee has had more presidents than any other state? Sparta became a stop-off place and these dudes built The Rock House. It was like The Hard Rock Café, but like back in the day. Drinking, smoking, fighting and fuckin', that's the American way, baby! Everybody was wearing a gun or two on their hip, drinking moonshine and bad beer. Then, once everybody was feeling fiery, they'd start fighting over prostitutes till one of them shot another, or they both shot each other dead! Nothing's changed in America in one hundred and fifty glorious years. The land of the free, gotta stand your ground. The second amendment basically means that my gun's bigger than yours, or you better draw yours quicker than me or I'm shooting your ass dead, motherfucker."

Frank paused, laughing at his own humour.

"The first amendment means I can call you an arsehole while I shoot you," Frank exclaimed. "We don't like to make things too complicated. That's all you need to know about America! We kicked your asses outta there, along with the French, Spanish and the Mexicans. The Indians was another story. We either killed them, then stole their land, or we stole their land then killed them. Either way, we fucked them up. Then we killed all the wild buffalo to extinction."

"Shit," I said.

"That's what I said," Frank started to laugh. "There was this dude from Sparta called Erasmus Lee Gardenhire. Great name, huh? He was a well-respected politician and judge who served in the Confederate States Congress and Tennessee House of Representatives. Good ol' Erasmus, you don't meet too many Erasmuses these days."

I touched the brakes and changed down a gear as I guided the car round a sharp corner. I spotted Roger leaning against the gate of his large field. Roger was a lovely old boy who always had a *Gitanes* cigarette permanently stuck in the side of his mouth. His hips were bent to the side and he could hardly walk. He propped himself up, dragged his legs forward, then stopped to position the crutch in front of himself before moving his legs forward. He would then repeat the process. Progress was slow, but it allowed him to walk and see his horse, his faithful friend that he had worked with until he no longer could. He had never traded up for a tractor. The manure was the best compost for growing his tomatoes, courgettes, onions, potatoes, runner beans, lettuces, radishes, cucumbers, cauliflowers, and huge marrows. He had given me boxes of vegetables, and his chickens laid the best eggs I had ever tasted. He used to be completely self-sufficient. He now lived in the house opposite and was looked after by a neighbour since losing his wife.

I slowed the car so I didn't frighten him, and wound down the window.

"*Ça va,* Roger?" I enquired.

"*Ça va, merci, je me promène, mais je ne cours pas vite maintenant.* I'm going for a little walk, but I don't run that fast anymore," he said with a wry expression that broke into a toothless smile. He hadn't put his teeth in. I noticed the car behind us flashing its lights.

"I'll pull over," I said to Roger, and parked the car in the entrance of his house.

"Get out and meet this dude, Frank," I said, opening the door. "He only ever farmed with horses. He rode horses all his life. He hobbles out here once, or maybe twice, a day to check on his horse in the field. Come and say hello to a real French peasant."

We walked over to where Roger was standing by the gate. We all shook his hands. Roger was calling out to the French Ardennais working horse, which was walking up the field at a brisk pace.

"I used to use four of them, sometimes five, for all the farm work, ploughing, cultivating, and haying," said Roger. "In the winter months, I would log with them in the forest. I would pull fifty cords or more of oak, or whatever they were chopping down that season. I had a contract with the château over there behind those trees." He pointed in the direction of the large château partly hidden behind tall trees.

"Draught horses have held on well in this area," he continued. "They're good for our poor soil, long winters, and the muddy land."

The huge Ardennais sauntered towards us and eventually arrived at where we were standing. He bowed his head and blew through his nose as he greeted Roger. The horse was happy to see Roger and he, likewise, was pleased to see the horse. Roger tapped the big horse on its neck and the horse dipped its head down in acknowledgement. Roger was a little man, bent over. His worn beret sat on the top of his head, and he wore a dark blue cardigan with a paper handkerchief sticking out of the pocket. We took turns to pat the horse.

"He's a handsome beast, isn't he?" I said to Frank.

"Yeh, he's beautiful. He must be sixteen, maybe eighteen hands. What's his name?" Frank asked, and I translated.

"Elveez," said Roger smiling.

"Elvis!" Frank laughed out loud. "That's so funny."

Roger chuckled too when he saw that it made Frank laugh.

He wiggled his hips from side. His lips wrapped around his toothless gums holding his cigarette, its wet end stuck to the corner of his mouth like glue. He started to hum the song 'Jail House Rock'.

"Went to a party at the county jail," Frank sang the first line of the song. "What breed of horse is he? He's really handsome. He's a big boy."

"*Oui*, he's officially called a Northern Draught horse," said

Roger. "Back in 1965, they changed the name of the breed to Northern Ardennais. They were crossed with Belgian Draught horses and eventually became known as their own distinct breed. They are more robust and have a brighter step," he added with authority. "They are one of the oldest breeds of horse in France and thought to be a direct descendant of the smaller Solutré horse. The French Ardennais has been used in war, from the Roman days of Julius Caesar through to Napoleon," Roger continued. I translated as best as I could.

"You can see the power in him. Look at you," Frank said, caressing the monstrous beast. The horse rubbed himself against the gate.

"Sadly, today, the demand for draught horses in France is primarily for meat production," Roger said. "But some small farmers still use them to work the land. Not many, though."

"How big is he?" Frank asked.

"They have an average height of fifteen to fifteen and half hands. He's slightly bigger and nearer sixteen," Roger said.

"What a great physique," Frank said. "Look at his head – it's small for such a big horse. His eyes are lively and bright." Frank admired the graceful animal. "Look at his muscular neck. He's well muscled. Is this the only colour they come in?"

"The traditional colours are chestnut, like him, as well as bay and roan," Roger replied. "Do you have horses, then?" he asked.

"*Il est American*," I said to Roger. "He's from Tennessee, not far from Graceland, chez Elvis, in Memphis," I continued. "He has horses, he's a cowboy and raises beef, grass fed. He likes your horse."

"Chez Elvis, *c'est chez moi*," said Frank in his limited French. I did my impression of lassoing a calf.

"A cowboy, *un vrai*, a real one? We have many breeds here in France." Roger turned his head and looked at Frank, adjusting his beret as he continued. "There's a breed that comes from around here, just up the road, but I have never had one." Roger turned his head from side to side. "They're good for riding, but I'm too old for all that now. Just up the road there." He pointed with his cane while holding onto the gate. "Henson, you should take him to see them while he's here. The stables are in the Marquenterre, in the marshlands of the Bay of Somme. You can go for a nice walk through the dunes. See some rare birds, too."

"Really? There's a breed from around here? I didn't know that," Frank said surprised.

"Yeah, Henson," replied Roger. "They are a really handsome, rustic-looking breed that was created pretty recently in the late 1970s."

"Where does the Henson breed come from, Roger?" I asked.

"Ah, the breed is a cross between Norwegian Fjord ponies and a wide variety of saddle horses. They get their dun colouring and white mane from the Fjord horses," he said.

"I've been to the stables in the Marquenterre a number of times," I said. "I watched them play their version of handball, which is like basketball on horseback in a small, confined paddock. It's really dangerous. They're sturdy, robust horses, light and very agile."

"How big are they?" Frank asked Roger.

"They have an average height of fifteen to fifteen and a half hands, an average size head with a slight concave profile. The eyes are lined with black, like ladies' eye liner," Roger chuckled. He was in his element and his love for horses was evident. Roger stroked his horse as it nibbled at his greasy beret. He liked to give out his knowledge and we listened with interest. Roger tapped the neck of his horse again.

"The Hensons have a fairly large base, then it tapers at the top," he continued. "They have strong shoulders, and short, straight legs with strong joints. That's why they're good to play that crazy sport they do up there. Medieval jousting with a leather ball with handles." Roger flipped his hand in a half-circle movement. "They're *fou*, someone will get really hurt one day. I know the guy that started the sport here. I had land around where they have their stables, anyway." He looked at Frank and eyed him up and down.

"A cowboy, you say?" He looked up at Frank, towering over his little frame. "Does he know about the horses down in the Camargue in the south of France?"

"Have you heard of that breed, Frank?" I enquired for Roger.

"They live in the wildness," said Roger. "It's a beautiful horse, one of the oldest horse breeds on the planet."

"Yeah, I've heard about that one." Frank nodded his head in confirmation.

"Yeah man, you should go down there one day, you'd love it," I said. "The area is amazing and the horses are wild. The marshland is right on the Mediterranean. It's where the gypsies go. The ancestors of the Carmargue horse date back to prehistoric times. They found ancient cave paintings of the horses in southern France. They've been left to let nature take its course for the last hundred thousand years or so, till man came along."

"Yep, we just turned up at the party yesterday! Them *critters* been stompin' around on this planet way before we decided to crawl out from under a stone somewhere in Africa!" Frank said.

Roger changed the subject. "I'll tell him about the gypsy ceremony at Saintes-Maries-de-la Mer in the Camargue." Roger steadied himself and lifted his arm as high as he could. "Every year the gypsies go on a pilgrimage there, it's a religious event. It takes place on the twenty-fourth and twenty-fifth of May. They take the statue of Sara la noire," he said, staring Frank in the eye.

"The statue is black, black as the ace of spades. They carry it from the church down to the sea." Roger cackled. I finished translating and we both laughed with him.

"Really? They should bring it over to America," said Frank. "The church would make a fortune from people paying come to see it. Damn!"

"What's he doing over here? Visiting the war graves?" Roger enquired.

"No," I replied, "he's just come up for a couple of days, before going to Lyon to see his girlfriend who works there."

"*Mademoiselle est jolie?*" Roger's face lit up.

"Is your girl pretty, Frank? Roger wants to know."

"She's Venus with arms," Frank tittered.

"*Ah bon, c'est bien ça,* tack, tack, tack." Roger pumped his little fist back and forth quickly. He hadn't lost his mojo.

"Before we go, tell Frank your story with the horse, Roger," I said. "When you were ill and your wife had to take the horse to the fields." Roger put his hand up to his ear. He didn't hear my question. I spoke more slowly for him.

"The horse, when your wife didn't know why it took so long for you to get back from the fields," I said again. He understood.

"Listen to this, Frank," I said.

"One frozen morning," began Roger, "while I was getting the horse ready to go to work in the fields on the outskirts of the village, I slipped on black ice and twisted my ankle. I couldn't put any weight on it and had to put it up and rest it. My wife made a dressing and sat me in the chair in front of the fire. She ordered me to rest or there would be trouble. She knew what I'm like, I can't sit down. Look at me now, I can hardly walk, but I always try to go for a walk, get out, get some fresh air."

A sad air came over him as he thought about his beloved wife. "She said she would take the horse to the fields and work the land. The horse was tacked up and I would see her at lunchtime. She left and headed to the fields. When she came back at lunchtime, she stormed into the house. She was mad, ranting and shouting. I was sleeping in front of the fire. I'd had a few." Roger put his thumb up to his lips like a baby sucking on a dummy. He continued with vigour.

"So, she rudely wakes me up, screaming. I didn't understand what was going on. She was angry and I was confused. I asked her what the matter was. She said that, on the way to the fields, she was passing the café and the horse veered to the right and promptly stopped in front of the café. It would not move for half an hour. The horse eventually responded to her commands and she made it out to the field. So, on her way back at midday, she's walking past the café again and the same thing happens. The horse veered towards the café and promptly refused to go any further for another half an hour, because I always stopped for a little drink. She left in the afternoon and the horse did the same thing, so she came back by the long detour in the evening. She was so furious with me after learning that I was spending so much time in the café." We all exploded into laughter.

Roger started to move in the direction of the house. "I'm going in, that's enough for me. *Allez, au revoir*," he said.

"*Au revoir* Roger, *à bientôt*."

"Goodbye, Roger. Thanks for the history lesson on horses, very interesting," Frank said and shook his hand. Roger raised his beret and turned to me with a serious look on his face. He grabbed my jacket with his free hand.

"Take him to see the big war cemetery at Étaples. He will be very impressed. They keep it very tidy and clean," Roger said to me, "but I haven't been past there in years. Many Americans, Canadians and English like you came here to fight, to liberate us from those dirty Germans." He turned to Frank.

"*Merci*, thank you America," Roger said sincerely. I translated for Frank as Roger brought his hand up and saluted. Frank saluted back.

"*C'est bon*," said Frank with a broad smile. Roger looked up at Frank and gave him a toothless smile back.

We turned and walked over to the car. I saw Roger waving his arm in the air in the rear-view mirror. I wound down the window and stuck my hand out to acknowledge him. I beeped the horn and the Alfa clawed its way on the wet surface. It roared into action and we sped off down the narrow lane.

"He's a nice old guy, that Roger. Knows his horses," Frank said.

I stopped at the junction and waited for a car to pass, then pulled out onto the main street. I drove past L'Escale café. It was full and the local beauty queens were lounging on the terrace.

"Damn, she's mighty fine lookin', pretty as a dove," Frank said.

"Do want to get a beer, Frank?" I said, pushing on the brakes.

"Yeah man. Damn, she's a dove. *Oooooui, bonjour* baby! I'm in *luuuuve* with that gal," Frank said. "Yeah, let me buy you a beer for picking me up. Thanks again, saved my life."

"Let's move on," I said, having second thoughts about stopping. "That place will only be full of a bunch of drunks holding on to the bar until it closes. You can buy me a beer up the road. They've got France's biggest rap star playing on the beach for free tonight. MC Solaar, his song '*Bouge de là*' is the big hit record this summer. It'll be fun. There's plenty of cafés and restaurants – we can get something to eat, too." I accelerated down the road.

"Yeah man, OK," said Frank. "It's your call. I'm just along for the ride. By the way, I made some cassettes of CDs I just bought in the US. The new stuff that you guys haven't heard yet." He took a cassette out from his rucksack. "Here, play this shit. It's gonna blow ya mind, man, guaranteed."

Frank passed the cassette to me. The sun was starting to set. The pink and blue sky coloured the white houses. The low sunlight reflected in my eyes off the window of the PMU café. I had to stop suddenly in the middle of the road and waited for a car to pass.

"That should have been your right of way," said Frank. "We're on the main road. They should have stopped, no? He didn't even brake, that was mad." He seemed astonished. "In America, he would be roughed and cuffed for that."

"It's crazy, isn't it?" I said. "Priority on the right. The cars just jump out at you from these narrow little streets. You don't see them, and then suddenly they are in the middle of the road. You have to stamp on the brakes and screech to a stop. It dates back to the days of the horse and cart, the right to turn, something like that. Napoleon laying down the law probably," I said. "*C'est la France, c'est la vie!*"

I put the cassette into the tape machine. It clicked into place as the heads pushed up on the celluloid and the tape started to turn. The sound of Snoop Doggy Dogg's 'Who Am I (What's My Name?)' came out of the speakers.

We turned off the main road and along a smaller road through fields in the direction of the beach. We drove past the road sign for the village.

"*Quend*, like when?" Frank asked me.

"Not exactly. *Quand* is with an A. This is *Quend*, with an E."

"All sounds French to me," Frank said.

We entered the pine forest. The tall, northern pines left a carpet of needles and pine cones on the ground. We drove past the entrance to one of the campsites. It was the height of summer and they were all full. The holidaymakers meandered back from a day on the beach. Shirtless teenagers on mopeds passed on both sides of the row of cars, waving their arms and shouting to girls as they drove past. We waited as the queue of cars slowly filtered through the narrow passage, marked by yellow tape, into the parking area.

"*Pomme, pomme,*" said Frank through the music.

"Apples?" I asked.

"No, pom, pom, pom, pommmmmm!" he replied. "Like the beginning of a film, a Universal or Paramount theme tune, the opening of the film, like that. Yeah, *pomme* is apple, what's the French for melons?"

"*Melons,*" I said.

"Alright, *des grands melons,* check...it...out," he said, leaving a pause between every word as two teenage girls wearing bikini tops walked past. "Check-it-out ol'cuz, *les melons sont incroyables, n'est pas.* Look at those things, *très bon,*" he said, enjoying the view.

"You are almost fluent now, Frank. You don't need much more French than that," I said. The girls looked in our direction. The music was loud and boomed from the car.

"Gin and juice," said Frank turning up the volume.

People walked past the car and stared at Frank from the other side of the road. He lifted his hand to acknowledge them. The English number plate gave away our identity.

Nobody had a copy of this album yet, not even the radio stations. The music boomed from the six speakers. We eventually arrived on the main road and turned left. The constant flow of people coming from the campsites and other parking areas filed past the car.

"Snoop Doggy Dogg, what's his motherfucking name?" Frank said out of his rolled-down window. "Better recognise! Snoop Dogg in da hood. Biiiiatch."

The car rolled forward slowly, down a gentle incline. We

turned the corner and could now see the sea at the end of the long road. The village was packed.

The young *Gendarmette* signalled to us to turn right and follow the other cars into the parking area.

"No cars beyond this point, except emergency vehicles, pedestrians only," the young policewoman said with authority as I slowly rolled past her.

"Arrest me and take down my par-tic-ulars," Frank said, smiling at the young lady. *"Laid back, sippin' on gin and juice, with my mind on my money and my money on my mind, laaaid back..."* Frank sang along to the music.

We followed the other cars through the pines and further into the forest. We were flagged into a slot, and I manoeuvred the car carefully to avoid hitting a tree. It was a tight squeeze.

We walked back towards the main street through the trees. The bed of pine needles was soft under my feet. We followed people heading towards where the loud music was coming from and climbed up the large sand dune near the beach.

MC Solaar was already on stage accompanied by four dancers and a DJ. The small stage was lit by cheap lighting, but the speakers were serious. The music boomed as we watched the show. He thanked the crowd and left the stage, people clapped and cheered. A few minutes later, he returned for an encore. I recognised the song immediately. The summer hit was played regularly on every radio station.

"Bouge de là, it's his big tune," I yelled over the loud music.

"This is France's answer to New Kids on the Block," Frank said. "He ain't no Snoop Dogg, that's for sure. He would have this guy shot," he shouted back and turned his head to look at the stage.

"Yeah man, that would make him a legend," I said as the song came to its finale. "Let's *bouge d'ici* and go and get some food."

"I'll buy you dinner, I've seen enough of this dude," Frank said.

"With all these people here, I don't know if we're going to find a place in one of the restaurants," I said. "It's going to be hard. Let's get a drink and see if we can find somewhere."

"They're coming, *les Indiens vont arriver*. Everybody watch out!" shouted the municipal policeman loudly, splaying out his arms like Jesus Christ to control the crowd.

We stopped to see what was happening. From the depths of the forest came an almighty roar and gunshots, but we couldn't see exactly where it was coming from. Suddenly, twenty to thirty mounted, bare-chested Indians with war markings, feathered headdresses, necklaces, beads, wooden spears, or bows and arrows, cantered towards the people crowded along the road. Holding their reins, squeezing their legs tightly to the horses' flanks, they flashed past us. A troupe of cowboys and soldiers on horseback followed behind, blasting blanks as they shot their guns and rifles in the air. The thunderous sound of the charging posse was ear-splitting.

The first wave of Indians reached the end of the road, stopped, and they jumped off their horses. The crowd was thrilled by the authentic American Wild West show and people started to clap and cheer. The Indians on foot started fighting with the cowboys. Uniformed American soldiers play-acted fighting with swords and daggers. More mounted cowboys galloped towards us at speed, carrying flags, the long poles balanced on their feet. Their polished stirrups shone brightly as they fired their pistols in the air. A soldier blew a bugle. The deafening sound of the hooves clopping on the tarmac and the screams of the war-painted Indians echoed down the street.

I tugged Frank's arm and bobbed my head to move on. We walked past a couple of restaurants; the terraces were full. From the corner of my eye, I saw two people stand up as if about to leave. I ran through the crowd and up the wooden steps of the terrace, Frank following behind me. I looked at the server to see if it was OK to take the table. He nodded affirmatively.

"We're good, what a bit of luck," I said happily, as I pulled the chair from under the table.

It was the best table on the terrace, overlooking the heaving crowd below on the main road. We had a clear view of the happenings on the street and could clearly see the beach front and the sea at the end of the long street.

"I'm hungry after all that," I said.

"I have a raging thirst. I need a beer, quickly," Frank said.

"Me too."

We ordered two large beers, a bottle of wine and steak and chips for both of us. The beers arrived quickly.

Frank had barely swallowed his beer before he burst into loud laughter. Heads turned in our direction.

"What is so funny?" I asked, but it was impossible to understand his reply.

I turned my head towards the front door of the restaurant. The owner had come out onto the terrace to talk with his customers wearing an Elvis wig, sunglasses and a shirt with stones and sequins all over it.

"Damn, he's still alive and well," Frank exclaimed. "Working in a restaurant in northern France, who would believe that? I've only been here about four hours, but I've just about seen everything now."

Two teenage girls, seated on the table next to us with their parents, joined in laughing with us. The waiter looked towards our table with a stern face, perhaps thinking we were laughing at him. We gathered our composure.

Elvis approached our table with two plates of food in his hands.

"Is everything OK with you?" he enquired, placing our

meals before us. His immaculately quaffed wig protruded from the middle of his head, the grease reflecting the lights.

"*Merci*, everything is perfect," I managed to say. "Another bottle of wine, please." I bit my lower lip to control my laughter.

"*Bon appétit*, Frank," I said.

We tucked into our steak and chips. Frank started to hum 'Hound Dog' as the owner approached our table with the second bottle of wine.

The elevated wooden terrace gave us a bird's-eye view of the crowded street below. The mob of sun-tanned faces squeezed past each other, banging shoulders as they filed past. The shops selling everything for the beach were doing a roaring trade. Inflatable rings, buckets and spades, espadrilles, and T-shirts with designs of flying eagles and American trucks adorned their shop fronts. Kids held up their hands as their ice creams melted down their forearms.

The cowboys and Indians, accompanied by their squaws and children, rode past for the last time, and disappeared back into the forest.

"I feel like I'm at General Custer's last stand, or more like Custer's last supper!" said Frank. "They say 'only in America', but this is beyond unbelievable. I was expecting to see dudes on bicycles with stripy shirts and bunches of onions round their necks, clutching a baguette while smoking untipped black tobacco cigarettes. Instead, I've met a horse called Elvis, been attacked by Cheyenne and Sioux Indians, saved by cowboys, and had my food served by The King... Boy, it's like a vaudevillian show, but all in French."

"Welcome to 'Piccardee' Tennessee," I said in my best southern accent.

THE LANGUAGE OF FOOD

I parked the car and walked over to the café. I pushed the door open and greeted the owner, Fred, who was behind the counter drying glasses.

"*Bonjour*," I said and closed the door behind me. He reached out across the bar and I shook his hand. Patrick was sitting on a stool.

He was short, with a pot belly. He wore black, national health-style glasses with thick lenses to correct a wandering eye. He wore a crumpled suit with a white shirt that always had a stain of wine, sauce or soup dribbled down the front. I had seen him in the café before, but never spoke to him. He was quiet and kept to himself.

"What would you like?" asked Fred, draping the tea towel over the washed glasses in the tray on the sink.

"*Une demie*," I said.

He took a glass from the counter behind him and glided it under the beer pump, precisely tilting the glass to minimise the foamy head. He gently straightened the angle as the beer filled to the top. He pushed the lever forward and stopped the flow of beer and placed the glass delicately on the round cardboard coaster depicting a green and white Perrier advert.

"*Ça va?*" Patrick said to me.

"*Oui, ça va*, apart from the cold," I said, then lifted the glass to my lips and took a large sup of beer. The cool liquid hit the back of my throat. "*Ça va mieux*, I'm better now," I said, putting the glass down on the counter. I pulled a packet of cigarettes from my pocket and offered one to Patrick.

"*Fumes-tu?*" I enquired.

"I stopped," replied Patrick. "I used to smoke, but I've been told by the doctor to stop, so I stopped. I like a cigar now and again, at Christmas, after the big dinner. My brother and his wife always do too much food. I just can't eat all they prepare."

Fred leant on the counter listening to Patrick.

"With all the food he has, all those delicious recipes and meats, I can well imagine, but magnifique, *délicieux, non?*" Fred said, walking over to shake a customer's hand.

"*Oui*, the food is amazing, that's true, but there's so much!" Patrick turned his head and looked in my direction. "He has the butcher's just next door to the bank, on the other side, before the little garage."

"That's your brother? *Le monsieur là-bas*, the butcher's just down the road?" I pointed in the direction of the shop.

"*Oui*, Jean-Michel. He's been there for over twenty years. Before that, my dad was a butcher, too. That was in another place, where they live now. They closed the shop part. The old shop was on the road leading down from the train station behind the café, the road that runs parallel to this one. And, before him, my grandfather was also a butcher. At that time, they would slaughter the animals behind the store." Patrick lifted his glass.

"Patrick and his family are the local mafia. Watch out!"

Fred said jokingly, tapping Patrick gently on his forearm on the counter top.

"I've been in there and bought some things," I said.

"You should, not because he's my brother, but because I know what he puts in his food, sausages, and terrines," replied Patrick. "He deals with a wide variety of animal types, not just pork. He prepares all his meat cuts, and the quality of cuts you get there is not like at the supermarket. He only uses the best products. He's a maniac, a true perfectionist."

"It's true," Fred said, butting into the conversation as he floated behind the bar. He tapped on the till and the drawer slid out. He stopped it with his hand and the coins rattled against the plastic compartments. He pulled out the correct change and pushed the draw in, turning around like a pirouetting ballerina and handed the change to the customer.

"*Merci, bonne journée*," Fred said to the client, then turned in our direction. "I always buy my pâté and charcuterie there. He's the best butcher in the area," he said with sincerity. "You really should taste what he makes."

"Let's drink up and I'll take you down there and introduce you," said Patrick. "That way, he'll know you're a friend of mine. I'll get him to show you how he makes all his pâtés and sausages. He's a member of the guild of sausage makers, blood sausages," he added, stepping down from his stool. "We're serious about our sausages here in France. You know us and food." Patrick smiled. "He's been in competitions, and he has won awards for his pâtés. He makes traditional dishes and recipes from the region. He's also a traiteur."

"A traitor?" I enquired.

"*Un trai-teur*," Patrick pronounced the word phonetically so I could understand. "He does catering for weddings and events, canapés, hors d'oeuvres, but also the main dishes. He gets asked to roast a pig on the spit, whatever you want – anything from a pig, sheep, or cow."

He asked Fred for his bill.

"I'll pay for this one, too," Patrick said pointing to my glass.

"Thank you," I said.

"Let's go. Merci, Fred, we'll be back. Just going to show him my brother's place, we'll come back after." Patrick opened the door for me and waved his hand.

We walked past the bank and arrived in front of the narrow shop window adorned with culinary specialties. Pheasants and rabbits hung from hooks.

Patrick waved to his brother and pushed the glass door open. I followed him in and the door clattered behind me like it was about to shatter into a million pieces. Inside, high glass-fronted cabinets stretched back to a large, cold room door. The cabinets were full of different types of charcuteries, pork products, smoked and dried sausages, pâtés, duck and game terrines, and prime cuts of meat and poultry.

"*Voilà, mon frère*, Jean-Michel," Patrick said, lifting his arm in his brother's direction. He was a hearty fellow, with a large round face. His white overalls were clean and you could see that he liked to eat what he sold. Jean-Michel moved round to the till, pushed a wheeled table aside and bent down and kissed Patrick on both cheeks. He held out his hand and I shook it.

"I found this Englishman in the café, he wants to know everything about how you make your sausages, pâtés and all the rest," Patrick said. "Show him around. Give him the royal tour, the VIP sausage-making experience. That way, he won't go and buy that *merde* that they sell up the road." Patrick slapped his older brother on the back.

Jean-Michel was a heavyweight, his huge carcass enveloped in white overalls and a neatly pressed apron. Patrick was a flyweight.

"Well, come this way, follow me," Jean-Michel said, as he passed through the narrow passageway that led to the back of the shop. We followed him into a clean room with two large metal doors.

"Let me show you in here," he said, pulling the heavy door of the cold room open. I could see all the different meats and cuts hanging on large hooks. The neatly arranged terrines and rolled meats were stored on metal shelves.

"I make everything that you see in here," Jean-Michel announced proudly.

The shiny metal working tables were spotless. Sharp knives, cleavers and cutting utensils hung on the wall, stuck to large, magnetic bars.

"This cold room is devoted to my meats, such as bacon, ham, and smoked sausage," he continued. "Originally, it was a way to preserve meat before the advent of refrigeration. The different flavours are derived from the preservation processes, that's why I store them in here, let them sleep a bit, to get more flavour." Jean-Michel smiled at me. He could see I was impressed by his meat collection.

"My terrine is similar to a pâté, but it's made with more coarsely chopped ingredients. Terrines are usually served cold or at room temperature. Most terrines contain a large amount of fat as well as pork, although it is often not the main ingredient. I also make terrines with game meat, like deer and boar, too."

Spurred on by the interest I showed in his produce, he continued.

"I make all types of pâtés, for example *pâté de lapin* – rabbit. I mainly use the liver and heart and mix it with a good dose of brandy, fresh bacon, sausage, chopped onion, bread crumbs, eggs, juniper berries, bay leaves, thyme, salt, and pepper. I also do it as a *pâté en croute*. *Pâté aux pommes de terre* is a kind of pie containing sliced potatoes and heavy cream. It's a Picard specialty, and it can serve as an appetiser, main dish, or an accompaniment, but it's good to eat with a green salad as a starter. This one is *pâté de Champagne, mousse de foie de canard au Porto*. I make it with chopped duck liver mixed with cream, eggs, and port. It is all mixed until it forms the smooth consistency of a mousse. I add spices and seasoning, then place it in a mould and bake it in water in the oven. When it has finished cooking, it must be topped with jelly or grease. I use duck fat to prevent oxidation.

"This is port duck liver, which is less refined than the mousse. I use a third duck meat to two-thirds of fatty pork and chicken livers. They get cooked up in a salty and spicy broth, to which I add the port and thicken it up with maize flour and some vegetables. Another one is *pâté en croûte*, I make many variations – baked in a crust as a pie, or some people call it a loaf. The regional and traditional way is to use rabbit, to which I add calf, pig, or poultry. I then add a mixture of flavoured stuffing, with either mushrooms or pistachios.

"For *rillettes*, I use pork, cook it for a long time in its fat, mash it up by hand or machine and season only with salt and pepper. Some people like to add herbs and spices, but I've added Calvados to it, too, but that's usually around Christmas."

"His *rillettes au Calvados* is incredible," Patrick added.

"What do you know? You never eat anything, look at you," Jean-Michel said to Patrick.

"My *rillettes* is easy to spread," he continued. "You can also have duck rillettes and rabbit rillettes. I know a farmer who still makes his own crow rillettes from the crows he shoots on his land. I personally like *rillettes de poulet* and venison is very good, and fish rillettes is nice, too. I have some *rillettes de saumon* in the shop, but my favourite is trout rillettes, when I can get some. In here," he said, swinging open the other huge door.

"I make gratins, and crackling sometimes. It's been a regional tradition in the north for years. You can have it hot, but most often it's eaten cold and served with an aperitif or a salad. I take pork bards, which are cuts of back fat from a pig, with lean cuts of pork rind that I cut into strips and make a confit over a low heat in a casserole with very little water. It's really important not to add too much water. The fat must remain white, without burning or scorching. You have to keep it on a low heat. After about five to six hours, it's drained, pressed and seasoned with salt, pepper, spices, a few drops of vinegar, garlic and chopped parsley. It takes fifteen kilos of pork fat, lard, the neck, and flare, to make about three kilos of pork scratchings, crispy and crunchy. It's very good to eat." Jean-Michel pulled out another large terrine and placed it on the inox work table.

"*Fromage de tête*, or head cheese. It's a type of charcuterie that consists of small pieces of pork, especially the head, the cheeks, the snout, and tongue, cooked with small carrots, pickles, shallots, onions, and moulded jelly. I then add parsley, garlic, pepper, thyme, and cloves."

He was in his element.

"I get a whole pig's head that I debone and cook overnight in brine, but without the ears, eyes, and cartilage. Here in Picardy, and in the Nord-Pas-de-Calais, the 'cheese' is flavoured with crushed juniper berries. I also do it when I get a wild boar, my customers go crazy for it. I just can't make enough of it, but obviously I can only make it during the hunting season."

"Show him the *foie gras*," Patrick said. "Taste this one. His most famous pâté is probably his *pâté de foie gras*, made from the livers of fattened geese. *Foie gras entier* is fattened goose liver cooked and sliced, not made into pâté."

Jean-Michel dived into the cold room and came back with a red-coloured dish and placed it on the table in front of me and took off the lid. He bent down to smell the aroma, then invited me to do the same.

"As far back as 2500 BC, the ancient Egyptians learnt how to fatten birds through forced feeding. By French law, *oui monsieur, attention, par la loi*, the popular delicacy, called *foie gras* belongs to the protected cultural and gastronomical heritage of France." Jean-Michel put his finger in the air.

"*Foie gras* is defined as a liver from a duck or goose that has been fattened by force-feeding corn," he continued. "They stick a feeding tube down their necks; this process is known as *gavage*. Like the verb *gaver*, to stuff yourself." This was serious stuff. Jean-Michel didn't joke when it came to talking about his pâtés and meats.

"Around here, there are a lot of ducks, around the bay area," he went on. "I buy my duck and goose from a producer just the other side of Favières. He does the best in the area. His ducks are force-fed twice a day, for twelve and half days, and his geese three times a day for around seventeen days. The Romans ate fig-stuffed liver, made by feeding figs to enlarge the goose's liver. Ancient Greece inspired Roman luxury cuisine. What else can one say? All washed down by litres of strong red wine. They knew how to have a good time back then!"

"Taste this one," Jean-Michael said. "This is duck *foie gras*. I made it a couple of days ago. It should be just right."

He cut a small sliver off the putty-like mass of yellowed liver *pâté*. I stuck it in my mouth and it melted on my tongue as the flavours poured out into my mouth.

"Wow, *c'est fantastique*, delicious," I said as the rich, buttery, delicate flavours covered my taste buds.

"The ducks are slaughtered after a hundred days, the geese after a hundred and twelve days. That's how we get this," he said. "Traditionally, *foie gras* was produced from special breeds of geese. However, these days, geese account for less than ten percent of the total of all the *foie gras* production in the world. Here in France, it's only five percent of the total production. Ducks account for ninety-five percent. About ninety-five percent of duck *foie gras* production comes from *moulards* and the remaining five from the Muscovy duck. That's why goose *foie gras* is so much more expensive. The process is longer and more costly, plus there isn't a lot of it. The two goose breeds used are the grey Landes goose and the Toulouse goose.

"That served as an accompaniment on a big steak, formidable," Jean-Michel added, holding his fingers up to his lips, then opening them like a firework exploding.

"I flavoured that one with truffles and mushrooms. You can add brandy, Cognac, or Armagnac. I take it out when it's ready and wrap it in a towel, then I mould it into shape and slow cook it in a *Bain-Marie*," he said. "These slow-cooked forms of *foie gras* are cooled and then served at or below room temperature."

"And your specialty, that you are most famously known for is...?" Patrick was trying to speed up the tour.

"OK, just quickly. This is where I make my sausages with this machine, *la voilà*," Jean-Michel said, moving over to a big lump of metal. "As you can see, you came at the right moment. I was preparing sausages. Look here, where it comes out, I'll show you." He slipped the tube of intestines on to the nozzle of the machine and switched it on.

"This is my mix. The primary seasoning I use is salt, no sugar, along with various savoury herbs and spices, onions, and garlic. A sausage typically contains seventy-seven and a half percent of meat, ten percent butcher's rusk, ten percent water, and two and half percent of seasoning. However, my sausages have a meat content of eighty percent," he said with pride. "I only use lean meat, not all that fat like those sausages that you get in the supermarket. You just don't know what they put in them, all the scraps, various tissue, organs, and nasty bits that they can get away with these days. I don't want to tell you what else they put in them, you will never want to eat a sausage ever again." He looked at me seriously.

"Look, now I take it like this." As he twisted the long cylinder with his hands, the machine kept pushing the long skin as it extended in length, producing the characteristic cylindrical shape. Jean-Michel switched off the machine. There was already more than three metres of sausage rolled up on the table next to the machine. Jean-Michael made equi-spaced sausages with precision by twisting the huge, flaccid tube of pink meat.

"I make them to an old, traditional Picard recipe," he continued. "I've been playing around with the ingredients I put in them. I like to combine fruits such as apples or apricots with the meat. However, I buy my Toulouse sausage and chorizo directly from a guy in Toulouse; he delivers in the area once a month. He also brings me the wine I have here, his brother-in-law makes it. You should try it, it's very good." He concentrated on what he was doing.

"*La voilà!*" He presented me with six finely prepared sausages. "I make merguez, too, with lamb, beef, or a mixture of both, not pork. Then I flavour them with a wide range of spices, such as sumac, paprika, and cayenne pepper. For the extra spicy ones, I add harissa, a hot chili paste that gives it a fiery red colour and taste. I use lamb casings rather than pork. Grilled or with a couscous, *fantastique!*"

He was so passionate about his food, it was making me hungry. "And I can't leave without showing you this. *Voilà, le boudin noir*, the blood sausage," he said proudly. "In the shop you will see, hanging on the wall, my certificate from the French Confrérie des Chevaliers du Goûte-Boudin, the 'Brotherhood of the Knights of the Blood Sausage'. Every year, they hold an international contest for all types of blood sausage specialties in Mortagne-au-Perche in southern Normandy. I have won certain categories over the years. I've been going to it for at least fifteen years," he added imperiously. "Haggis in Scotland is similar."

"In Britain, it is called 'black pudding', but to be honest I don't like it," I said. "You can find it in a café for the big *petit-dej Anglais*. We eat eggs, bacon, sausages and baked beans and sometimes black pudding."

"Do you eat that with mint jelly?" Jean-Michel asked.

"No, only with lamb, roast lamb, lamb chops, not for breakfast," I replied. "Orange marmalade or strawberry jam on toast. However, get some mint, cut it up finely, mix it with vinegar, try that with some lamb sometime and see."

The shop's door buzzer sounded and Jean-Michel stopped what he was doing.

"*Excuse-moi, un client*," he said and left in the direction of the small passageway that led to the shop. Patrick and I followed. I took my place in the queue behind the woman and looked at the various dishes in the glass-fronted refrigerated cabinets.

I already had enough to eat in my fridge at home, but I bought some *pâté* and pork chops. Jean-Michel placed the tightly wrapped packets on the counter next to the till.

"*Avec souci?*" Jean-Michel bellowed in his heavy Picard accent. I was confused for a moment.

"*Avec sauci, saucisse*, with sausages?" It was logical that he would ask, as we had just spent fifteen minutes talking about and making sausages. *Yes, of course*, I thought to myself, *I must have some of his delicious sausages, how rude of me.*

"OK, *deux merguez et metez six aux fines herbes*, please," I said, hoping I had not offended him for not buying some.

"*Bien sûr*," he said reaching into the cabinet. He put the sausages in the weighing tray and wrapped them up.

"Thank you for the tour and the sausage-making class," I said shaking his hand.

"See you soon, bye," Jean-Michel said as Patrick and I walked out of the shop.

Back on the street, I thanked Patrick for inviting me. "It was interesting to see that. I'll be going back there to buy my meats and, of course, his wonderful sausages," I said.

I stopped in front of the bank.

"I have to go in here. I'll see you in the café and buy you a drink. I just have to do something." The automatic doors slid open as I approached.

"OK, see you in a minute," Patrick said and walked towards the café.

I joined the queue inside. The three counters where manned by two of the cutest girls in town and a huge, morose oaf who everybody called 'Carlos', after the rotund French singer and TV personality.

I had said '*bonjour*' to the girls in the café next door on a few occasions. I was hoping to get one of them, not Billy Bunter in his non-matching clothes. His red and white check shirt was accompanied by a purple and blue tie encased in a horizontal striped jumper, probably knitted by his colour-blind great-great-grandmother.

I counted down the grannies in front of me and tried to estimate which counter would finish first, hoping the granny directly in front of me would go to the oaf, and I would be served by one of the banking angels. The counter on the left, with the smiling face, finished first and the old lady shuffled over. An old lady moved away from the counter in the middle.

I had seen 'Carlos' in the café next door, but never spoken to him. He ate there regularly at lunchtimes, hunched over the table in his ill-fitting clothes, stuffing his round face. His black-framed glasses were held together thanks to a large blob of woven tape that looked like a growth.

I approached his counter. I had already written out the

cheque and passed it to him. He took it, turned it over and passed it back to me.

"*Signature,*" he said in an obtuse manner.

I signed the cheque on the back and passed it back. He snatched it with his chubby fingers, stamped it and took out the notes from the drawer. He counted the six one hundred Francs notes out in front of me and I counted them with him. He put the printed receipt for me to sign next to the counted money. I signed my name in the small box at the bottom and put the pen back in the well, and he snatched the signed receipt.

"*Merci,*" I said.

I waited for 'Carlos' to give me my receipt. Normally, they split it in two parts, keeping the original and handing me the copy. I waited for a couple of seconds. I smiled and started to explain my dilemma to him in my very limited French.

"*Je veux mon slip.*"

His eyes opened wide. He looked like a fat rabbit in its final seconds, frozen by fear before an oncoming car explodes its head. I continued to look at his blubbery face. He obviously hadn't understood. I presumed I wasn't pronouncing slip correctly.

"*Slip, mon slip,*" I said again. I looked at his swollen fleshy cheeks. I tried to be sincere, polite, and eloquent in my delivery of the words, paying careful attention to my pronunciation and rounding my words off correctly. "*Mon sleep, mon sleep,* slip of paper," I repeated louder.

I pointed in the direction of the paper receipt sitting in front of him on his desk. The whole of the bank looked at me as I leant over the high counter and tried to direct his eyes to the slip of paper. He just froze and went as a red a tomato.

"Paper slip," I said, "*le papier!*" I was almost shouting now, trying to get 'Carlos' to understand me. I saw the relief on his face as his brain clicked into motion and he realised that he hadn't given it back to me. His hands were shaking as he ripped the two sheets apart and handed me my copy.

"*Merci*, thank you," I said, relieved.

I had another thing that needed to be done at the bank. I received my debit card in the post, but I had not yet been sent the code, so I couldn't draw out money. Coming into the bank to draw money was time consuming and I had to deal with this buffoon.

"*La voilà*," I said showing him the card.

He grabbed it with his chubby fingers without saying anything. He looked anxious.

"OK, I got the card in the post, *c'est bon*, but I haven't got my PIN number yet. My PIN," I said.

'Carlos' looked at me and his eyes expanded wide again. His eyebrows stretched up so high on his forehead they resembled a clown's over-exaggerated makeup. The lines on his forehead rippled into tubes of horizontal blubber. He just stared up at me from his slouched position. His football-sized head went tomato red again. I could see his rounded ears starting to turn purple.

I tried again. I pronounced my words with perfection, paying close attention to my phonetics. My internal dictionary had slowly been built, brick by brick, drink by drink. I accentuated my mouth movements to get my accent perfect.

"PIN, I haven't got my pin, for the card, P-I-N," I said and started tapping my finger on the counter so he could understand. "Personal identity number." *It was obvious, everybody knows what a PIN is, you fucking idiot*, I thought. I tapped my finger like I was tapping on the keys of an ATM. His reaction was the same, he was frozen in shock. His mouth drooped wide open as I kept tapping my finger on the counter.

"*Peen, peen, peen, le code*," I started to get annoyed. His ginormous frame deflated into his chair. I could see the relief on his face as he sat up and passed my card back to me.

"*La poste, la poste, le code arrive par la poste, bientôt,* soon, *ze poste*," he said as he stood up, turned around and waddled away from his desk towards the door in the corner.

I turned around and walked towards the electronic doors. They whooshed open. I walked back to the café next door and pushed open the heavy door. Patrick was sitting with a small group of friends at the bar. They all turned their heads simultaneously to look at me as I entered.

"*Ça va,*" Fred said. "*Demie?*"

"*Oui, merci,*" I said, quickly followed with, "That fat guy at the bank next door, Carlos, or whatever his name is... that big oaf, he just doesn't want to understand me."

"Why, what's the problem?" asked Patrick sympathetically. "Can I help? I know the people in there."

"Well, I received my card, carte blue, in the post nearly a week ago, but I haven't got my pin yet."

The café exploded into laughter.

"*Pin,* pronounced peen, is your dick, *la penis* in French slang," said Patrick. "Pine is a type of tree. You mean a NIP code, *Número Identication Personel.*" He was laughing profusely. Fred had tears pouring out from behind his spectacles.

"He said it was going to come in the post," I said. "He didn't understand me when I asked for my slip, either. I asked him for my slip, slip of paper," I said seriously. The café again exploded with laughter. People were doubled over, their red faces beaming like traffic lights.

"*Slip,*" Fred tried to speak. "You asked Carlos for his *slip?*"

"*Un slip* is underpants, boxer shorts, *un caleçon,*" Patrick said laughing loudly.

"Ah, OK," I said timidly, thinking about what I had asked the eight-hundred-pound gorilla next door. How was I going to look him in the eye again? He probably thought I was trying to cruise him.

Fred and the rest of the café roared again with laughter.

Two days later, it was Sunday and I was heading home through the wildness of the Picardy countryside. I stopped at the Café-Tabac to buy cigarettes. I entered the bar and awaited my turn in the short queue. The café was packed and the Sunday lunchtime drinking team hovered around the bar. The cigarette counter was perched at the end of the bar next to the Lotto machine and the chewing gum stand. I waited in line as I prepared my words, *Je voudrais...* Every moment of communication was a process of preparing my thoughts and words.

The woman turned to me. *"Bonjour, monsieur."*

"Bonjour, madame. Two packs of Marl-bar-o rouge, please," I said in my finest accent. The woman grabbed two packs of cigarettes from the shelf behind her; she put them on the counter and tapped in the price on her till and smiled at me.

"Avec souci, monsieur?" the woman said politely.

I froze like a statue, my eyes transfixed on the woman's smiling face. I had only heard this phrase once before, from Jean-Michel in his butcher's shop and, obviously, I wasn't in a butcher's shop now. *Avec souci,* was something to do with sausages and I was well aware that I was buying cigarettes. I knew that she didn't have any sausages for sale because you buy fucking *saucisses* in a butcher's.

My lexicon rolodex spun at full speed, the little cables of blue and red veins pumped and the lethargic linguistic structures of my brain tried pairing the meaning of *souci*.

I knew all about *saucisse sèche, saucisson, saucisse crue* or *à cuire, saucisse fumé.* I knew all about *saucisse de sang,* I knew that was called boudin noir and I knew all about *boudin blanc, saucisse de gibier.* I knew every type of fucking sausage. Jean-Michel had shown me!

I quickly concluded that this woman was taking the piss.

I counted the money out and looked her in the eyes. She was smiling at me, waiting patiently. This smiley old cow was taking the piss out of me, in front of all these people, I couldn't believe it. She was asking me if I wanted some sausages with my cigarettes! The cheeky bitch. I scowled at her as I slammed the right money on the plastic money tray between the scratch cards.

I was fuming; my honour and ego had been dented. I turned quickly on my heels and pushed past the people waiting in the queue that stretched to the door. I pulled the door open and stormed out of the café, mumbling under my breath. I walked quickly back to the car and jumped in. I pulled out of the parking space with stones and dust flying out from behind the car.

"Cheeky cow," I spoke out loud to myself. "Fucking old crusty old bitch. I'm never stopping there again, she can stick her cigarettes up her ass!" I shouted out as I drove down the road.

I arrived at the house and parked at the gate. The small café was still open and the array of bicycles, mopeds, and parked cars outside meant that the joint was rocking. I needed a drink.

I pushed the café door open and it stuck on the tiles and rubbed across the floor. I shut it firmly behind me. The bar was in full motion and the posse of young hoodlums were playing French billiards on the pocketless table. The cloth had a number of cuts in it where the players rammed the head of the cue under the ball into the cloth. The cuts had been stuck back in place with superglue.

I shook hands with the mob that was scattered along the bar and muscled my way into a place.

"*Bonjour*," said the daughter of the owner. I made a hand

signal to her mother who was working in the shop next door, through the archway.

"I want a *cent-deux*, a double dose of Pastis," I said.

I opened the new box of cigarettes. Unravelling the plastic covering made me think of the woman who handed me the cigarettes. My drink arrived and the young teenage girl behind the bar passed me the glass decanter with water. I poured a slop of it into my glass. The dark amber colour hardly changed. I took a large swig, then another and the whole glass slipped down my neck. The girl looked at me from behind her round glasses. Her expression of amazement lit up her face.

"Another one, please," I said, putting the glass on the zinc counter. I felt instantly better as the alcohol rushed through my veins.

"*Ça va Anglais?*" Jean-Claude was on form. His stained flat cap was tilted to the side and his eyes were glassy. It was only five-forty, but everybody had started early. There were another two hours and twenty minutes to go until closing time.

"*C'est la fête ce soir,*" I said.

"*Oui,* it's Alain's son's birthday, that's why there's so many people here tonight," he said.

"I've never seen so many people in here," I shouted. Normally, we were only five or six 'Knights of the Zinc', but tonight there were at least thirty people in the small bar. Nearly all the tables were taken. The young kids sipped on multi-coloured drinks such as beer with grenadine and Pastis with peppermint. Others drank beers straight from the bottle.

I turned to Jean-Claude. I had to get it off my chest, as it was still annoying me.

"I stopped at the café on the main road in Vron, up the hill, the café that sells cigarettes. Not the other café, the Café-Tabac. I asked her for a couple of packets of cigarettes and then the old bitch asked me if I wanted some sausages, '*avec souci*'!"

I was mad just repeating the story. I accentuated my feelings about the woman. Jean-Claude burst into laughter, spitting out the large swig of beer he had just taken as I said my last words. He sprayed me and everybody in the vicinity.

Everybody in the café looked in our direction. All thirty faces were concentrated on Jean-Claude, who was now doubled up, nobody knew why. His face was cherry red, his eyes were watery pools, and tears cascaded down his stubbly face.

"What's so funny?" I asked. "What did I say?"

Jean-Claude was trying to get to grips with his hysterics, taking deep breaths.

"What's so funny?" he began. "'*Avec souci*' means 'with anything else' and not 'do you want sausages?'" The rest of the café burst into laughter with him.

I realised my mistake – not quite a Freudian slip, but yet another misunderstanding. I was glad I had not been rude to the woman and called her a 'bitch' to her face. I always thought she was a nice lady.

A week later, I was driving back home and stopped at the Café-Tabac to buy cigarettes. Madame greeted me with a smile.

"*Bonjour, monsieur,*" she said as I walked over to the counter.

"*Bonjour, madame*, a packet of Marl-bar-o cigarettes, *merci,*" I said in my most perfect French and smiled politely. I thought of all the bad things I had said about this hard-working, charming lady. I felt bad, but glad I hadn't said it to her face.

"*Avec souci?*" she asked me, putting the cigarettes on the counter. I smiled back, I knew exactly what she was enquiring. I had learnt a new expression, a new word! I had expanded my lexicon. I was one word further down the road on my sociolinguistical voyage. I pulled my best smile. *She's so nice*, I thought.

I remembered that the little AAA batteries in my transistor

radio had run down. I had seen batteries on the shelf the last time I came in to buy cigarettes. My mind raced. I knew the word. I had looked it up in the dictionary when I placed the batteries on the kitchen table. The word was...

My brain spun into motion as I tried to remember the word. Then it came to me.

Pile. I could hear it in my head. I had written it down on a little bit of paper, which was still on the kitchen table. I could see the letters, P, I, L, E, S.

The café was busy for a late afternoon.

"*Est ce que vous avez des...*" I began, as I concentrated on the word in my head.

"*Est ce vous avez des poils*," my mouth opened up on the second half of the word. I brought my arm up in front of her face as her mouth opened wide with shock. I opened up my fingers to the length of AAA battery, an inch and a half long.

"Like this," I said holding my fingers apart.

The woman looked at me in sheer horror. She had already changed the money and put it down on the counter.

"*Non, non, non.*" She moved away from the counter and scampered quickly towards the bar, looking at me over her shoulder like I was possessed. I could see the batteries on the other side of counter, but clearly she didn't want to sell them to me and that was OK. I would leave it. I'd go to the supermarket. It was her loss.

A short drive across the fields and I arrived at the house. It was that time of the day, and the usual legion of alcoholics were standing in their places at the bar.

I walked across the road as the sun started to dip behind the copse of trees that surrounded the water tower on the crest of the knoll behind the village. But what does *poils* mean? I pushed the door open and greeted the crowd.

"*Bonjour, ti'zaute.*"

I shook everyone's hand.

I turned to Jean-Claude. He had one of those faces. You never quite knew how much alcohol he had consumed.

"I went back to the café over in Vron. I bought cigarettes and then the woman said to me, '*avec souci*'." I felt proud of knowing the expression.

"I now know what that means, and then I asked if she had *poils*, you know, for my r..."

I couldn't finish my sentence as Jean-Claude and the old boys exploded with laughter.

"*Des poils?*" Jean-Claude managed to say. Everybody in the café roared with laughter. I opened up my fingers about an inch and a half wide.

"Yes, *longue comme ça*," I said naively.

Jean-Claude opened up his fingers. "*Comme ça?*" He doubled over, holding himself, his laughter turning to coughing. He eventually gained control of his speech and panted heavily.

"*Tes poils, c'est les cheveux sur tes couilles*," he pointed to my crutch. "Hair, there."

I could feel the blood rush to my face, and the heat coming out of me as I realised what I had asked that nice, charming women. He burst into laughter again.

"You asked madame if her pubes are long," he panted, "long like this!"

The bar roared loudly again.

I never went back to the Café-Tabac ever again.

ADAM AND YVES

The reception area of the Hotel Lion d'Or was always neatly presented, with a vase of fresh flowers on the front desk counter top. The small, family-run hotel was clean and smelled of lavender. The newly mopped tiles shone in the morning sunlight. The steep, narrow, wooden staircase by the reception gleamed with polish. I went through the opening in the dividing wall next to the stairs and walked into the bar.

"*Bonjour, Madame,*" I said.

The owner, Brigitte, was drying up cups and saucers behind the bar. She wiped her hands and laid the tea towel over the bright white coffee cups on top of the coffee machine.

"*Bonjour, Monsieur*, did you sleep well?" she asked, greeting me with a sweet smile. She shook my hand. She was petite and her little body was eloquently squeezed into a matching skirt and jacket with a white and red dogtooth design. Her hair was trapped behind her head by a large clip.

"*Oui, merci,* is it still possible to have breakfast?" I enquired.

"*Oui, oui,* no problem. Please, over there, it's all for you." She waved her arm in the direction of the only table with crockery on it in the corner. *"Teee or coffeeee?"* she asked in English.

"Café au lait, si'il vous plait," I said, with one of my limited phrases. Seven words at the same time. I was impressed with myself.

"Straight away, Monsieur. Please zit down," she said.

I assumed I was the last person to have breakfast. Only one space was laid out with a plate, cup and saucer and a mountain of sugar in a bowl. The large glass windows at the front of the hotel looked out onto the main high street.

Brigitte returned with my coffee, two croissants and half a baguette in a wicker basket. She placed the jam and butter, served on little teapot-shaped saucers, on the table. I dipped the croissant into my coffee and lifted it to my mouth. The coffee dribbled out of the croissant and down my chin. To avoid the drips going down my shirt, I lunged my head forward, just as a woman with a young child walked past.

The woman looked at me like I was going to vomit over the table. Our eyes met and she raised her eyebrows in judgement.

I wiped my chin with the serviette and ate the croissant without dipping it in the coffee. I thought about what the woman had seen and I laughed to myself. I reenacted the split-second comedy in my head as I stared out of the window into the street.

The little bell above the front door of the café pinged and Yves, the estate agent, entered. He clutched his little leather bag under his upper left arm. He lifted his forearm in the air and waved his chubby fingers like he was playing an air-keyboard. He spun around on the balls of his feet and closed the door with his right hand.

Brigitte bent down to open the dishwasher and a huge cloud of steam puffed out and steamed up her glasses. She used a tea towel to wipe them.

Yves waved to me, then he dipped his hips at Brigitte, curt-seying to her in greeting.

"*Bonjour chérie, coucou. Comment ça va?*" she enquired.

"*Ça va, merci,*" Yves said, smiling.

Brigitte replaced her glasses back on her nose, put down the towel and ran around to the other side of the bar. Yves was not tall, but she had to push herself up onto her toes to kiss him on both cheeks. Kiss, kiss – they moved their heads like swooning swans. Again, they simultaneously repeated the same question.

"*Ça va?*"

"*Oui, ça va, merci,*" they replied to each other's question at the same time.

They talked for a couple of minutes. Yves ran his hand up her arm in a friendly gesture. He turned around and started to walk over to my table.

"*Salut, Monsieur, comment ça va?* Are you well, everything OK?" he said from the middle of the room. He arrived in front of my table and we shook hands.

"How are you? Did you get here OK? The boat wasn't late? Were you held up by the roadworks?" Yves asked me in quick succession.

"No problems, it was easy, I drove down in good time. The traffic lights were flashing yellow, so I didn't have to wait," I said.

"What time did you arrive here at the hotel?"

"About eight-thirty, I think, nearly nine o'clock," I replied. "I put my stuff in the room, had something to eat first, then I checked in. Everything was great. Thanks for reserving the room and setting everything up for me."

"It's all part of the service," Yves smiled. "What did you have to eat? Everything is good here."

"I had a *ficelle picarde* to start with, I love those. Then steak and chips with a bottle of wine." I licked my lips at the memory of it all.

"The Picardy pancake, I like them too. They do a good one here," Yves said.

"It was yummy. I was hungry by the time I had got here," I said.

"Yes, it's not far, but all the getting on the boat, off it, then customs control, it takes time," said Yves. "It will be a lot quicker when they eventually build the motorway from Calais. When the tunnel is open, it will be lightning fast and really easy, they say, but we'll see. They need to build it first." He laughed at the end of his sentence.

"Yes, let's hope so," I said. "I like the drive down, though, the little villages, it's OK." I folded my serviette and laid it next to the plate.

"Do you want a coffee or something?" I asked Yves.

"No, thanks." He looked at me with a serious look on his face. "Have you finished your breakfast?"

"Yes, I'm done here," I said.

"Well, I had a phone call from the notary this morning while I was in the office. The meeting has been pushed back to three this afternoon. I'm sorry about that. However, I have the car outside and I thought we could go for a drive and have some lunch, then go to the notary at three."

"OK, great," I said.

"I have to go and take pictures of a lovely house," continued Yves. "We just got it on the books. I know the house. I sold it to them about three years ago. The people are moving to Dubai. The guy is in the property business and he's been posted out there. They want me to sell the place quickly. It's been renovated, but I haven't been there since they bought it and worked on it. Maybe you'll fall in love with it and buy another one. It's comfier than yours. They obviously want more money for theirs, though."

"OK, cool, I'm easy," I said.

"Hopefully, I'll sell it again, make more money on it now they have done some renovations," Yves said, rubbing his hands. "Then we can go for a nice lunch in Le Crotoy, OK?"

"I'll go and get my passport for the notary – you said I needed it," I said.

"No, we'll come past here on the way back," he replied. "The notaries' office is only three hundred metres up the road, where you signed the *Compromis*." Yves indicated to the door. "Let's go, come on. Adam is waiting in the car. He'll start moaning if we take any longer, you know what he's like."

Yves scurried quickly towards the door, the plastic soles of his deck shoes squeaking on the freshly cleaned tiles.

"He's really looking forward to seeing you again," Yves said as he pulled down on the door lever.

I could hear cars beeping their horns outside.

"*Au revoir, Madame, à tout à l'heure, merci*," I said as I followed Yves through the door into the morning sun. Brigitte waved to us from behind the counter.

"*A tout à l'heure, bonne journée*," she said, smiling.

I stepped onto the narrow pavement and saw the huge, burgundy red whale of a car parked in front of the hotel. The right-hand drive Rolls Royce Corniche convertible was twenty percent on the pavement with eighty percent of it in the road. I noticed the British number plate, ROLL5 128. The roof was down and Adam was in the backseat wearing a Panama hat, a white jacket, and a radiant blue shirt, which matched his piercing blue eyes. He looked handsome, an immaculately and impeccably dressed effeminate man in his mid-sixties. He was waving at the beeping cars as they drove past, like he was the Queen of England.

He was a queen, but today he was playing the Picard Prince Charming.

"I love these people and they love me!" Adam shouted in his

broad South African accent. "My people, they have never seen anything like me before, they're so inter-fucking bred even the women have beards. It's always so fucking dull and grey round here, I'm livening up their lives. Coooweee," he called, smiling broadly at his fans.

The large carcass of the cardinal red boat blocked the flow of traffic. There wasn't enough room for two cars to pass. Cars wanting to turn right onto the main road were blocked from doing so by the cars backed up behind the Rolls. Adam waved his arms more vigorously in the air to the cars driving past, and at the people who stopped on the pavement to look at the commotion as they came out of the Tabac and Maison de la Presse opposite the hotel.

As I approached the car, I got a whiff of Adam's sweet-smelling aftershave wafting over to me in the wind. The distinctive smell of the classic vintage formula stimulated my senses.

"I'm keeping the peasants happy as you block the fucking road, Yves," Adam quipped. "Otherwise, they will revolt and start chopping off heads with a fucking guillotine again! You know what they're like, no fucking patience."

Car horns were beeping in quicker succession. As I stopped in front of the passenger door, Adam looked me up and down. His piercing blue eyes matched his huge sapphire ring and Cartier Pacha watch. Its sapphire stone on the winder flashed in the sunlight as he waved his hand.

"*Quelle boykie*," Adam said loudly. His vocabulary was as unique as he was. He used words and expressions from a collage of languages, including Afrikaans and Zulu. He'd grown up in the bush in South Africa, but he also threw in a bit of French and English, including Cockney rhyming slang. All his sentences were scattered with swear words.

"You look fabulous, did you lose some weight? Look at your

lovely long blond hair. Those big shoulders, big and strong. Ummm, get in," he ordered me.

We shook hands and he held my hand for what felt like an eternity. "Get in man, *waaai* ('let's go' in Afrikaans)."

There was now a small crowd looking at the car from the opposite side of the road. The drivers of the cars that had stopped behind the Rolls were getting impatient and the honking of horns seemed to get louder with every second. Five or six cars were all beeping their horns with rage. Adam continued waving at the beeping cars and the people on the other side of the road. Some waved back.

"Ooooowee," Adam cooed.

Yves scurried round to the driver's side door as he raised his little hand and typed his fingers in the air to wave at the waiting cars.

He swung the huge heavy door open, climbed in and jumped up and down a couple of times until he was comfortable. He turned the key in the ignition and the powerful engine roared into life.

Yves pulled the gear lever into position and the Rolls rocked forward. He looked over his shoulder and nodded to the beeping cars. He gripped the large wooden wheel with both hands in a ten to two position, then he beeped the loud horn as if to say 'good bye'. Adam and Yves were as close to royalty that these people were going to see today.

The large wheels spun on the light gravel and the front left-hand-side suspension bounced gently as the car bumped off the kerb onto the road.

The sun shone through the clouds as we passed an old warehouse on the left, the rusty corrugated roof still dripping from the early morning showers. Adam stretched out across the large, hand-stitched sofa in the back. The Rolls bounced vigorously as it crossed a little bridge over a stream.

The car was huge in comparison with the little Twingos, Fords, Citroen AXs, and Renault vans that we passed. The deep red burgundy colour blended serenely with the autumn colours and the earthy browns of the soil freshly washed by the rain.

The car floated a foot above the road like a magic carpet. The suspension cushioned any bumps or dips in the road, which still had patches of rain gathered in elongated ponds. The large wheels sliced through the water, which splashed outwards as the Rolls whooshed through the countryside.

I saw a small car coming towards us on the other side of a humpback bridge. Yves did not slow down; he beeped the horn and flashed the headlights.

"There's not enough space for both cars," I said, anticipating a head-on collision.

"Don't worry, they always stop!" replied Yves. "They don't want to pay for the damages. Anyway, it's our priority – look at the arrow on the signpost. I know this road."

He accelerated and the 6.2-litre engine opened up, the speedometer needle drifting upwards. I was pushed back into the smooth leather seat and my hair was flattened by the wind.

"Yee-haw!" shouted Adam from the backseat divan. I could barely hear him with the wind in my ears. I looked back at him; he had both his arms stretched up in the air. The wind blew his jacket and shirt around his skinny frame. His head was tilted all the way back and he yelled out loudly into the wind, staring up at the sky.

"Ooow," he yelled.

I turned around to look at the road ahead; I hoped that the little French car had stopped on the other side of the bridge. The two-door 1971 drophead coupé powered on down the road. The four-wheel independent suspension's coil springs bounced up and down, absorbing the uneven surface. The three-speed automatic transmission pushed the one hundred and twenty inches of chrome and aluminium down the road. The turbo-charged HydraMatic engine purred like a lion on the Savanna. Adam had no idea of the danger ahead, oblivious to everything as he cried out in ecstasy at the fluffy cumulonimbus clouds above.

The little car stopped abruptly and pulled over on the grass verge next to a ditch. Yves puffed himself up and looked over the front of the long bonnet that stretched out in front of the car. The driver's seat had been pushed as far forward as possible so that his little legs could reach the pedals. He guided the car between the brick pillars of the small humpback bridge. We all bounced in the air as the car lifted off the road.

"Ooow!" shouted Adam.

The heavy car came down with a cushioned bounce and flew past the petrified faces in the little car as Adam waved at them. His blue-tinted Foster Grant sunglasses stretched across his fine face, hovering above his chiselled cheekbones. His white jacket flapped in the wind, matching his teeth, and his blue cotton shirt clung to his skinny, tanned torso. His shirt was unbuttoned to below his chest. Two gold chains hung around his neck, one as thick as my little finger, the other thinner and bearing a large sapphire.

It was a glorious day and I could feel the heat from the sun on my forehead. The countryside was spectacular, an endless Constable painting passing by on an escalator. I was mesmerised by the beauty of the undulating fields stretching to the horizon. The car glided through the lanes and people stared as it drove through small villages. To Adam's delight, Yves beeped the loud horn to the people by the side of the road.

With his hat in one hand, Adam leant out of the car and waved energetically at the people.

"Cooowee, *bonjour*, oooohuuuuu! Beep, Yves, beep!" he ordered Yves.

Astonished faces stared at the car, their fly-trap mouths opened wide and their heads turned to follow it down the road, as if they were watching a tennis match where the ball never returns.

"Ugly old cow. Don't wave back, see if I care. People are so fucking ugly round here and they dress like they come from Bulgaria or Estonia, somewhere cold and depressing," Adam declared.

We entered a small village where a white Renault Express van was pulled up on the kerb selling bread, croissants, and the local paper to a gathering of women.

The tiny village square was like a red-bricked courtyard and the sound of the Rolls' horn bounced off the high walls, sounding like a ship's fog horn.

We whooshed past the women, who clutched their baguettes to their chests, and the Renault van rocked from side to side.

Yves caught sight of Adam in the rearview mirror. He was sitting with an unlit cigarette in his mouth.

"You won't light it without the cigar lighter," he said.

"Shut up and drive, chauffeur," Adam said. "Yebo ('yes' in Zulu, pronounced yeahbaw), light my cigarette, Yves, now! Pass it back to me instead of passing me the lit cigar lighter!" He passed his cigarette forward.

"I'm only good to light your cigarettes, am I?" Yves said.

"Pass me the cigarette already and I'll tell you what you are good for. Then we can discuss all your faults. Keep your eyes on the fucking road, man! I don't want to die, not today anyway!"

We arrived at the house.

Yves parked the car on the driveway in front of the closed gates. The car was so long it stretched onto the grassy verges either side of the gravel driveway. The grass had not been mown and the garden was overgrown. Yves's door almost touched the locked gate as he got out. I stepped out and walked round to the back of the car.

Yves held a large bunch of keys in his hands and was frantically looking for the right set of keys. Eventually, after trying five different keys, he found the right one.

"*Voilà*, at last. I put them all on this bunch of keys. Just have to go through the ones I'm not sure about. You can't lose this number of keys." He put the key in the padlock and unlocked it. He lifted the metal latch and pushed the gate open and I followed Yves through.

"I'm going to stay in the car and wave to any cars that happen to drive by," said Adam. "If I get kidnapped by a bunch of gorgeous men, don't bother to come and look for me." He took a puff on his cigarette, blew the smoke in the air, then put his hat back on his head and turned to look at the open fields opposite the house.

We walked towards the front door of the old farmhouse. The exterior had been completely restored and painted. The lush green grass at the end was overgrown. Yves searched for the front door key amongst his gargantuan bunch of keys. He found the right one and the old lock clicked open.

He pulled down on the metal door handle and stepped into the room. There was a damp, musky smell. There were spider webs everywhere, and lots of dead flies on the floor and window sills. Yves took out a small torch from his coat pocket and switched it on. He walked into the room immediately to the left of the door and pushed a switch, turning on the electricity. The oven in the kitchen started beeping and various machine lights started flashing.

"Open the shutters and windows to get some air in here. I'll go upstairs and start to take photos," Yves said, turning towards the narrow, steep stairs in the corner of the room.

I walked into the dark living room and searched for the light switch on the wall.

The VHS machine made a churning noise like it was going to throw up. The cassette tray repeatedly lifted up and retracted down in quick succession. I found the switch and turned on the central light that hung down from the centre of the ceiling. I walked over and unplugged the video player.

I opened a window, unlatched the shutters, and pushed them open. I crossed over to the other side of the room and did the same thing. Sunlight poured through the windows onto the fireplace. The house had been tastefully restored. The large, sanded beams and stripped wooden floorboards were stained a rich dark brown. I could hear Yves moving around upstairs. I walked into the bedrooms that led off from the living room. The shutters creaked as they opened. The house was clean, but had not been lived in or visited for a couple of months. The unlived-in smell was dispelled as fresh air blew into the house. Yves walked into the living room.

"What do you think? Have a look upstairs, they've renovated it. Two lovely bedrooms and a bathroom with a toilet, so you don't have to come downstairs at night," he said.

I walked up the narrow, winding staircase and ducked my head under the crossbeams. I looked into the bedrooms and bathroom quickly. I peered out of the Velux windows at the fields opposite. I saw Adam in the car, leaning back, his arms stretched out along the top of the backseat looking up at the sky. I heard wooden shutters clatter as Yves tugged them shut.

I walked down the stairs, across the kitchen and back into the living room.

"OK, would you mind shutting those other shutters and I'll do the kitchen and the other rooms at the other end," Yves said, scampering through the doorway.

I closed the windows, turning the handles into a vertical

position and pulling gently to make sure they were properly locked in the grooves. I put the latches of the shutters on their hooks and turned the heavy cross bars into place. I walked into the entrance room of the house as Yves stepped from the kitchen.

"I'm all done here, just outside to do, the garden and the barns," he said. "I just need a few new photos. I have all the measurements in the dossier." He skipped down the steps into the courtyard and walked in the direction of the garden.

I locked the door and walked over to where Yves was standing holding the huge bunch of keys.

"The house has three sides made from local stone," he said. "And then, on the courtyard side, it's wattle and daub, like your place. Good old cow shit! They just scraped off all the rendering to have the beams showing. It has three hundred and ninety-five square metres in total of habitable living space. Four bedrooms, two bathrooms and that barn could easily be a garage for three or four cars. It's nice, don't you think?"

"Yes, it's a beautiful house, nicely renovated with every comfort. I can't wait for my place to look like this," I said.

"They've put a lot of money into this place since they bought it. It was in ruins at the end there." Yves pointed along the building. "They've completely rebuilt that end. Look at the landscaped garden. They've fenced it off from the field at the back, too." He turned and walked towards the car.

"It has new electrics, a new septic tank, a new roof and floors. They're leaving all the furniture and the new equipment – the fridge, freezer, and the washing machine. The water heater is brand new. Imagine hot and cold water, what a luxury! It's a pleasant location, an ideal property for staying with family or friends." He took photographs as he spoke, reeling off his sales pitch. "Set back from the road. The house has a relaxing atmosphere to it, it's situated at the end of a small village and ideally located in the heart of the Bay of the Somme. The intersection at the end of the lane gives you a choice of the beaches of Saint-Valery, Le Crotoy, Saint Firmin, Saint Quentin en Tourmont, Quend-Plage-les-Pins, and Fort-Mahon. They are all accessible from here in five to twenty minutes by car."

Adam watched us walking towards the car. We arrived at the gates.

"Right, I've nearly finished taking photos," said Yves. "We're publishing our new brochure that I'm taking to the French property trade show in London. Hopefully, sell some houses. Everybody overlooks this area, but you'll see. Once they finish the motorway, the trip down from Calais will only take an hour and half. The Channel tunnel will make the trip so much quicker, too. This is the first place you arrive at. Get off the train in Calais, then down here for fresh mussels and chips, oysters, fresh fish, and lovely sandy beaches with no one on them. It is undervisited. OK, there's the rain, but – hey – English people love the rain. You are always talking about the rain!"

"We lived in London, did he tell you?" Adam said, butting in.

"Yeah, Adam worked in a pub, but I fired him and stopped him from working there," Yves said, laughing.

"You fired him?" I asked.

"Yes, I came in and said to his boss, the landlord, 'He's not coming back to work here anymore, fire him!' The landlord wouldn't fire him, but he said to me, 'It's true, he doesn't do anything – he doesn't pour drinks, he just sits on a stool and talks to people and buys the whole pub free drinks.'"

"I was in charge of customer relations," quipped Adam.

"Customer relations my ass," replied Yves. "He just bought everybody in the pub a drink. Whoever comes through the door, even if he doesn't know them, he says, 'Hello, lovely to see you, how are you doing, can I get you a drink?' Then he shouts to the barman to pour the drinks. When the people ask him how much, he says, 'Don't worry, darling, it's on the house. Enjoy yourselves, have a good time.' He'd order a large one for himself, then sit with the customers and drink with them, no work."

"Cheers, bottoms up, darling!" Adam said sarcastically from the car.

"He was costing me money to go to work," continued Yves. "He owed about five hundred pounds after just two weeks."

"He doesn't buy me anything anymore, he's such a Jew," Adam said.

"I might be Jewish, but you are going to hell! You are way past saving," Yves said sternly.

"My maker will judge me on how I look," said Adam. "He's going to see me drift up in my suit and nicely cleaned shoes, with no socks. You won't need any socks up there. I'll be polite. I'll say, 'Hello, it's Adam here,' and they'll say 'OK, come in, the bar's open.' I'll float over to the eternal open bar. 'Coo-ee, I'm here! They'll have my favourite tipple ready, with a handsome barman with no shirt on, flapping his little wings. With Yves, he'll get to the pearly gates and the angels will be there with a huge bunch of keys, just like Yves. They'll be there, trying to stay afloat on their little clouds because the fucking keys are too heavy and they can't find the fucking right key to stick in the hole to open the gates! A bit like Yves – he can't find the hole, either! Yves's angels – imagine, little fat fairies in big, oversized nappies, buzzing around with big bunches of keys dragging them down!"

Adam looked at Yves. This was all part of their daily banter. Adam was on flying form.

"I need a fucking drink, look at the time. Yves, Yves, Yves, come on, let's go. I'm thirsty," Adam shouted. Yves was taking the last photos of the outside barns and the overgrown garden.

"I just want to get one with the view from the road, with the gates, the house and courtyard," replied Yves, looking through the lens of his camera. "Bugger, I can't quite get all the house in the frame. Can you move the car out of the way, so I can take a photo of the whole house?" he asked me. "Do you want to drive?"

"Er, wow, are you sure? You don't mind? Thanks, with pleasure," I said.

"Yes, of course he does! Who doesn't want to drive a Rolls fucking Royce! What a stupid fucking question. He knows how to drive," Adam said. "Anything is better than your driving! You always drive in the potholes, on the verges of the narrow lanes, and you brake so late on the corners it scares me to fucking death!"

I opened the heavy door and got into the driver's seat. The key was still in the ignition.

"Do you know how to drive an automatic?" enquired Yves. He seemed concerned.

"Er, yes," I lied. I had only driven an automatic once, in the field next to my grandmother's house. The corn had just been harvested and the short stubble was ideal. But that had been ten years ago and this was a Rolls Royce, not a Ford Corsair Estate.

"Don't crash. We haven't got any fucking insurance for it," Adam said from the backseat.

"What's the point if we don't use it?" replied Yves. "What a waste of money. Anyway, it was you who suggested we go for a drive, have lunch. 'Let's take the Rolls,' you said." Yves had the camera up to his eye as he focused. "I have a perfectly good Renault Nineteen, all insured, paid for, taxed, vignette, with a new air filter and oil filter, oil change and it had a complete check-up only last week. So, don't talk to me about not paying, and it's you who wants to be seen in the Rolls."

"Ah, I won't be seen dead in a fucking French car," Adam said.

"You ol' queen, he's so vain," Yves said. "You just complain all the bloody time, you are never happy. Yves this, Yves that!"

"You're lucky I don't give you the 'Yves-ho' the way you prattle on, you ol' fart." Adam started to shout. "I'm bored, I'm bored – come on, hurry up!"

"We're done now," said Yves. "Let's get a drink."

Adam leant forward between the leather seats and whispered in my ear.

"You do know how to drive an automatic?" he asked seriously. "You're not going to put us in the ditch? He'll be fucked off if we end up in the ditch!"

"I know, don't worry, we won't end up in the ditch – at least, if we do, it won't be my fault. I'll drive nice and gently," I said, reassuring Adam.

He reclined back into the cream leather bench seat. I started the car and it purred into life.

"Ronnie Corbett must have gone for a drive in this car, the seat is so far forward," I said to Adam, searching for the lever under the trim piping of the cream leather chair. I pushed the seat back.

"He's a fucking Swiss midget. They could put him in one of those cuckoo clocks. All you have to do is attach a big spring to his arse," said Adam. "Cuckoo, cuckoo, cuckoooooo!"

I pushed my foot on the brake and moved the lever over, making sure that it arrived in the right position, and looked attentively where the little arrow stopped. I gently pushed down on the large accelerator pedal and the car lunged forwards. It rocked as it came out of the rut it had made under its own weight on the soft wet verge. I turned the wheel and put on the warning indicators, so any cars that came along would see us.

Yves took the last pictures of the outside of the house. He opened the gates so he could get the whole courtyard and the house with the gate posts. He closed the gates and pushed the metal spike into the hole to hold it in place. He wrapped the chain around the gates and closed the padlock. He walked around the back of the car and arrived at the passenger's side door and opened it.

"OK, let's go. Drive on, chauffeur," he said, climbing into the car and closing the large door with a loud thud.

I put the seatbelt over my shoulder and clicked it into the shiny metal holder. I looked in the rearview mirror and saw Adam combing his hair with his hand. He flicked off some ash that had fallen onto his shirt. I looked in the side mirror and saw there was no car coming. The large beast of a car moved smoothly forward and air started to flow through my hair as we gathered speed, bouncing smoothly over the uneven surface.

"There's a junction up ahead, we're going to turn right," Yves said.

The brakes were severe and the car jerked forward. The seatbelt flexed as our heads bobbed.

"The brakes are very sensitive," Yves said.

"Yeh, I can see that, sorry," I said.

"Just press lightly and she stops," Yves said.

"At least they work," I said.

I tried again. This time, I pushed more softly and the large boat of a car slowed down quickly. I eased my foot off the brake and let the car cruise up to the stop sign and stopped. The road was clear and I pushed my foot down. I was enjoying myself. The car quickly reached ninety kilometres an hour as we flew through the open fields, the hedgerows whipping by.

"Only fifty in the villages," said Yves. "They just changed the laws for the speed limit in villages."

"Stop nagging him, he's doing alright," Adam jeered, leaning forward.

I eased off on the accelerator; the car was going fast enough.

We breezed into a small linear village. The vernacular architecture of different shapes and sizes built with different materials lined the road. Buildings made with red bricks, wood cladding, wattle and daub, and white chalk stone houses mixed with the large farms, with their expansive courtyards and large, brick pillars holding up tall, heavy wrought iron gates. A round, brick-built *pigeonnier* stood proudly in the middle of a dirty farm courtyard.

"I love this farm. Look at that pigeon castle, a family could live in it. Picardy is a fancier's fancy," Yves said through the wind. I looked at the impressive tower and the pigeons pruning themselves on the purpose-built perches.

"It's all part of the culture round here," added Yves. "The more decorative and bigger the *pigeonnier*, the richer the family was. They have some really elaborate ones. Pigeons are a sign of class and stature. Everybody looks at your pigeons and judges you accordingly."

"They just shit on everything," Adam shouted out from the backseat. "They're just shitting machines, fucking things!"

Some of the houses' front doors opened directly onto the pavement, their red brick facades all identical. Smoke rose from chimneys. The rainwater from the storm the night before was still lying along the side of the road. The sun shone directly onto the windscreen, it was a glorious day. I accelerated as we left the village and passed the village signpost. There was a red line through the name. We drove past a farm and the smell of manure enveloped the car.

"Christ, man! Who dropped a *klankie*? ('fart' in Afrikaans)," Adam shouted as he got a nose full of the country air.

"It's the pleasure of driving in a convertible," Yves said. "Breathe in... Ah, wonderful!"

We drove past a handwritten sign on a wooden spike knocked into the ground, on the side of the road.

"*Ball-trap*," I said, reading it aloud. I beeped the horn.

"That's what Yves needs," hurled Adam. "I need to trap his balls, but they're like prunes now, shrivelled prunes, all dried up! No juice left in them!"

"It's a clay pigeon shoot," explained Yves. "They get drunk, shoot guns and win prizes. Probably the closest thing you get to being American around here."

"I want to win a prize!" shouted Adam from the backseat. "I'll trap all the balls in my hands. Give them a little squeeze. See if they've got it in them. I doubt they do, I'm too handsome for them. They need a bearded hag with no teeth to turn them on." Adam laughed while coughing at the same time.

"Why not call it a shoot?" I said.

"*Ball* comes from *balle*, which literally means bullet or cartridge. A trap is what they call the machine that launches the clays," Yves explained.

"Just coz you're old and boring, doesn't mean I can't dream," yelled Adam. "He's so old and boring now. He used to be fun and we had a *jol* ('good time' in Afrikaans), but not now," he said poking his face between the head rests.

I slowed down for a junction and the car rolled to a stop. I indicated and slowly moved the car further into the road, the long nose of the car advancing. I could just see round the edge of the brick wall of a large house on the corner.

"They always build walls where you don't need them," said Yves. "There have been so many accidents here. Cars come flying down that road and the people can't see them until the last minute and bang! More dead people for no reason." He looked both ways down the road. "Be careful, it's OK, all clear, drive on."

We drove down the narrow, winding lanes, the light blue sky mixed with large, grey clouds. I slowed to a stop to let a tractor with a wide plough behind it cross the road into a field.

"All I see now is tractors, I hate fucking tractors! They look like monsters. Big square blue and red monsters, green ones, too," Adam said grumpily. He crossed his arms across his chest as he fell back onto the backseat.

I turned right and drove past a row of three cottages. I suddenly recognised where I was.

"I see where we've come out. That's the direction to the town, I see where we are," I said, pleased with myself.

"That's a shortcut and the way to come back from the beach. If you go out and have a drink, come back this way. Your house is just over there," Yves said and pointed with his arm.

"OK, I'll remember that, thanks," I said.

"That way, you don't bump into any *kêrels* ('police' in Afrikaans). The boys in blue, darling," Adam tapped me on the shoulder.

"*Les flics*," Yves added.

"I like my boys dressed in a nice black or grey suit, something dark and mysterious," Adam moved forward. "Or, I like nice earthy colours during autumn. As you know, I only wear whites, white trousers always, with either a white shirt, which is the best, or with a splash of one bright colour in the summer. Say, a pink polo shirt with a pink jumper, it's always got to match. It can be a different hue or tone, but it has to be the same colour," Adam continued. "You have to make an effort, some less than others, hey Yves?" Adam moved his head forward so Yves could hear what he said.

"Yves doesn't have time for any beauty sleep," continued Adam. "His ship left port donkey's years ago. He better start swimming after that ship, coz it's a way away, on the fucking horizon." He slapped me on the shoulder as he laughed out loud, throwing himself back onto his voluptuous leather sofa.

"I don't have the time to stop working, keeping you in gin,

vodka and wine," Yves said, turning around and looking sternly at Adam, beginning to get pissed off with his digs.

"He's got too much catching up to do, to try and make himself look any good!" retorted Adam. "See, all that effort isn't working! It's all sunk down to his big, wobbly beer barrel of a paunch."

"Oh, that's below the belt," Yves said. Adam missed the joke and continued his sermon.

"He grew that thing on his face to make himself look thinner, but it doesn't work. He's always saying he's going on a diet, but ends up eating profiteroles filled with ice cream and he has creamy sauces with everything. He never eats a salad, never, never! He doesn't really eat vegetables anymore, do you?"

It was a rhetorical question. All that counted was that he had won the debate hook, line, and sinker.

Driving the car was pure delight; the steering and comfort were matchless. The Rolls Royce Corniche is a true masterpiece and was probably the best car that money could buy when it was launched. It had stood the test of time, too. We drifted past the cemetery and the large monument to the fallen from the two World Wars.

I slowed the car and steered it round the gentle corner. The large cross of Jesus had been recently repainted.

"They gave him a coat of paint, that'll help him stay warm this winter," said Adam. "Poor thing, having to stand, well... hang, up there all winter in just his underpants, imagine that! I wouldn't like to be stuck up there in just my underwear."

As we approached the level crossing, the yellow lights started flashing and the warning bell clanged loudly. I slowed down and stopped next to the flashing light. The wooden barrier lowered and bounced into a horizontal position. I put the car in 'park' and waited for the approaching train. The house on the corner blocked our view of the tracks.

"Oooow, a train! Yves, a train, look," Adam said sarcastically, tapping Yves hard on the shoulder repeatedly. "A train, a train's coming!" He shouted into the air in excitement.

The train rolled past us rapidly. Adam stood up in the back of the car, holding onto Yves's seat with his hand. He waved his arm from side to side vigorously, with his hat in his hand, at the passing train.

"Coooooo!" He was happy, smiling broadly. "Coooooooooweee!"

People on the train waved back at him. The air whooshed by as the train sped past above us. Adam slumped back onto the backseat and put his Panama on his head.

"That was fun. I need a drink now, I'm exhausted," he said firmly. The security bell stopped ringing. "Thank God for that! Fucking racket." He lit a cigarette with his own lighter.

A loud clunk came from the white metal box holding the barrier and it started to lift up. I moved the gear lever, aligning it with the 'D' and eased my foot off the big brake pedal. The car rolled forward. I accelerated and we moved up the slight incline. I looked left, then right, just to make sure another train wasn't coming. We passed over the railway lines and bounced down on the other side onto the road. The ditches were full of water and the road was slightly elevated above the green fields on either side of the narrow lane. I hoped that no car was coming in the other direction, as there was barely enough room for the Rolls Royce.

We passed the campsite entrance.

"He-di-hi! They're so camp in there," Adam screamed from the back of the car.

"You had a smashing time in there. Do you remember, you and your driving?" Yves ribbed Adam.

"You should have shut up. That reminds me, play some

music. Put on that cassette of Village People, Yves," Adam ordered.

Yves looked for the fabled Village People cassette in the glove box.

"The cassette must be in there somewhere, man," said Adam. "Go on, man, look harder."

"He always wants to hear Village People when we're in the car," Yves said. "I found it, OK! Look, here's the cassette box." He flipped it open, pulled out the tape and pushed it into the slot.

"I'll rewind it so you get the song from the start. Are you ready?" I said. I glanced in the rearview mirror and saw Adam propping himself up in the back.

The cassette clunked and stopped. I pressed play and there was a short silence, then crackling static. The music started and the drums kicked the song into rhythm. The thumping disco track resounded from the huge metal bass bins. Yves leant forward and turned up the volume by at least fifty decibels.

"Let's teach the natives how to dance. 'Village People for village people!' Dance, you boring bunch of morons. Dance, come on!" Adam shouted at the top of his lungs in the wind as the music boomed from the car.

"Village people has another meaning around here!" he continued to shout. "Instead of being a disco group well known for their catchy tunes, suggestive lyrics and on-stage costumes depicting pure masculine wonder lust, it means toothless old women in aprons, house coats and slippers – gossiping about other people's business, while standing in the fucking rain. *Les miserables, les miserables!* Bunch of fuckers!"

Our eyes met as I looked in the rearview mirror, his deep blue eyes piercing mine. He had a slight smile and winked at me.

"I want to hear 'Macho Man' or 'In the Navy'," Adam ordered.

"They're all on the tape, you know that," Yves said.

"Yves couldn't get into the Navy, not even the Swiss Navy, imagine! He's got flat feet and he can't swim!" Adam threw his cigarette in the air.

Adam never let Yves win. He was in charge, and Yves was his slave and accountant. Adam smoked his Dunhill International cigarettes with a long cigarette holder, held lightly in his delicate, manicured fingers. His hands had never seen a day's work in his life. They were only used for holding crystal glasses and lighting cigarettes with his gold Dunhill lighter.

I slowed the car down as we approached a sharp right-hand corner. I knew the road well. The junction to turn to Villers-sur-Authie was just after this corner. The straight road led directly into the village where I was buying a house at three o'clock. The car slowly rounded the corner.

"Stop!" Yves shouted suddenly. "Look, she's there. Stop."

I braked and the car came to an abrupt, skidding stop. We all lunged forward. Adam's head appeared between the front seats and he grabbed the smooth, leather-piped upholstery to steady himself.

"Ah!" he cried out.

"Are you OK?" I enquired.

"No, I'm going to die," Adam jested.

"No, you're not. Stop being a baby. She's at home, she's there," Yves said happily.

Adam pushed himself up and automatically combed his hand over his hair to put it back into place.

"Who, for fuck's sake? It better be Sophia Loren or the Queen of fucking England to stop like that!" Adam scowled.

"Reverse up and turn into those gates of that house over

there." Yves pointed his hand at the gates. "Look where we are," he said to Adam. "Corinne's house."

"She's lovely, gorgeous," said Adam. "She's a good friend of ours. Yves sold them the house. We used to have dinner parties here and they'd come over to our place. How long ago did they buy it, Yves? Five, maybe six years ago, I think," Adam said.

"Eight," said Yves. "It's been eight years since I started the agency, this was one of the first houses I sold. Time flies when you're having fun."

"So, that makes it ten years since we left Paris for this hell hole!" Adam moaned.

"You are never happy anywhere. Anyway, we're having fun today, aren't we?" Yves said. "Now stop, let's see if she's there. I think I saw her car, or maybe it's the cleaner lady. If she's there, she'll buy us a drink," Yves said.

"I fucking hope so, man. I'm gasping," Adam shouted.

I turned the large car in through the gates and it rolled down the gravel track that led up to the impressive, renovated Picard *fermette*. The branches of a large weeping willow tree in the middle of a well-manicured garden bowed down to the ground.

"Stay here, I'll go and see if she's in," Yves said, opening the car door before it had come to a stop. I pushed on the brakes and the car stopped, skidding slightly on the deep gravel. Yves skipped over towards the front door, which opened before he reached it.

Yves kissed the woman on both cheeks. She smiled and waved her hand in the air to Adam. Yves minced quickly back down the stone pathway to the car.

"Come on, I'll pull the chair forward to make it easier for you to get out," Yves said, opening the driver's door. He pulled the chair forward. I switched off the engine and pulled the key out. As I walked around the front of the car, I looked at the large chrome radiator and the Spirit of Ecstasy bonnet ornament. I rubbed my hand on the graceful metal statue and handed the car key to Yves. Adam took short steps towards the door.

"Thanks for letting me drive. It was great," I said. Yves turned his head and grinned at me.

"Glad you enjoyed it, and you didn't put it in a ditch, like someone I know," he replied, pointing with his head at Adam.

"I was blinded by that bitch who didn't dip her lights," said Adam. "And the other time, I told you, one of those big water rats jumped into the road and scared me to death! I was so frightened, it looked like it was going to jump up and kill me with its two big front teeth. Turning the wheel was the obvious thing to do!"

"No – you don't turn the wheel for a rat," replied Yves. "You brake, stop, and then carry on or speed up and kill the fucking thing! Run it over. It's going to run away anyway and, if it doesn't, tuff shit!"

"Lovely to see you," Yves and Adam said in unison.

An attractive woman in her mid-fifties stood in the doorway. Her black jumper and tight black trousers hugged her slim hips. Elegant and fine, she stood tall in high-heeled shoes. Her light makeup accentuated her high cheekbones and strong, refined jaw. Her hair was perfectly groomed. I noticed a large ring on her wedding finger. She held out her fine-fingered right hand with manicured red nails and squeezed mine firmly.

"*Bonjour Madame. Je m'appelle* Max," I said.

"*Bonjour* Max. Corinne," she replied, holding my hand for much longer than was normal.

"Come in, please," she said. "Come in and sit down. Make yourselves comfortable." She waved her arm in the direction of the sitting area.

"We don't want to take up any of your time, or put you out for too long. Thank you for inviting us in," Adam said, wiping his shoes on the mat.

I walked into the huge living room with a large fireplace.

"It's my pleasure," she replied. "I'm here on my own. I literally just arrived from Paris for the long weekend."

"Ah, gay Paris," Adam drew out every syllable. "We love Paris, don't we, Yves? We used to count how good a night out was by how many bottles of Champagne we drank. We used to go everywhere, all the hot spots." He was lost in reminiscence. "An average night out was three to five bottles of Champagne, not less than three. Eight to ten was a good night, but anything above fifteen was a really great night out!"

Large paintings and prints adorned the walls. I looked at one that was directly in front of me, recognising the view.

"Ah, Saint-Valery, *le petit port*," I said in my minimal French.

"*Oui, j'adore* Saint-Valery, *le port*," replied Corinne. "I go to the market every Sunday, when I'm here. They always have good fresh local products. The view is lovely, whether the tide is high or low. The bay has so much charm. I always stop and have a coffee at the Casino Café afterwards. The café restaurant on the quay, next to the market square, on the front. I like to look out at the lovely bay and daydream"

The large room opened up to the roof, with bannisters running around an internal balcony. Bookshelves covered the walls and all the oak woodwork was stained dark brown. Also hanging on the walls was a big hairy boar's head, a pair of antlers and a huge stag's head above the fireplace.

"Wow, you have a very nice house, it's gorgeous," I said.

"I told you," Adam said, happily.

"*Super*," said Adam. "*J'adore, tu sais, j'adore chez toi* Corinne, *mon amour*."

"What would you like to drink?" she asked.

"Ah, *en fin, quelle bonne question*. What a great question," said Adam. He was finally close to getting something wet down his neck.

"I have everything, Pastis, Martini," replied Corinne. "I think I have a Chardonnay and a Sancerre in the fridge. There's beer, Leffe, Heineken and Export Thirty-three... um, there's rosé, too. Then there's whisky, vodka, gin, you name it, I have it. My husband is never here to drink any of it. OK, who wants what? Adam, you are the thirstiest person I know."

"I want a double Pastis. *Un cent-deux*, a one, zero, two, like Serge Gainsbourg," Adam said.

"OK, Pastis. Yves?" she enquired.

"*Allez un Pastis*, but a small one for me, not like that old soak," said Yves.

"That's true, you've got a small one," Adam elbowed me in the arm, and giggled.

"Max?" she said to me.

"A Leffe beer, please," I said.

"Where are you going for lunch?" she enquired as she walked towards the kitchen.

"Chez Jean," said Adam.

Corinne left the room to get the drinks.

"No, we're going to René's place, on the front. You like it there," said Yves.

"But I want to go and chow at Chez Jean, I like it there. It's great and it would be so nice for Max," Adam said, nodding in my direction. "The food is delicious."

"No, we're going to René's on the front," replied Yves. "The food is great and it's more of a lunchtime place. Chez Jean is too stuffy and formal. You have to get dressed up to go there. It's fantastic for dinner. We have to get there, eat, and then get back in time to be at the notaries' office for three. Look, it's already twelve-thirty. It takes twenty to thirty minutes to get there from here. Then we have to eat and get back to Rue for three. Plus, I'll have to drop you off before. We can't be late."

"I want to go to Chez Jean. I want to eat a *bouillabaisse*," Adam said, starting to sulk.

"But you know we have to order it in advance, and it's not a lunch place. Stop acting up! We're going to René's. I've already booked a table, so stop it," Yves said.

"You don't want to go there coz it's expensive, more expensive than Chez René," Adam snapped at Yves.

"It's not that, you know it's not," Yves affirmed.

"If you can't afford a lover, don't bother!" Adam said, turning his head at forty-five degrees in the air. A large cloud of smoke wafted above his head. He kept the cigarette in the side of his mouth. Crinne came back into the room with glasses and nick-nacks on a tray. She walked elegantly with a graceful sway of her slender hips. She had poise and grace like a model.

She put the tray down on the table and handed out the various drinks.

"*Voilà*, a real Serge Gainsbourg-sized Pastis for you," she said, handing over the glass to Adam, who wiggled forward on the sofa. He took the glass in his shaking hand, the ice cubes clattering against the sides.

"Max," she passed me the bottle of Belgium beer and a rounded glass. The bottle was already open and I poured it into the glass.

"*Merci Madame*," I said.

"Corinne, please call me Corinne," she said smiling at me.

She held a Martini Rosso with ice and a slice of lemon in her hand. It was the right type of glass for a Martini – the glass fanned out at the top.

"OK, *allez, santé*," she said and we all raised our glasses. They chimed as we touched them together.

"Cheers," everybody said in unison.

The beer was refreshing and the white froth gave me a moustache.

"Max is buying the house on the corner opposite to the little épicerie and café in the village," Adam said.

"We were supposed to do it at eleven o'clock this morning, but it was put back to three this afternoon," Yves added. "So we've gone for a little drive and we're going to lunch."

"That's nice," Corinne turned to me. "There must be a lot to do in that house. It's been closed up for years. I don't think I have ever seen the shutters open, the whole time I've been here."

"Yes, there's everything to do, but it's not expensive. A bit of elbow grease and an inside toilet," I said.

"Ah, there's no inside toilet?" she said, horrified.

"No, just a brick outhouse," said Yves. "A big plastic tub collects the rainwater from the roof and there's a ladle to scoop up the water to flush. It always rains here, so there's no danger of it never being full."

"Really, it rains nearly every day. It's worse than England," Corinne said to me.

"Yes, there's lot to do to it, but the house has a lot of potential. There is an apple, pear and a cherry tree in the garden," I said.

"You need a goat or a sheep to mow the lawn, then you can eat it afterwards, like back home," Adam said.

"Yes, I need a good lawnmower. It's a bit of jungle," I replied. "I have some help coming over from England – some friends are going to help me for a week. We'll get loads done and put a coat of fresh paint all over the place, inside and out, and give it a big cleanout, too."

"Yves can lend his broom, the ol' witch," Adam said and smiled, pleased with his jab. We all laughed.

"You should clean that foul mouth of yours with bleach and floor cleaner," said Yves.

"Are you going to live here full time, or just use it as a holiday home?" Corinne asked me.

"I'm going to try and make it liveable in four to five months, then see where I am," I said. "See if I can handle the hustle and bustle of the village."

"This is definitely not the place if you are looking for somewhere to have a fun time," she said, looking at me. "Everything closes at nine o'clock. Everybody shuts their shutters and locks themselves behind them until the next day."

"Tell Max and Corinne about that time you were in Cannes. Go on, Adam, you love to tell that story," said Yves, egging on Adam to tell his story.

"You mean before I got caught in your spider's web. When I was handsome and the world was my oyster, then I met you and everything went down from then on," replied Adam.

"Go on, quickly, and then we have to get going," Yves said.

Adam took a large swig of his Pastis.

"Which story? There are so many."

"You know the one, the one about the watch and the movie star at Cannes," Yves said.

"Oh, *that* one, with the 'shush, nudge, nudge, wink, wink'. Him?" Adam brought his finger up to his lips. "That well-known French ladies' man, the French heartthrob." He didn't need prompting and started his story, making sure everybody was listening to him.

"It was just before the film festival in Cannes," Adam said seriously. "I was at Nice airport picking up my bags, he'd been on the same flight. So, he chats me up and says he's staying at the Carlton. If I wanted to come over and have dinner, he'd book a room for me. I was actually going to see the Monaco Grand Prix.

Some South African friends of mine had a huge house there and they invited me every year. They are good friends from back home, a cousin of mine. They were married – he was white, of course, and she was black, which was unheard of back then."

"That didn't stop you," said Yves.

"The big black cock was only ever used in emergencies, a great cure for a hangover," Adam said proudly, then laughed out loud.

"Yeah, a hangover with you is every morning – or should I say afternoon," Yves said.

"OK, maybe it was used on more than one occasion, but it was purely medicinal! Like voodoo or seeing a witch doctor, they all do it. Anyway, where was I?" Adam took a large gulp and finished his drink. He turned to Corinne with his empty glass in his hand and passed it over to her.

"Can I have another one please, Corinne?" he asked.

"OK, but continue your story. Who is the actor? Is it a well-known person?" she enquired.

"He's very well known. He was at the top of the big actors' tree at that time. He's French, of course, the dirty sod," Adam said, flapping his hand in the air. "So, I called him up and he says he'll book me a suite next to his. So, I get a taxi and go over there."

"Go on, tell us who it is," Corinne insisted. She stopped and turned around halfway to the kitchen. "Go on, who is it?"

"No, I won't say who it is. Not even now! He'll sue me or get me killed," said Adam.

"It was so long ago, nobody cares now," Yves said.

"It would ruin his career," Adam said seriously. "And anyway, I won't do that. It's part of the contract."

"You had a contract with him?" Yves said mockingly.

"Of course not," replied Adam. "It wasn't as crazy as it is today, but there were still the paparazzi everywhere. They would be sneaking around, but today with all those lenses and cameras that can see up your ass all the time, they can see what you have had to eat from miles away. Nobody is safe anymore. Anyway, I don't have to bother about that and I don't care, they can come around and take as many pictures of me as they want – naked, if they like."

Corinne came back with another large double dose of dark yellow Pastis. She lifted the water jug and turned to Adam.

"Tell me when," she said, as she poured the water into his glass. The water barely touched the Pastis.

"Stop," Adam ordered abruptly.

She put the jug back down on the tray. Adam took his freshly charged glass and took a large swig of it. He licked his lips as he tasted the alcohol. He crossed his legs and looked at Corinne.

"It's amazing how voluptuous your figure is," he said. "I watched you walk back from the kitchen. Wonderful, darling."

Corinne pulled on the pleats in her trousers and looked at the chair behind her before she sat down. She grabbed her glass from a small table and took a sip.

"Come on, what happened?" Yves said.

"So, I was in this huge suite. There was a large bed, big enough for five people, it was massive. There's a knock on the door, I open it and there's this bellboy standing there with an envelope in his hand. All of a sudden, my dressing gown falls open and I'm naked underneath, of course. You should have seen his eyes, they popped out of his head like he had seen a ghost. So, I said to him, 'As you can see, I don't have any coins on me for a tip, the only tip is on the end of my cock, darling,' and slammed the door. The little handwritten note wished me a good morning. Then it said I should have breakfast, then go down to the hotel's private beach, where there would be a little surprise waiting for me. He would see me later, as he had a full morning of interviews and meetings. I was to meet him on the beach at one o'clock, for lunch."

Adam took a large sip of his drink, then placed the glass on the table.

"Imagine if it had got about that he was seeing me," he continued. "He was doing more than seeing me, I can assure you, love," he chuckled and gave a wry smile. "He never had it so good, I can tell you! The media would have gone into a feeding frenzy. It would have been the end of his career. He was playing with fire, he knew that, but hey, he just couldn't resist the cherry on the cake! Men are all the same! Look at Yves, he couldn't resist it, either." Adam turned his head and looked at Yves, who shyly looked up at the ceiling. His eyelids blinked quickly and he smiled timidly.

"*Ag*, man, I ordered breakfast on room service," said Adam. "I wasn't paying, that was on him, he invited me. They came up to the room with a lovely breakfast on a little trolley thing with flowers on it. They clattered it along the wooden floor over to the large French doors that opened up onto a tiny balcony, if you can call it a balcony. They put the table just in front of the doors. The view was fabulous, looking out on the sea, the bay with all the boats bobbing up and down. Anyway, I drank the fresh orange juice and a cup of tea, then nibbled on the breakfast. I had a bath and got dressed for the beach. I went downstairs, through the glorious reception area and crossed over the road. I arrived on the private beach and introduced myself to the manager chap, as instructed in the note." Adam lit another cigarette, blowing out the smoke above him.

"'*Monsieur*,' he said, 'come this way, please,' all very smart and correct. It's the fucking Carlton, darling, what else – nothing but the best. So, I follow him to the deck chair with its parasol, a little table to put your drink on. The two garçons busily raced around, cleaned the sand off the deck chair, dusted down the little table. Of course, everything was already clean and spotless. They bought an ice bucket and a bottle of Champagne. I lit a cigarette. The garçon clicked his lighter in front of me before I could grab mine. You can imagine the service, three people racing around me, fantastic! He pops open the bottle and I start drinking the first glass of the lovely cold Champagne. So, I strip off. I had my cozzie on already, everybody was looking at me." Adam leant forward and flicked the ash from his cigarette in the ashtray.

"I was already brown, as I'd been in Naples with this gorgeous hunky Italian. We spent all the time on the beach, eating ice cream and lovely pasta and the most amazing pizzas. I tell you, I ate so much fucking pizza! It put me off it for life!" Adam leant forward to pick up his drink. "I can't eat it now, too much of a good thing! The back of my mouth swells up just thinking about putting it in my mouth, ooooow."

He took another sip of his drink and a puff on his cigarette, looking up at the ceiling.

"So, I'm there and I've rubbed on all this oil on my golden body. Everybody was looking at me, of course. I have another drink and then, all of a sudden, he turns up on the beach. He's got a small box in his hand and says, 'Voila, this is for you,' and hands me the box. It was wrapped in paper, with a bow, like a fucking birthday present. I asked him if it was a bomb. So, he's now sitting next to me on the deck chair bed thingy. He stripped off, too, and he's in his cozzie. It was his last half-day of relaxing before starting the marketing for his new film. He just wanted to relax and suck up some sun before the madness started. So, I rip off the paper on the box. It was upside down, I turned it over and opened it, and there it was... a Rolex. Imagine, a fucking Rooooooooolex." Adam stretched out the word for ten seconds. "What a cheap bastard, I thought! Really, a fucking Rolex. No, really, I was horrified, man." He took another sip of his drink.

"So, he says to me, in a quiet voice, coz everybody is starting to look our way. He's cowering, trying to hide his face so nobody recognises him. I'm genuinely livid! I'd never wear a Rolex. Ghastly, revolting watches sported by drug dealers and nasty second-hand car dealers, or people who have too much money and not one grain of brains. People who play golf. What a fucking waste of time that is! The nineteenth hole is the only hole I play, well, you know what I mean."

Adam paused to take another puff of his cigarette.

"Scummy low-life people, huh, just awful. No, never a Rolex, you must be kidding me, man. I wouldn't be seen dead wearing a fucking Rolex," he said with seriousness. "So, I looked at him and I said to him, right up close to his face, 'It's a fucking Rolex, you stupid prick!'" Adam laughed out loud; we all burst into a roar of laughter. I took a large swig on my beer.

"I said it loudly – you should have seen the expression on his face, pure horror! He must have thought buying a Rolex was classy or something, fucking French peasant. I think, he genuinely expected me to scream out in happiness. Imagine!" He took another sip on his Pastis. "So, he smiles at me and says, 'What's wrong, don't you like it? Do you already have one?' I butted in and said, 'No, who do you think I am? A cheap fucking whore? How dare you.' I knocked over the ice bucket, the little table went crashing onto the sand and the Champagne poured out of the bottle. I stormed down to the water's edge. We were right near the water, anyway. You can imagine, we had the best table!

"So anyway, I went to the water's edge shouting, 'A Rolex, a Rolex, a fucking Rolex!' Everybody was looking at me by now with all my shouting and ranting. My toes touched the lapping waves and I took a couple of steps into the shallow water. With all my strength, I launched the watch into the air. It flew for miles. I remember being surprised by how far it went. It seemed to fly through the air for hours. It eventually crash-landed into the water and made a splash and then it sunk, obviously."

Adam looked at us to see if we were all paying attention. His clear blue eyes flashed in the sunlight that streamed through the large windows.

"So, he sees me throw the watch into the water and came running down the beach, screaming something, I couldn't work out what he was saying. He ran past me at great speed and didn't stop until he could not run anymore. The water's not very deep and he goes out quite a way before there's a ledge. He ran across the water like Jesus Christ and dived into the deeper water. I walked back to my deck chair, grabbed my shirt and trousers, got dressed and went back to my room. Meanwhile, he started splashing about, sticking his head under the water looking for the watch, turning around, splashing his arms about like he was drowning."

We all laughed with him as he imitated the French actor splashing about. Adam lifted his arms, splayed them out and swayed them in the air like branches of a tree in the wind. He was in full acting mode. Yves must have heard the story a hundred times before, maybe more, but he listened attentively like it was the first time, smiling and laughing at the right moments.

"What about him in the water?" Yves asked.

"I heard afterwards he nearly drowned," replied Adam. "The lifeguards and the garçons from the café dived in to save him with their clothes on. They pulled him to shore and the lifeguard had to pump his chest until he spat out the water he had swallowed, cheap fucker! But he could have drowned, seriously, he nearly died. He swallowed a lot of water. *Ag* man, he should have thought about all that before buying that fucking Rolex in the first place."

Adam took another sip of his drink and stubbed out his cigarette.

"So, as I said, I went back to my room as he was splashing around. I thought it was very funny and laughed out loud when I got back to my suite. From my balcony, I looked at the charade of a guy diving down to look for the watch in the water. I sat on my balcony, drinking Champagne I'd ordered on room service. He thought he was a great actor, he had nothing on me. I had that little bitch wrapped around my little finger."

"What happened after that? What did he say?" Corinne asked. "Was he angry with you? Did he kick you out of the room?"

"No, that bitch came back, begging like a dog. I was acting all the time and that drove him crazy. He couldn't control me. Not that little bitch! So anyway, he comes up to my room later that afternoon, early evening, two or three hours later, I can't remember, it's become a blur. But anyway, he came back to the hotel. I locked the adjoining door. He started banging on it, ordering me to open the door, shouting, kicking it with his foot, pulling on the door handle. He was livid! He was like a spoilt child, he was mad at me. I laughed at him from behind the door. He banged really hard, so I composed myself and unlocked the door.

"He burst into the room, shouting. I told him if he was going to be like that, I didn't want to talk. He calmed down and said I had humiliated him down on the beach, and that he was an important star, and couldn't be seen in situations like that. The festival was starting and all the world was looking at him. He said the watch had been found, the lifeguard with a mask spent nearly an hour looking for it. He took the watch back to the shop on the front, on the promenade, just along from the hotel."

"And what happened after that?" Corinne asked. She was enjoying the story immensely.

"He excused himself for buying such a cheap gift. He had another box in his hand behind his back. He smiled and moved his hand from behind his back and handed me the box. I took it and opened the box and there was this lovely Cartier." Adam proudly showed everyone the watch on his wrist.

"Look, isn't it gorgeous!" he continued. "It's a Cartier Pacha with a large sapphire on the winder. I think he paid ten grand for it, back then. I said, 'OK, I forgive you' and we had a lovely dinner. It works like clockwork," he laughed. "It must have cost him double what the Rolex did, the ol' fag! That'll teach him to be a fucking cheapskate."

Adam looked at the watch and lit another cigarette.

"No doubt he woke up the following morning with a hangover," said Yves.

"That's for me to know and you to never find out! One of my favourite expressions that I like to use is *'bubble ass'* – it means hangover in Afrikaans," said Adam. "As I keep on telling you, Yves, if you can't afford a lover, don't bother. At least he could afford it, but I couldn't be bothered with him. He loved himself too much. Women loved him, but he was more in love with himself. The bigger and more well known he became, the more he fell in love with his own ego and image. He was too wrapped up in his looks, the vain queen. Pretending to be straight, he got married not long after our brief affair," he added knowingly. "He was actually a heartthrob in Italy and France, even around the world. He became very famous, the old poof."

"Who is it? Tell us who it is," Corinne insisted. "Go on, tell us who it is."

"No, I can't tell you, it will ruin his myth, and you'll be too upset," said Adam. "All your teenage dreams will be shattered if I tell you who it is."

Yves looked at his watch.

"Talking about watches, we must be going now. We have to

get over to Le Crotoy for lunch and we can't be late for the notary at three o'clock." He stood up.

"Do you want to see the biggest bird in Picardy before we go?" said Adam. "It's not like those ducks they shoot in the bay. This is a real bird, a bird with balls, it's true." He rolled his shoulders as he spoke. You never knew what was going to come out of his mouth next.

"I'm serious," Adam said. "He's gorgeous, if he doesn't bite me!" He leant back in the sofa. "Would you mind showing him your parrot before we go?" Adam said to Corinne. "Where is it from again? Somewhere exotic, where the fucking sun shines."

Yves stood up and flexed his legs. He flicked his right leg out like he was highland dancing.

"Yves is warming up for a bit of Cossack dancing, watch out!" Adam said. "What are you doing, for fuck's sake, Yves? You'll break something with that carry on."

"Getting my circulation going," Yves said, heading for the toilet off the hallway.

"Let's see this fucking bird," Adam said to me as I placed my glass on a tray. "Give me a hand up, man. Ag, I hate getting fucking old. Once you sit in these sofas you can't get out. You just have to sit there and drink until you fall asleep."

I pulled him to his feet. He held my arm for balance as we followed Corinne into the large, open-plan kitchen with sliding doors that led out onto a covered patio. The bird's cage took up one whole corner of the kitchen. The large windows gave the parrot a panoramic view of the garden, the kitchen, and a clear view into the main room.

The cage was oriental in design and intricately decorated, with ornate sculptured metal birds and animals welded to the bars. The large bird was perched on a thick stick that traversed the cage from one side to the other. A round mirror spun on a chain behind him.

"It's an Amazon parrot. They are some of the most beautiful parrots in the world. They mate for life, unlike my husband, the bastard," Corinne said with an element of sadness in her voice.

"Ooow, he's at it again, *encore? Non, oh chérie*," said Adam, mincing over to Corinne. He put his arms around her shoulders and hugged her tightly.

"*Bon, le perroquet est toujours là.* At least the parrot is still here," Yves said as he arrived in the kitchen. Adam was still consoling Corinne with his arm around her shoulder, his head tilted to towards hers.

"He's the first thing I look forward to seeing when I arrive here from Paris," Corinne said with tears in her eyes. "I have a person who comes in to check on him every day, to look at the water and his food and give him his treats. She puts him on the phone to me so I can speak to him over the phone. She puts the speakerphone on and I talk to him. He understands my voice. He knows it's me talking. He speaks back to me. I promise you, it's true, he loves me. Ah, chérie, my adorable bird." Corinne turned around and looked at the bird as she was speaking. "You won't leave me. Truly, this time I have had enough. Excuse me." She turned in my direction and looked me in the eyes.

"Carry on, I don't understand, anyway." I lifted my hands up to gesture that everything was OK with me.

"*Une autre bière?*" she asked me, opening the door of the fridge. As Corinne bent over, her pert bottom stuck out in front of Adam. He spanked it with an open hand, the sound resonating around the room. The parrot let out a loud squeal and jumped to the side of the cage. The bird squealed again, bouncing from side to side and the cage shook with his weight. The mirror bumped into the chains that held various nibbles.

"Ooow!" Corinne turned around briskly and lunged at Adam. She lightly slapped him in jest. "You brute, you," she said, pretending to be angry with him.

Adam shuffled backwards, holding his arms up to his chest to protect himself. He bumped into the back of the heavy, wrought iron chair under the round Moroccan tiled table. The weighty chair scrapped across the sand-coloured terracotta tiles. Adam steadied himself with the table.

"Ooow, that hurt," he said and made a sad face, like a scolded child sulking. Then a beaming smile quickly returned to his face. "*T'es mechant!*" he barked, smiling. "You have a good bottom, nice and firm, *chérie*, like a peach, still yummy."

Corinne smiled and moved her head like a girl who had just won her first gymkhana and was posing for the obligatory photos.

"Wonderful, very good bottom, bravo!" Adam clapped his hands together.

"We don't have time for another drink, we have to get going. OK, let's go," Yves ordered, and walked towards the front door. "Corinne, merci for the drink."

I followed Yves, and Corinne helped Adam walk down the pathway to the car.

"Thank you for the drink," I said and held out my hand. Corinne gently shook it and leant forwards, kissing me on each cheek.

The car seat was still pushed forward and Adam climbed into the back.

"*Au revoir,* Max," she said looking into my eyes. "Bon courage, good luck with the house," she added.

Yves started the car and turned it around in a three-point turn. The large car rolled down the gravelled driveway and Yves slowed the car as we drove between the tall, red brick gateposts. He looked to see if a car was coming round the sharp corner, then accelerated out of the driveway, stones tapping the underside of the car.

"That was fun, wasn't it? She's adorable," said Yves. "Her

husband is a stockbroker banker guy in Paris. He earns a fortune. He bought that place to put her up here while he goes off with his secretary. He's been doing it for years. She knows about it, but won't leave him for some reason." He turned his head briefly in my direction, then looked at the narrow lane ahead.

"What is it you call her, Adam?"

"The parrot woman," said Adam. "She loves that fucking parrot more than her husband, that's for sure."

"Let's have lunch and go and buy a house," Yves said.

"I want a drink. Hurry up, for Christ's sake man, I'm gasping," Adam shouted into the wind as we cruised across the fields in the big Rolls Royce.

THE PARROT WOMAN

I was up a ladder, again. The guttering on the gable end of the house needed looking at. Yet another emergency. I was endlessly stopping leaks, blocking icy cold draughts, doing anything I could to stay warm at night.

For over a week it rained constantly. The water spilled over the top of the plastic guttering on the corner of the house. The down spout had cracked and split. The fasteners had come away from the rotten cant and the rainwater dripped through the broken pan tiles on the eave of the roof.

The projecting edge of the roof extended beyond the supporting exterior wall by three pan tiles, at a slightly different angle to the rest of the roof. The field of the roof was in fairly good condition considering it had been bombarded by rain, snow, and hail for over two hundred years.

The perimeters and all the flashing needed looking at. Many of the overhanging tiles were cracked, split, or dislodged by the wind, exposing the wood to the rain. This had caused a lot of water damage to the wooden supports nailed onto the rafters. The north-facing gable end wall took the brunt of the rain. The downspout that captured all the runoff water from the roof had exploded and water poured out of the broken joint and cascaded down the newly painted walls. The old metal channel that ran along the downslope perimeter of the roof was rusty and leaked. The whole guttering needed replacing, but I had more important things to do to the house first.

The gutters had not been cleaned out in years. I scooped up the leaves, twigs and the heavy black sludge that lay along the bottom of the groove. I scooped it all up with my hand and plopped it into a plastic bag that I had attached to the rung of the ladder in front of me. I kept my other hand free to hold on to the ladder. I started to look at the major problem with the down-pipe. It descended down the wall and water then flowed into the large drain on the corner of the street.

Jean-Claude, the *garde champêtre* of the village, stopped his old Renault Twelve estate on the pavement next to the ladder. The car was badly parked with the boot sticking out into the road.

He climbed out of the battered car, and looked up at me with his *Gitanes maïs* cigarette stuck in the corner of his mouth. He was employed by the mayor and acted as a rural policeman and road sweeper. He was responsible for the upkeep of the village. He only wore his ill-fitting uniform for the village fete and Christmas drink at the mayor's office.

He lifted his hand and waved.

"How's it going?" he enquired.

"OK, thanks. I've got leaks all over the house after that heavy rain last week," I replied, looking down at him.

"You haven't finished yet, there's a lot to do to that place," he said. "I used to patch up the roof for him every winter. He didn't want to spend any money on the place."

"One thing at a time," I said. "An inside toilet and a hot shower is the next thing."

"You have to put up a flag or something brightly coloured –

a tea towel or a tee shirt on a stick – so people see you up the ladder," he said.

"OK."

I climbed down the ladder and shook J-C's hand.

"You have to warn the drivers that you are using a ladder on the street, so they see you and slow down. They drive through the village so quickly these days," he said, climbing back into his car. "See you in the café later."

"*Bien sûr.*"

I tied an old tea towel to a bamboo cane and attached it to a wooden wine case that I found in the garage. I placed it in the road on the corner and climbed back up the ladder.

I hadn't moved in straight away after buying the house.

I came over from England with a van and two friends. I brought furniture, cooking utensils and some tools, and we spent a week working on the house, cleaning out the old junk. John acted as bonfire monitor in the garden. We piled up the junk with a lot of dry wood, dead branches, and bushes from the garden.

The long, dry grass caught fire and it quickly spread to the wall at the end of the garden. We rapidly filled buckets with rainwater gathered in the three-hundred-litre plastic drum outside the brick shithouse. We managed to douse the flames just before the large pine tree caught fire.

We worked hard. In our breaks, we drank cheap wine, Pastis, calvados, *bon prix* brandy and cases of little stubbly green bottles of beer.

After two thick coats of fresh white paint on the exterior walls, the old house suddenly looked lived-in again. Richard prided himself on his ability to climb onto the roof. He sat on the gable and painted the chimney stack.

Mums on their way to collect their kids from the small school at the end of the road looked up at him in shock and amazement. They spoke to us and used sign language that translated to, "He is crazy!" I agreed, but told them not to worry, as he had drunk six bottles of beer, a bottle of wine, and three large glasses of calvados for lunch. He was flying, literarily!

Returning with their children, they stared at him again. The kids thought it was cool and looked up at the man perched on the top of the roof. Richard was showing them what Father Christmas does at Christmas, it all made sense to them now. If 'Monsieur Anglais' can get up there, then old red pants and his big beard could breeze it.

The school run always seemed to ignite the village into action. Suddenly, there would be a commotion of cars, tractors, delivery vans (driven by alcohol-fuelled drivers), mopeds, bicycles, and a group of up to seven mums and their troop of different-sized kids on foot.

The mums would curiously inspect what I was doing as they walked past the house. If I had opened the street-side shutters, they would peer through the thin curtains and comment on how nice it was to see the house being lived in after being shut up for so long. My minimal communication skills were accompanied by hand movements and international hand signals for painting, hammering and cutting.

Time passed quickly, and I'd now been living in the village for six months. I had cut back the overhanging trees and painted the breeze-block wall that ran along the grass verge that led to the church.

The brand-new black BMW 525tds six-cylinder diesel engine roared up the road. I could see it racing towards me with its lights on. The four headlights shone in the early afternoon sunlight. I was outstretched on the ladder as I tried to push the new guttering into the rounded lip on the old metal guttering that I had cut with a disc saw. I concentrated on trying to line up the plastic guttering without breaking it. Unfortunately, the new guttering was slightly smaller.

The revs of the 143bhp engine growled as the lump of German-styled metal rolled quickly towards where my ladder was in the road. I looked at the fast-approaching car.

Do I hold on to the rotten wood or jump if the car hits the ladder? I thought.

The car glided past, missing the legs of the ladder by thirty centimetres.

The driver was a woman wearing large, black sunglasses. The car pulled up on the low kerb and stopped abruptly. The driver's door flew open and I saw it was Corinne, the 'Parrot Woman'.

She was wearing a black roll-neck jumper with a waist-length fur coat. She had changed her hairstyle since I met her with Adam and Yves almost a year before.

"*Bonjour* Max," she said above the sound of loud music coming from inside the car.

"*Bonjour* Corinne," I said and started to climb down the ladder.

"Ah, you know how to do that," she said, pointing up to the roof.

I pulled off my right-hand glove as I walked towards her and held out my hand. My thoughts raced: *Do we do the kissy thing? Do I say vous to her, or, as we've already met, I could use tu? But she's older than me...*

She shook my hand.

"*Ça va?*" she asked.

"*Oui, ça va, merci,*" I said.

"I have a problem at my house." She twirled her hands round and around in circles. "*Oh là là avec la pluie!* With all that heavy rain we've had over the last couple of weeks, it just hasn't stopped. This is the first time it's let up, but they say it's going to rain again tonight."

I looked up at the sky to give my expert advice.

"*Oui, peut-être,*" I said.

"I have a problem like you with the *gouttières*, the guttering," she said. "Water was pouring everywhere when I went outside earlier. I'm worried that it will ruin the wattle and daub façade. Can you come around and have a look, I'm really concerned."

"OK, *quand?*" I asked. I was getting the hang of the lingo!

"*Tout à l'heure.*" She pushed back the sleeve of her fur coat and looked at her gold Omega watch as she fanned out her fingers. Her large diamond on her wedding finger beamed in the sunlight. "*Vers*, five, *allez*, five-thirty, later this afternoon, OK?" she enquired. "I will pay you for your time," she added. "I also have a ladder, so you don't have to bring yours."

I had nothing planned, just doing my thing, trying to get the house fixed up. "OK, no problem," I said. Did I have a choice? "*Cinq heures et demie,*" I said, to confirm that I had understood the right time.

"Super, I must go now! I have to go to Abbeville, but I will be at my place later." She pointed in the direction of her house on the outside of the village. She turned and smiled at me before lunging into the car and slamming the car door. She had left the engine running and the music blaring. The car accelerated away quickly and I watched it disappear round the bend.

I finished working on the guttering at around four o'clock. I put the ladder in the garage and made a cup of tea. I drank it while looking at the work that needed to be done the next day.

I took a shower and dressed in clean working clothes. I picked up a few tools and my working gloves.

I closed the front door and turned the old key in the lock. It was about four inches long and the teeth were finely and precisely cut by hand. The ornate bow had a small ball of metal welded in the middle. It pressed into the palm of my hand as I applied pressure to turn the key. The one hundred and eighty-year-old mechanism made a metallic 'click' sound as the deadbolt slid into the strike plate.

I put the tools and gloves on the passenger's seat of the car and walked over to the small café. I pushed the door open and it stuck on the tiles. I knew the routine. I had pushed and pulled on that door for the last six months. Jean-Claude stood in his usual place by the window on the right-hand side of the door. He had finished for the day. I had seen him with his wheelbarrow, large broom, and a spade as he had passed in front of the house twice as he swept his way down both sides of the straight road through the village. I shook his hand again.

"*Salut*," I said to the legends of the bar.

Jérôme turned his whole body in my direction and shook my hand. He had to turn his shoulders and all his body as his neck muscles didn't function any more, and his head was stuck in one position. The rest of his carcass was not in a much better condition. He had jumped out of planes or crash-landed more than three hundred times.

He was an ex-paratrooper who had served with the prestigious and versatile 3rd Parachute Regiment based in Carcassonne. Apart from crashes, he had never landed in an airplane; he had taken off, but always jumped out. I asked him why he hadn't taken a plane to somewhere just to see what it's like to land. He told me he didn't like flying, and now that he was older there was no way he would get in a plane. After many operations on his back, knees, and neck, there was nothing more they could do for him.

He got early retirement and a disability pension and spent his days drifting from café to café. He told me his stories about being sent all over the world. He jumped out of planes at night with over a hundred kilos of gear tied to him. He recounted how he crash-landed into the deserts of Mali, the mountains of Corsica, and the jungle in French Guyana. He told me stories of how they were taught how to catch and eat snakes and bugs and drink their own piss during a jungle training exercise. He was a generous and enthusiastic person, who had deeply loved his job and was proud to have served his country in extreme circumstances.

"Want a drink, *Anglais*?" Jérôme asked me. "Jean-Claude, *un tit coupe*?" he shouted down the bar.

It was a rhetorical question, asking Jean-Claude if he wanted a drink. This was J-C's chillaxing time before he had to get home. If he didn't walk through the front door of his house at precisely eight o'clock when the evening news started on TF1, his wife would ring the café. He would be passed the telephone and his wife would shout at him to come home immediately. Even with all the loud background noise in the café, you could still hear her screeching voice coming from the earpiece of the heavy, canary yellow Bakelite telephone that dated back to the fifties. The café would erupt into laughter at his expense.

"*Oui merci, une bière*," J-C and I said in unison.

"I can only stay for one," I said. "I only popped in to buy some cigarettes. I'll have to buy a round tomorrow."

"No problem, *Anglais*! I know where you live," Jérôme said jokingly.

J-C's happy hour lasted from five to eight and it was spent at the bar, standing in his place next to the front door.

He relished his three hours of freedom. Standing at his place, he could carry on a conversation and 'curtain bash' at the same time. He liked to look out and observe who was going where, who was driving past, keeping a vigilant eye on the homeland. Fridays and Saturdays he was allowed to stay until nine o'clock.

Many a time I found J-C slumped over his steering wheel at eleven o'clock when *Madame* would close up. His baby blue Renault Twelve estate had many bumps and dents due to his expert driving skills. He reversed into walls, ditches, street lamps, gates, and sign posts regularly.

Madame put the three Vega Pils beer bottles and two tall glasses on the counter. J-C drank from the bottle. Why waste time pouring beer into a glass when he could pour it down his neck and save his precious drinking time?

"Can I have a packet of Marlboro red, please, *Madame*," I asked.

She took a small key from its hook on the wall next to the wooden till drawer and walked over to the glass medicine cabinet. She unlocked it, took out a packet of cigarettes and closed the door. She put the packet in front of me before replacing the key in its place on the small hook. I put a twenty Franc note on the counter, she turned around and pulled out a five centimes coin and put it on the cigarettes.

I finished the refreshing beer. The old clock above the archway that led to the small shop next door showed I had five minutes to get to the house.

"*OK, merci Jérôme* for the beer," I said, shaking hands. I turned to Jean-Claude and he shook my hand briskly, as he always did.

I drove the short distance to Corinne's house, which was about three kilometres from the village. The house was situated on a sharp bend, the large gates to the exquisitely renovated Picard *fermette* were open.

I turned into the entrance, past the red brick pillars and drove down the white gravel driveway, bordered by a meticulous garden with fruit trees and a multitude of plants and bushes of various types.

The front of the house was about a hundred metres across with roses climbing up the exposed timbers.

I parked next to Corinne's BMW. I could see her moving around inside the house through the large kitchen windows. The front door sprung open and she greeted me with a broad smile, waving her arm in the air vigorously.

"Come in," she beckoned.

I walked across the gravel and stepped onto the stone pathway that led to the steps at the front door.

"*Merci*," I said, holding out my hand. She shook my hand and kept hold of it.

"*En se fait les bis t'as déjà venu ici, en se connais*," she said, kissing me on both cheeks with her lips.

"Thank you for coming," she said.

"That's OK. What is the problem with the guttering?" I asked, standing in the entrance. "I'll get my tools and things from the car."

"Don't worry," she replied. "I saw the rainwater gushing over the plastic gutter in the corner by the downpipe, it's where all the rainwater from the roof goes down. I noticed it the other day. It must have been blocked with leaves or something. When I came back, it wasn't doing it again, so maybe all the rainwater flushed it all down the pipe and unblocked it. Really, I'm sorry for wasting your time," she said sincerely.

"I'm glad it's resolved itself," I said.

"Anyway, it's far too late now," she said. "It's getting dark and I'm sure it's not as bad as I thought. Maybe you should come around one day when it's raining and see if it overflows, but really, I'll mention it to the gardener who cuts the lawn and trims the trees." She promptly reached for her handbag on a little table next to the front door. She took out her purse, from which she produced a two hundred Franc note. She thrust it into my hand.

"I'm so sorry, please take this, I really I don't want to waste your time. This should cover your expenses."

I pushed the note back into her hand, but she firmly pushed it back at me.

"No, really," I said. "I haven't done anything. It's not very far from my house. Please, I don't want this, please take it back," I added, holding out the note again. She closed her handbag and placed it on the table.

"I insist. I asked you to come by because I thought there was a problem, but *voilà*, no problem now! So, let's have a drink, shall we? Do you have time?" Corinne walked into the house, walking through the large living room towards the kitchen. I put the money in my pocket. I was confused. She had seemed so anxious when she had stopped earlier.

I followed her across the living room. The fire was roaring with three large logs. As I looked around at the collection of artworks on the walls, I noticed a tray with chips and peanuts on a table placed between two large sofas.

Was she waiting for someone to turn up? I followed her into the kitchen and her high heels tapped on the terracotta tiles.

"Have you seen Adam and Yves?" she laughed and held her hand up to her mouth as if she had said a bad word. "That's so funny, like all mankind comes from those two, God forbid," she said, imitating Adam's South African accent, throwing out her hand the way Adam did. We both laughed.

"I saw Yves at the supermarket in town the other day." I said. "He looked well, running around as ever. He said business was good and he's selling lots of houses to keep Adam in vodka."

"*Oh là là,* Adam, *il boit pour deux,*" Corinne said tapping me on the arm. "Talking about drinking, what would you like?" she asked, with one hand propping herself up on the kitchen counter. "As you know, I have everything! Pastis, beer, white wine, rosé, Muscat, gin and tonic, vodka, whisky, or Champagne?" she recited. "*Allez*, Champagne, I've decided for you! It's always a good time to drink Champagne." She turned her head to me and smiled. She lunged towards the fridge door and tugged it open.

"OK, Champagne, thank you," I said.

She pulled a bottle out of the fridge and showed it to me proudly.

"Veuve Clicquot rosé. It really is my favourite Champagne," she declared. "Would you mind opening the bottle, please?" She passed it to me. It was nicely chilled.

"Did you know that, all the way back in 1775, it was the first Champagne house to produce rosé Champagne. Fourteen years before the revolution."

"I didn't know that," I said. "I like the Brut, I have drunk a few of those! I know they hold a royal warrant from the Queen, so she drinks it. If it's good enough for her, it's good enough for me," I added and Corinne laughed.

"*Bien, bien,* she's got good taste, your Queen," she said. "I bought a case of it at the supermarket the other day. It should be nice and cold by now."

"Yes, it's just right," I said, looking for the little tag on the metal sheath.

"Veuve Clicquot is the Champagne that is served at Rick's Café American in the film Casablanca," she said, "with Humphrey Bogart and Ingrid Bergman. I love that film. It's now over fifty years old, but it's still a wonderful love story. It's so sad. I always cry at the end when she leaves Rick."

I looked at the huge parrot in the ornate cage. It screeched at me. Holding a large nut in his pointy claws, he ripped the top off the shell and screeched at me again.

Corinne took a sack of ice from the freezer and poured the cubes into a metal Champagne ice bucket. She turned around and opened a cabinet door and took two glasses in her hand. I pulled the metal paper off the top of the bottle and untwisted the wire muselet and pulled it off.

She saw me looking at the parrot.

"Do you know anything about parrots?" she asked.

"Not really. I know that they live in the Amazon jungle and they can talk. They can also become aggressive and their bite can cause serious injury," I said.

"Parrots don't suit everyone as a pet because of their natural wild instincts such as screaming and chewing," she said. "You have to know how to talk to them, make them feel at home. Although parrots can be very affectionate and cute when immature, once mature they can turn nasty, but that's mainly due to mishandling and poor training. He's never bitten me. Let's go through to the living room. I have the fire going, it's more comfortable in there."

Corinne placed the glasses in the ice bucket and picked it up. She walked into the living room and I followed her with the bottle in my hand.

"What type is it?" I enquired as we walked over to the sofas.

She placed the ice bucket on the low table next to a large glass ashtray.

"It's a blue-and-yellow macaw. They are generally regarded as the best imitators and speakers of the parrot world," Corinne informed me. "Go ahead, make yourself comfortable, sit down." She pointed her manicured fingernail in the direction of the tan leather sofa. There were three, three-seater sofas in a U shape around the long, low rectangular table in the middle of the huge living room. The dining table was behind the sofas and ran along the windows.

I sat at the end of the sofa furthest from the roaring fire. Corinne manoeuvred herself around the table and sat next to me. Her fine form slid gracefully onto the sofa and she crossed her legs with poise.

I slowly turned the bottle in my hand and pointed the bottle away from us. The cork gently came away from the bottle in my hand in a controlled manner. I poured the Champagne and waited for the bubbles to settle before filling the flute glasses to the top. Corinne picked up both glasses and passed me one with her left hand. Again, I noticed the large diamond ring on her wedding finger.

"Cheers, as you say in England," she said.

We chinked our glasses.

"*Santé*, as you say in France," I said and we laughed.

I took a large sip and the tiny little fizzy bubbles hit the back of my throat.

"Delicious," I said.

"Champagne makes me feel totally euphoric and bubbly," Corinne said.

"France in a glass," I said jokingly and she giggled.

"I must confess that there has been a parrot in my life," I explained. "I have never owned one, but this parrot was the coolest bird in the world and I loved him like a brother. I gave him all my crisps and spent all my pocket money on dry roasted KP peanuts for him." I had never admitted my love for the old bird to anyone. "He was called Nelson, as he only had one eye. He lived in the pub that my mother used to drink in."

My childhood memories flashed back to me. I could see Nelson perched in his cage. I could smell the stale cigarette smoke permeating from the walls, curtains, and well-worn carpet of The Wheatsheaf pub in Old Oxted.

Peter Crick ran the small, narrow pub that had been converted from an old watermill after the war. He was a member of The Magic Circle, and looked like Tommy Cooper. He never combed his hair and always wore a black suit with a white, wrinkly shirt, often with a stain of beer down the front, and a thin black tie.

"The man who owned the parrot was a magician," I told Corinne. "My mother booked him to do a show for my birthday party at our house. He turned up in his Rover V8. He parked by driving up on the verge outside the house and knocking over the dustbin. He staggered up the small slope, carrying his props in a suitcase with a scarf hanging out of it, and fell through the front door. My mother guided him into the living room and he set up on a small, collapsible camping table.

"She gave him a brandy to calm his nerves. He slurred his way through a couple of tricks, then dropped his playing cards all over the floor. When he bent over to pick them up, his body-weight went past his balancing point, and he crashed head first into the wall. His foot knocked away the leg of the table and it crashed to the ground, scattering his props all over the floor. The rabbit hiding in his top hat started bouncing away to freedom. All the children roared with laughter. That was his best trick ever!"

We both laughed and I took a sip of the Champagne.

"With the help of one of the other mums, my mother managed to roll him over on his back," I continued. "He looked dead. He was knocked out cold and blood poured from a cut on his head. They managed to sit him up against the wall as the blood kept pouring from the wound. The blood rolled down his face, and dripped off his chin onto his white shirt. My mother got bandages, a basin full of warm water, and a large brandy which she waved under his nose. He came around, but the show was over. He'd gone out with a bang! A true professional."

"*Quelle finale!*" Corinne said, bursting into laughter.

"His pub was split into two bars. The saloon bar and the public bar opposite."

"Before you continue, what type of parrot was it, do you know?" she asked.

"He looked just like yours. He was old. I remember hearing that he was like a hundred years old in human years," I said.

"They can live for a long time," Corinne said and reached for the bottle and charged my glass.

"*Merci*," I said. "I was allowed to go inside the pub, but only to go to the toilet. I remember how that old urinal reeked, the smell was overpowering. The odour from the cubes of bleach would sting my eyes." I made a gesture with my hand and pulled a long face. "I would have to walk past the parrot. He had his place next to the counter in the quieter saloon bar. The tiny counter was an opening in the wall, no larger than a trap door. The parrot was fed on a diet of Guinness, English brown bitter, KP peanuts, Planters dry roasted peanuts and cheese and onion crisps. The customers would ram things through the cage bars, trying not to get their fingers caught by his sharp beak. The parrot was renowned for his bite and his vulgar vocabulary. He didn't like being locked up and would get angry. He was in a large cage, nearly as big as the cage your parrot has." I reached for my glass on the table.

"The bird only lived on beer and peanuts?" Corinne said horrified.

"That's all I ever saw him eat and drink," I replied. "I would feed him all my crisps or peanuts. I had seen people trying to provoke him to get a reaction, or get him to say his famous 'naughty' words. The pub closed at three o'clock for the whole of the afternoon, but my mother was part of the 'in crowd' who would be locked in for the afternoon session. Then I was allowed inside as the pub was officially closed, and it was Peter's private gathering.

"He let the big bird out of the cage, and I would watch in amazement as it flew back and forth between the saloon bar and the public bar. Nelson would launch himself from the bookshelf. The books, small porcelain ornaments, and other objects placed on the shelves would crash to the floor. He'd land on tables, smashing glasses and ashtrays that would get pushed off with his claws or wings.

"His weight would rock the small, round wooden tables scattered around the pub as he landed on them, or flung himself into the air. His huge claws would grip the wooden beam above the fireplace. He would re-launch himself down the bar, swooping above the heads of the drunks sitting on their stools. People would duck down or fall over each other, the intoxicated customers ending up in a pile on the ground. The bird would cause so much chaos and damage in the pub. I thought it was hilarious. But the best bit was when he would perch himself on the shelf that ran along the back of the bar. He would stand up straight and look down at everyone and say, 'Fuck orrrf, fuck orrrf, fuck orrrf.'"

Corinne laughed as I imitated the parrot's voice. The image of him flashed into my head, and I could see Nelson winking at me with his only eye.

"That used to make me laugh so much. A parrot saying those words! I certainly wasn't allowed to say that, but he got away with it. Parrots are cool!" I said, smiling after my trip down memory lane.

"That is so funny. Would you like some more?" Corinne asked me. She had already finished her glass. I took a large swig and finished my glass. I placed it on the table in front of her. She emptied the rest of the bottle into our glasses.

"*Ah, zut,* we need more Champagne. Oh dear, it's finished," she exclaimed, looking at the empty bottle. "I'll get another bottle from the fridge," she said, getting up from the sofa.

"Er, *encore?*" I said. My French was improving as the Champagne flowed.

She wanted another bottle, I had no choice.

Corinne walked towards the kitchen with the empty bottle

in her hand and rapidly returned with a full one. She passed me the bottle to open and sat down.

I twisted the cork and the popping sound filled the room. I poured the Champagne and placed it back in the ice bucket. I grabbed a handful of peanuts from the tray.

"There are many different exotic bird species that are commonly kept as pets, like macaws, Amazons, cockatoos, and then there are African greys, cockatiels, budgerigars, parakeets and, of course, lovebirds," Corinne said, staring directly in my eyes.

I looked away towards the garden. I could feel that she was coming on to me. I felt uncomfortable – she was a married woman. I didn't need any extramarital bullshit. I looked up at the stuffed animal heads on the walls. They were probably shot by her husband.

"Cheers," we said and clinked our glasses.

"You know, I love parrots," she said, "but it's funny because I got given my first parrot because of the English! I love the Monty Python's 'dead parrot' sketch. *J'adore*, I love it!" She took another sip from her glass.

"I have had the parrot for ten years now," she continued. "I was asked what I wanted for a wedding present. I jokingly said 'a parrot'. My friend was so crazy, he turned up with it in that huge cage all wrapped in paper. I couldn't believe my eyes when I ripped the paper off and saw it!" Corinne laughed with delight. "He's been in our life – or, should I say, in my life – ever since. I brought him up here from Paris two years ago. He can get out and can fly around the house. That's why we bought the house, so he had enough room to fly about. The house was bought really as an excuse for my husband to get me to bring the bird up here. Then he hoped I would move up here, because he knows how much I love that bird."

"You bought the house for the parrot?" I asked. I didn't quite understand what she had just said to me.

"Yes, more, or less. That's why we cut out all the floorboards here." She pointed up to the ceiling, which was open to the ridge beam of the roof. "I wanted to have a large, open-plan space, lots of volume, no walls, or doors, but still with the look of an old Picardy farmhouse. I can never stop talking about parrots, I love them. Parrots have featured in human writings, story, art, humour, religion, and music for thousands of years. They have been our friends since time began."

"Dominica, the little island in the Caribbean, just next to the French island of Guadeloupe, has a parrot on their flag," I said.

"Humans and parrots have complicated relationships, but it is nothing compared to the impossible relationships between humans and humans. He's my little companion, and he's so *mignion*." Corinne looked over her shoulder in the direction of the parrot's cage and blew him a kiss. "You know, they only have one mate during their life, so he's like my fluffy boyfriend. He talks to me and I talk to him about everything!"

"There is an expression in English, we say you are as 'sick as a parrot' – do you say that?" I asked.

"*Moi, je suis malade comme un parrot* because of my husband," Corinne said seriously, then burst into laughter. I could see she hadn't laughed like that in a long time, probably since the last time I was here with Adam and Yves.

She finished her glass in one large swig, I followed suit. I pulled the pink-labelled bottle from the ice bucket and wiped the bottom with the tea towel that hung from one of the handles. I poured two glasses and passed her glass back to her.

Corinne took her glass and held it and looked at me straight in the eye.

"My husband, the bastard, is having an affair with his secretary, *la salope*, the bitch," she continued. I could feel the wrath in her voice. She wanted to get something off her chest.

"I've seen his bank statements. He takes her away for romantic weekends in Honfleur, in Normandy, Paris, Rome, Venice and London. He thinks I don't know anything about it, but I know everything!" she said with anger in her voice. She took another large swig of her Champagne. She slammed her glass down hard on the table. "He's no longer interested in me. He makes it home every now and again just to change his wardrobe, change his suits, and then he heads off again." She spoke quickly without stopping between sentences. "I want him out, out of my life. I want him gone! I have had enough of his lies, his cheating. Here I am, a good woman, I clean the house, I still look after myself and he has no interest in me. I want that bastard out of my life." Her voice rose with rage.

I didn't know what to think or say. She had got me round to clean her gutters, but she was now telling me about how her husband was having an affair with a woman young enough to be his daughter. I filled her glass and poured the rest into my glass. The last of the bubbles flowed over the top of the glass and ran down the side onto the coaster.

"You will be married before the end of the year," Corinne said.

"I don't think so," I said firmly, moving my head from side to side.

"It's a thing we say in France. When the last of the Champagne in the bottle pours out and overfills the glass, we say you will get married. Don't worry – I wasn't proposing to you." Corinne tapped me playfully on the shoulder. "I want to get rid of a husband, not get a new one, no thank you!" We clinked glasses and laughed before taking a sip in unison.

"The bottle is finished," she said, pushing herself up from the sofa. She finished her glass and put it on the table. "In that case, I will get another bottle, straight away, *toute de suite.*" Wobbling from side to side, she took a couple of steps and turned around.

"Do you know Jacques Brel, le chanteur? He has such beautiful songs," she said, stopping in front of her hi-fi.

"I don't know much about him – I've heard him on the radio," I said.

Corinne pressed play and the CD spun into life. The song, 'Ne Me Quitte Pas' came out of the speakers that were attached to the wall either side of the fireplace.

"Would you mind checking on the fire," she said. I watched her as she glided elegantly towards the kitchen.

"Of course," I said.

I jumped up from the sofa and walked over to the open fire. I took the poker from the metal stand and stabbed at the fire, prodding the large logs. The fire roared and the heat made it impossible to stand in front of it.

"It's working well," I said loudly. She couldn't hear me through the music.

I turned and, through the window, I saw a light flash on the back of the parked cars. The courtyard lit up momentarily, then went dark.

Corinne swaggered back into the living room with the third bottle of Champagne in her hand. I jabbed the fire. She walked onto the carpet and stood next to me in front of the fireplace, dangling the full bottle in her hand.

"I think someone has turned up, I saw a light on the cars," I said, putting the metal spike back on its hook.

"No, nobody is coming, here – open this." She waved the bottle in the air and headed towards the sofa.

"Really, I saw something," I said.

I heard the sound of the metal door handle and the front door swept open. A man entered and he was suddenly standing there in the middle of the room. He was a large man — monstrous in stature.

"It's me!" he bellowed.

"Oh, what are you doing here?" asked Corinne, walking towards him. "You didn't tell me you were coming."

"What's all this? Who is this man?" he said. His face reddened as he clenched his jaw and his bushy eyebrows lowered and joined together to form a huge, single moustache across his glaring eyes. His whole body was tense as he tried to control his rage. He closed his fists tightly and his breathing was heavy. "What's he doing here, drinking my Champagne? Tell me what's going on."

He spoke so quickly that I only caught a few words, but I could understand that he wasn't happy.

I noticed that they didn't kiss, which was not very French.

"*Bonjour*," I said timidly, putting out my hand. "I'm Max, nice to meet you. I was just leaving, actually," I added, shaking his hand.

"Corinne, *merci* for the little drink," I said. "I must be going. I have a dinner engagement with Adam and Yves. Thanks, once again."

Mentioning Adam and Yves was a stroke of genius conjured in a moment of terror. Her husband's face relaxed. I could see that he presumed I was on the same 'team' as Adam and Yves and, therefore, no threat to his pride. I kissed Corinne on both cheeks and she grabbed me by the elbows, pulling me closer as we kissed.

I shook the husband's hand again.

"OK, goodbye, *à bientôt*," I said, moving towards the front door.

"I'll put the outside light on for you," Corinne said, walking swiftly towards the switch by the door.

I walked quickly to my car. I got in and started the engine. I reversed up the driveway. Corinne waved at me from the front door and I flashed the headlights.

A few weeks later, Yves dropped by my house to show a client a 'work in progress' project. He told me that Corinne had called him in tears. The parrot had escaped and flown away. Her husband had flown off, too, with his young secretary, and they were getting divorced. Yves was commissioned to sell the house for them and she was moving to Nice for the sunshine.

I always looked out for the parrot as I drove through the countryside near the village, but I never saw it, or Corinne, again.

I like to think that he bumped into a feral 'lady' parrot and they created a new species, 'The Picardy Parrot', and lived happily ever after.

FISHERMAN'S FRIEND

I was told to be on the quay of the port at '*eeelevurn-zerty*' if I wanted to go fishing. Eleven-thirty – an hour before high tide. I didn't have a fishing rod or much experience. Years ago, I had caught newts and toads with a small net in a pond behind the house I grew up in.

When I did go fishing, I mostly spent my time untangling the hooks and lines I snagged in rocks, trees, and lumps of wood, or got caught in grass, lily pads, or my own arse.

It was the perfect day for fishing. The seagulls were screeching above my head as they glided and bounced on the breeze. The wind was up and I watched as the crews began hauling the sails as the boat captains steered out into the bay of the Somme.

In the marina of the small coastal village of Saint-Valery-sur-Somme, the putt-putting of the small engines and the sloshing of the waves against the quay created a rhythmic soundtrack. The fumes of marine petrol filled my nostrils and the residual oil left rainbow rings on the surface of the water. The temperature was climbing and I felt the perspiration accumulating above my eyebrows and gathering in a ridge at the top of my shirt collar.

I heard the ambulance approaching before I saw it roar around the corner, with its blue lights flashing as it raced down the quay, destroying the tranquillity.

I shifted my weight off the railing I had been leaning on, trying to see where the ambulance was headed. I could see nothing that suggested an emergency. The ambulance flashed through the trees and whizzed past the parked cars. Its wheels squealed as it turned sharply in my direction. It accelerated and barrelled towards me – it was a 1986 Citroen CX Quasar fitted out by Hueliez, not unlike the Ectomobile from the Ghostbusters movie.

Braking hard, the vehicle skidded to a stop a few metres in front of me. Gravel flew in all directions spraying my legs and dusting my shoes.

I jumped back as the wail of the siren fizzled out like a record on a turntable losing speed, and the small blue light on the roof faded as the engine went silent.

The doors burst open and out sprang '*Le Belge*', Didier and Alan.

Waving his arms around in the air, '*Le Belge*' raced forward from the ambulance and shook my hand. A large, bushy moustache covered the whole of his face, enveloping his toothless smile. His hair was styled as if he had been hit by lightning.

"Do you like it?" he said to me in English, gesturing toward the elongated white whale of a car. The blue lines that ran along the sides made it look even longer. The outline of the Star of Life was still evident on the bonnet and doors.

"*Oui*, it's huge, great horn," I replied.

'*Le Belge*' was actually called Patrick. I knew him from the café. He was lean, wiry, and never clean shaven. Always covered in engine oil or some product for cleaning engines or paint: white spirit, glue, plastic, or fibreglass. His fragrance was more chemical plant than human. His English was not good, but he liked to speak it. I would always reply in French and he would try to put another sentence together.

He had been to England on numerous day trips, which involved getting on the boat as a foot passenger from Boulogne, drinking continuously until the boat docked in England, then walking to the nearest pub, positioned at the gates of the dock. He would spend the day at the bar and catch the last boat back to France. That's all he knew of England, but he liked what he'd seen and he was happy with that.

"It's a decommissioned ambulance," he said. "I just bought it this morning in Paris. That's why we're late, we got caught up in traffic, a big accident. But I switched on the siren and the flashing lights and drove down the hard shoulder. *Et voilà*, no waiting! It's got a 2.4-litre petrol engine, 115 horse power, even has a 12-volt socket, radio-telephone, flashing emergency lights, siren, a road horn, electric windows, and H4 headlamps that light up the sky and blind oncoming drivers who don't dip their lights." He beamed proudly and put his arm around my shoulder.

He looked and behaved like the French comic strip hero Asterix, the cartoon character who had no respect for Julius Caesar and the conquering Roman Army. Like Asterix, he didn't give a shit for rules and regulations.

"Everything works on it! It was well looked after, you know, by those ambulance people. They make so much money driving dead people around. OK, there's a little hole in the exhaust, but that's nothing to repair. It has all you need in an emergency and you never know when there's going to be an emergency, so it's good to be prepared."

He had acquired the name '*Le Belge*' after his sudden disappearance from the village for a couple of years.

He had spent this time, not in Belgium, but a few kilometres from the border in one of France's largest prisons. His wife would visit him every other weekend, announcing to anyone who enquired that she was going to Belgium to see her husband who was working on a job there. Upon returning to the village, she would distribute the cheap cigarettes, Martini, and Belgium chocolates that people had requested.

Patrick had shared his story with me and said it had been a time of reflection – to ponder how not to get caught the next time.

The story goes that his garage was broken into one night when he was away in Paris on business. Only a few people knew he was going to be away for a week or so. When he got back, he found all his tools and various pieces of equipment had been stolen. The house insurance did not cover the contents of the garage or his equipment. He had lost everything he needed in his craft as a mechanic and was unable to work.

Patrick circulated a rumour that the insurance company had paid him in full for his losses and that he had now replaced all of his tools and equipment with shiny new ones. He spread the word throughout the bars of the area, describing his beautiful new tools in delicious detail to anyone who would listen.

Then he set a trap for the foolhardy thief who thought he could get the best of Patrick a second time. He placed blocks of wood just under the windows with fourteen-centimetre nails pointing upward.

When everything was perfectly positioned, he left the windows enticingly open. A few nights later, he was jarred awake by a noise coming from the garage. He dressed quickly and threw open the garage doors. He turned on the single, low-wattage bulb that was suspended from a bare rafter. He saw immediately that the upturned nails were bloody. There were drips of dark red spattered on the cement floor, but no sign of the intruder.

He rang all the local hospitals asking if his 'brother' had been taken in for emergency foot treatment, explaining that he had walked on a nail or two. It was confirmed that they had such a patient at the hospital in Amiens.

Patrick told the helpful hospital clerk not to disturb his 'brother' and that he would visit him the next day. He jumped into his car and, within the hour, was at the hospital, asking which room his 'brother' was in. He located the room containing the patient with the foot injuries. The man in the room had his heavily bandaged foot elevated in a complex contraption, which implied the injury was even worse than Patrick had hoped.

Patrick lumbered slowly and deliberately toward the injured man. In a flash, he punched the man in the face – pow, pow, pow! Then again – pow, pow! He broke the patient's nose and dislodged a number of teeth. As he turned to leave, he picked up the heavy metal chair next to the bed and slammed it down on the injured foot.

The patient's screams rang through the hospital corridors as Patrick quietly exited the side door.

"*C'est de la merde, de la merde... Allez*, get ze provisions on board, quick, quick, quick," he shouted to his two compatriots as he gestured wildly toward the boat.

His fishing boat, the *Belle Marie*, was his pride and joy. It was about seven metres long and nearly fifty years old. He had done a major refurbishment, replacing much of the hull with new timber and reinforcing the whole thing with carbon fibre. He had repainted and treated the teak decking, the wheelhouse and replaced a lot of the fixtures and fittings, often with parts dispossessed from other boats.

The galley was small, but serviceable. There was even a

'head' of sorts, not exactly a cruise liner toilet, but a flushing toilet nonetheless.

The boat was painted marine blue with white piping around the handrails and along her sides.

'Le Belge' had enlarged the engine housing to accommodate a Volvo Penta engine. This engine had been completely rebuilt after it was fortuitously salvaged in the port one night from a fishing boat that had sunk in the mud after a big storm.

No one could ever explain how or why the boat sank. 'Le Belge' was the first on the scene at the next low tide. He came with a crane and lifted the engine out of the submerged boat.

"Get on the boat, we have to get going. We're already late. We won't have much time to get the nets out, fish and get back here." Patrick raised his voice and turned to his crew.

One of the crew members was a rotund giant who resembled Obelix, Asterix's overweight sidekick with superhuman strength. His name was Didier, but everybody called him 'Ch'gros', which could be taken as either big or fat. He, like Obelix, took offence at being called fat. I'd seen him get angry with people on a few occasions. Only certain people were allowed to call him 'Ch'gros'. I think it depended on his mood and the volume of beer he had consumed.

One night, I watched him drink seventeen *bières de Noël* – sweet, cherry, super-strength winter-warmer beer. When he took a first sip of the eighteenth, he spat it out along the entire length of the bar. He claimed that it was too sweet and demanded a large Pastis instead.

The third crew member, Alan, had a long grey beard, a shining bald head with thinning grey hair on the sides, similar to the potion-making Getafix.

Didier picked up the four packs of beer (each pack containing twenty-four bottles) with ease and carried them to the quayside. I grabbed plastic bags containing bread, cheese, sliced ham, and four bottles of red wine from the back of the ambulance.

Patrick slammed the car door shut, raced in front of me and jumped onto the boat from the top of the steel steps that descended from the quayside. Once in the cabin, he frantically turned a number of buttons and flipped large, metal switches. The engine rumbled into life and a large black cloud of smoke billowed from the hatch.

"She always does that," Patrick shouted over his shoulder.

Asterix, Obelix and Getafix took their positions and undid the ropes that secured the boat alongside the quay. 'Le Belge' turned the wheel and the boat started to reverse. More smoke spewed from the exhaust, lighter in colour, but rich with the smell of diesel oil.

"We're late. All those little fish are waiting for us! Get me a beer, I'm thirsty," Patrick yelled to Didier.

"No time to waste," he said to me. I stood next to him, peering out of the cabin window.

The boat was now pointing in the right direction so that we could head out to sea. The wooden wheel had seen thousands of hours of use and was worn from the sandpaper hands of countless helmsmen. The control panel was a multi-coloured maze of dials, switches, gauges, buttons, and knobs.

'Le Belge' pushed the throttle levers forward and the boat powered through the water, racing past the harbour light.

The long quay follows the channel for nearly two kilometres. I could see other boats in the distance, proceeding in the same direction. Most had already passed the channel through the sandbars and were now in open water.

People walking along the quay looked at the Belle Marie as it powered through the waves. They were not accustomed to seeing a boat going at such a rapid speed. 'Le Belge' downed his beer in two gulps and shouted for another. Didier obliged and unscrewed the cap on a small green bottle and passed it to the captain. '*Le Belge*' waved at the people walking along the quay from the cabin and they waved back.

I found myself holding the rail, trying to keep my balance. The waves were becoming bigger as we headed further into the bay. A door clattered every time the hull of the boat thumped into a wave. We were catching up with the last of the sailing ships. The channel was marked by different-coloured buoys, which moved with the tides. If you went on the wrong side of the buoys, you would likely run aground on the sandbars.

"Take ze helm," Patrick barked to me and he darted through the narrow door held open by a brass bracket. I grabbed the steering wheel from him, puffed out my chest and stood more erect, feeling a sense of authority and responsibility. I tightened my arms and piloted a course through the waves, trying to judge the best path between the rolling tapestries of dark-grey water.

'*Le Belge*' burst back into the cabin clutching two beers. He thrust one into my hand. He pointed in the direction of the beach that lay directly ahead of us on the other side of the small bay.

"Keeping going straight, go for ze big trees zere, aim for zem in ze straight line." These were the orders he shouted above the deafening roar of the motor, punctuated with the deep, bass line of the hull pounding against the waves.

"Yes, captain." I saluted and squeezed the wheel more tightly. Waving his hand, '*Le Belge*' beckoned me to lean forward and look into the box that was positioned on the control panel in front of me.

"Looking in ear, zis tell you ze depz ov ze watur. You see ze bit ear, zats ze sable, ze sandbanks, zere's less than vivty centermetres of watur and we are fuck-ed and ze boat stay ear wiz uz," he said, his manner suggesting that this was a little bit serious.

I understood enough to know that a boat with insufficient

water underneath it is not going very far. I took a large slug of the beer and resumed my responsibilities at the helm. It was going to be my fault if we ran aground. My throat was dry and the sweat started to drip down my cheek. I took another large gulp of beer and intensified my assessment of the distance between me and the beach landing.

I dipped my head into what looked like a microscope. The wooden hull slammed violently as another wave smashed into the bow, causing my head to crash into the viewfinder.

"Ah," I screamed.

"*Merde, ça va, OK?*" '*Le Belge*' enquired.

"*Oui, ça va,*" I replied.

"Look in zere," he said, darting back out onto the deck. My arms flexed with the movement of the waves as I held the boat on course.

The sea was not going to get the best of me.

I peered into the viewfinder and looked at the green lines. The depth of the water was marked boldly across the top of the screen and there was an outline of the bottom of the sea.

The salt-stained windows obscured my view ahead. The boat rolled and tossed violently. Various metal fittings started to come loose and smash about in the cabin below. With every jerk of the vessel, plates, steel cooking pans, pieces of wood and plastic buoys of different sizes crashed into each other or against the surfaces of the sink, table, and walls in the galley.

This isn't the direction to the open sea where all the fishes live, I thought to myself.

"Errrrrrrr," I stuck my head out of the small side window and shouted, "*Toujours tout droit?*" I enquired.

"*Oui,* keep ze boat in zis direction." '*Le Belge*' pointed dead ahead, in the direction of the beach.

I steered us straight in the direction he instructed. The long sandbars were becoming more frequent as we got closer to the stand of trees that provided relief to the line of the horizon.

I peered back into the depth gauge.

"*Sable*," I yelled.

'*Le Belge*' bolted through the cabin door. His skinny arms grabbed the wheel from me and he turned it frantically towards himself. He tugged on the wheel in rapid jolts and thrust the two throttle levers forward. The boat veered to the left and the back spun round behind us, the sand spraying up with the water. Then a loud thud came from the hull. Patrick peered out at the coastline and then into the depth gauge.

"*Merde, merde, il faut faire demi-tour, on va essayer encore.* Turn around, let's try it again," he told me. I was the helmsman and I had to get it right. "We've got to make it through that channel in the middle of the two trees on the coast. You'll see what I mean."

He left and went to the back of the boat to continue preparing the nets. I turned the boat around and headed back towards the coastline.

"I've got to head toward the two trees and almost run the boat onto the beach?" I said to myself. This was crazy!

'*Le Belge*' came into the cabin again with another beer. "*Voilà, pacha*," he said thrusting another cold beer in my hand. He did his dance of peering out in front and diving into the depth gauge.

"Like zis, straight," he said, pointing straight ahead. "Ze trees, ze big ones, in ze middle, OK?" he reiterated, making sure I understood.

"OK, and then what?" I replied.

"We skim ze beach for ze baby *solettes,* very good pour ze eating," he reassured me. "But if we are stuck-ed on ze beach, remember, zen we are fuck-ed." He leant into my face while slapping me on the back. "Zis is not a pleasure cruise, zis is bizness!" He cocked his head backwards in laughter. His moustache rose and his last two remaining nicotine-stained teeth winked at me.

"*C'est bon, c'est bon.*" He repeated this phrase a lot when he was happy.

'*Le Belge*' explained that I would soon see what he meant and that everything would be OK. He ran back to prepare the heavy wooden plates that weighed down the net so that it would drag along the sandy bottom.

He was going to tell me when to turn around, he would give me the command and I would have to react immediately. It was important not to screw up. He was the Commander-in-Chief, and captain of this pirate ship. He knew what he was doing, and I simply had to execute his orders.

I looked ahead and again into the depth gauge. I shouted out the figure I saw on the screen. As I turned my head and looked behind me, I saw '*Le Belge*' waving his arms in the air, pointing to the left, jumping up and down as he did. I couldn't hear what he was shouting but understood his gestures. I pulled down on the helm and brought the boat alongside the beach.

We weren't far from land. You could swim it easily. The water was clear and I could see the sand below. The hull scraped along the bottom. I opened up the throttle and smoke billowed from the engine.

The smell of burning fuel filled the boat. '*Le Belge*' flipped open the hatch to the engine house and a large plume of smoke filled the sky. I looked through the window to see what was happening. Patrick's bare arms were plunged inside the open hatch. Holding his breath, he dived into the dark-grey smoke. He came up for air and grabbed a rag from his pocket. He wrapped it around his hand and dove back through the hatch. The smoke suddenly cleared and fumes started to billow from behind the boat again. The smoke cleared from the cabin. The two deckhands, Didier and Alan, helped close the hatch.

'*Le Belge*' grabbed a bottle from the bucket full of cold beers and cracked the screw cap. He downed it in one gulp and then wiped his mouth with the back of his greasy forearm. He turned to inspect the large fishing net being dragged behind us. He swung bare-chested, like Tarzan, on the steel cables, testing their resistance. The tighter the cables, the fuller the net and the bigger the haul, was the theory.

"*C'est bon, c'est bon*," he shouted at the top of his voice. He shouted profanities to the seagulls flying overhead, who had started to grow in numbers, following the boat. "*Comme c'est bon, quand tu n'as pas tous ces cons,* it's so good, when you ain't got all those idiots," he bellowed, pointing to the landscape with a dramatic broad gesture of his arm.

Ordering his two deckhands either side of the net lines, '*Le Belge*' took his place in the middle. He was going to guide the net in. Levers and cranks of steel were pushed and pulled and the winch started to turn. Cables tightened and turned on the large, steel spindle. The net lifted from the sea bed, and the heavy wooden guides swung dangerously with the roll of the boat.

The strained filaments of the net broke the surface of the water. Pulling hard on the cables, the crew guided the net over the back of the boat and the stuffed net dropped onto the wooden deck.

The net was full to overflowing with small, brown, speckled Dover sole and other varieties of fish. It looked like the intestines of a whale all neatly tied up in a hand-stitched shopping basket. At last, the net was safely landed.

'*Le Belge*' shouted that it was time to turn around and head out into deeper water. He gave me the sign, a turning gesture and pointed in the direction of the port behind us, in the distance on the other side of the bay.

I pulled the helm down hard, and the wooden wheel rotated in my hands. The boat slowly began to turn. I accelerated, intent on getting away from the sandbars, and the boat bounced across the waves to the safe haven of deeper water. With the haul in the net, the boat was heavier and the *Belle Marie* struggled against the powerful current of the changing tide. We needed to reach the channel before it was too late. If we didn't make it, it was going to be a long wait until the next high tide.

The crew attended to emptying the catch into boxes and throwing the small fish and non-edibles back into the ocean. Fish of different sizes and shapes littered the slippery boards of the deck. The seagulls plunged in the surf to snatch the fish that the crew threw back.

'*Le Belge*' ran into the cabin. "*C'est bon, c'est bon,*" he repeated over and over again. "We have to get back to ze port, quickly. Ze tide has already turned, look at ze current."

He took the binoculars from the nail on which they hung and put them up to his eyes and surveyed the choppy waters that surrounded us. He dashed from side to side around the glass-walled cabin and looked in every direction.

The majority of the boats that had accompanied us into the bay were back in the channel and on the right side of the markers that guided them back into port. We were only just starting to head back; the sandbars were still before us and the narrow channel looked a long way off.

"It's going to be ze close shaver," he garbled in English. '*Le Belge*' leant over me, his hand pushing on the throttle levers, but they were already at maximum. The engine growled behind us, giving its maximum. I held onto the handrail inside the cabin and bent my knees with every wave. The little boat was flying across the water. I was worried we wouldn't get to the first orange buoy without running aground. I could see the sand starting to rise up from the water. There was a sense of anticipation among all of us.

'*Le Belge*' concentrated on the water, and the boat smacked across the waves. Then an almighty thump hit the boat under our feet. I lost my balance and stumbled. The rear of the boat lifted out of the water. The engine started to howl as the propellers came out of the water.

We were skidding across a sandbar. I held onto the side of the door and the handrail. The boat continued to skid across the sand, then headed downwards with the slight incline. We had momentum and now gravity was on our side, but friction was stronger. The boat started to slow as its weight served as its own anchor. The boat began to shudder but continued to slide, slowing with every bump. The bow dipped into the water and, with a sudden jolt, we came to a halt.

The bow was now pointing downwards at nearly forty-five degrees. The sandbar had taken hold of the *Belle Marie* and her propellers were pointing to the sky. It looked more like a children's slide next to the beach than a fishing boat. The unpacked fish slid all over the deck and a pile stacked against the back of the cabin door. We all held our breath.

"We have to push and pull to set her free. Get into the water," Patrick instructed the crew.

We had to liberate the *Belle Marie* from the sandbar or we would be marooned with half a ton of fresh fish, which needed to be refrigerated.

The boat couldn't stay in the position it was in. The next tide could easily flip it over. We couldn't sleep on it at that angle. We had to move the boat into at least fifty centimetres of water so that she was flat.

We jumped onto the soggy sand. '*Le Belge*' tied ropes around the bow and the mooring hooks. We waded into the shallow water in front of us. It was not deep, but the current was strong. You didn't want to fall because you could be sucked out into the open sea.

"*Un, deux, trois,*" bawled '*Le Belge*', gritting his two remaining top teeth into his lower gums. He closed his eyes tightly as he heaved with all his strength. His muscles tightened on his sinuous arms. We all gave an almighty tug and the boat slipped forwards and downwards until the bow was nearly afloat. We ran to the back of the boat and positioned ourselves in the sand. The four of us crouched down and simultaneously dove toward the boat. We shoved with all our strength, the boat plunged forward and slid into the water. We all fell face-first into the wet, gritty sand.

The boat was now afloat again, but none of us were on board. The tide was going out quickly, and the lapping water started to carry the boat away from us. '*Le Belge*' pulled himself up and ran into the water. We all followed. I waded into the water thigh high. We used our hands to steady ourselves as we plodded through the strong current. None of us wore life jackets, just T-shirts and shorts, with soaked packets of cigarettes in the pockets.

The boat was now floating, but we were still in the middle of the bay. '*Le Belge*' jumped like a dolphin and grabbed the ropes and held them like it was an unbroken stallion at a rodeo. The boat spun around, away from him.

The tide was getting stronger and was starting to move faster than I could wade. I tried to quicken my step, but the water was deep and I could no longer lift my legs. I started to swim toward the boat, the tide carrying me closer. I was swimming toward an unmanned boat in the middle of the bay.

'*Le Belge*' climbed out of the water and was further up the sandbar. He was trying to reel in the rope and bring the boat to him. Didier was not made for swimming. He hated water and was shouting obscenities about how stupid an idea it was to abandon the boat.

I arrived first alongside the boat, panting. I had not swum like this in years. I held on to a tyre hanging on the outside of the boat for all I was worth, as the current pulled at my legs and the waves churned me up and down.

Alan also grabbed onto a tyre and used it to hoist himself back into the boat. He turned the key and started the engine, which roared into action with a dark plume of smoke.

I climbed aboard and took a beer. I offered one to Alan as he steered the boat towards 'Le Belge', who was marooned on his little sandy island. Alan forced the boat along the channel. I could feel it scraping the sides of the sandbars. We came closer to 'Le Belge'. He still had the rope in his hand. Alan accelerated and the boat darted forward near to where 'Le Belge' stood. He threw the ropes into the boat and started running alongside. He was slightly higher that the handrail. Waving his arms in the air, he shouted something that we couldn't hear through the noise of the engine and the wind. I went to the stern of the boat.

"Attention, attention," shouted 'Le Belge' as he ran as fast as he could, his feet sinking into the sand with every stride. With one last burst of force, he launched himself into the air.

For a moment, he was suspended in mid-air.

'Le Belge' landed between a large steel fitting bolted to the wall of the boat and the wooden trap door of the engine house. His fall was cushioned by the pile of fish that lay on the deck. As he landed, he slipped on the slimy fish and slammed into the wheelhouse with a big thump. I rushed to his assistance. As I reached for his hand, he started to laugh, picking himself up while imitating a seagull.

When he'd landed on the great pile of sole, his weight caused many of the fish to explode. There were bits of fish everywhere, even in his moustache. He turned, skidded again, and reached for the beers in the bucket. He threw each of us a beer. Thrusting his bottle in the air, he shouted to the skies, *"Vive la France, bordel!"*

'*Le Belge*' downed his beer in one gulp and brushed himself down as we pulled the boat up alongside Didier, who was still outside the boat, slowly wading toward us. He was screaming out obscenities and cursing relentlessly. He had had enough and didn't want to play anymore. Alan and I leant over the side and hauled him up. He used the old tyre as a step.

We just made it back to port with the hull skimming the sand.

At the quayside, '*Le Belge*' thrust a shopping bag filled with small sole into my hand, singing the famous children's song.

"Les petits poissons dans l'eau, nagent, nagent, nagent..."

MERDE! WATERLOO

Seven-thirty and the local market was already in full swing.

It was held every Sunday morning, come rain or shine, on the big square that served as a parking area during the week. The stalls sold locally produced food and flowers as well as kitchen utensils, clothes, gifts, cheap jewellery, and sunglasses.

"*C'est ma place. J'suis là mec.* That's my place, I'm there, mate," garbled the impulsive bald man with a strong Parisian accent behind a big, bushy moustache. "You'll have to move," he added aggressively.

His gravelly voice sounded like he'd smoked a packet of cigarettes in two minutes. "*Ça fait cinq semaines que j'suis là!* I've been coming here for five weeks, that's my place. You'll have to move, that's my place *mec*," he said again in an obnoxious manner.

I'd arrived early and said hello to Roger, the '*Placer*', the mayor's henchman who collected the placement fees. The regular sellers had already set up their goods in their usual places amidst the labyrinth of metal cages, tables, baskets, plastic containers, vans selling cheese or meat, the roast chicken machine, and the Chinese food seller.

I had already seen Roger at the mayor's office earlier in the week when I picked up my 'stamped' trading permit. I informed him that I would be selling my hanging baskets at the market every Sunday. He told me to set up my stall next to the fruit and veg stall on the corner of *Place des Pilotes* next to the public toilets. At least I wouldn't have to walk far for a piss.

I assembled the metal bars of the stall in my allocated spot. Roger had joked that he would be back to collect the fee at around ten o'clock, to allow me to make some money first.

"*J'ai vu Roger* and he told me to set up here," I said to the angry man. "If you have a problem, sort it out with him." I carried on sorting out the baskets and attaching the chains with a pair of pliers. I used a screwdriver to open up the clips at the end of the chains. I carefully counted out the same number of links so the baskets were balanced and hung correctly, then closed them tightly with the pliers.

The Parisian puffed out his chest, his body language accentuating his arrogance. The number plate of his silver Volkswagen Golf was registered in the seventy-eight department of Yvelines, in the Île-de-France region in the central Paris basin. The chi-chi suburb on the west side of Paris is best known for being the location of the Palace of Versailles. The car blocked the road and traffic was starting to back up. The drivers commenced a fanfare of blaring horns.

He marched back to his car and shouted something I didn't understand at one of the beeping vehicles. The narrow road was the only one through the village; the lower road along the bay front was blocked with stalls.

The man stormed past me, trying to look as intimidating as possible. He scornfully looked at my stock of baskets piled on the kerb behind my stall. He was what the French call a '*Faiseur*', someone who is arrogant and obnoxious.

Charging back to his car, he again shouted at the blocked

cars that continued to beep their horns in unison. Cursing at them, he waved his arms in the air like a traffic controller in Thailand. I slid a finished basket onto one of the broom handles I had attached to the traversal metal bars with heavy duct tape.

"You have to move. I've been coming here for five weeks," he said to me, more aggressively, his voice filled with rage. He was standing right behind me. I turned around and we were face to face.

I smelt alcohol on his stale breath. He lit a cigarette and puffed on it, blowing the smoke forcefully in my direction.

I clenched my fists. I was convinced he was going to throw a punch. I hadn't got up at six o'clock on a Sunday morning to have a fight. I wanted to sell some of my new hanging baskets and aluminium brackets. This was my new *petit entreprise*, my new business venture. I had invested nearly a thousand pounds in stock, bags of potting soil and flowers. Just sorting out the paperwork had been time consuming and costly.

"Where the hell am I going to find him in there?" he said, throwing his right arm in the direction of the main market.

"That's your problem, *mec*!" I said sarcastically.

My French wasn't brilliant, but I could now hold my own and this two-legged, snail-eating toad was not going to order me about. He could see that I was not intimidated by him as I carried on preparing my stall.

"*Ah, merde, merde, merde, merde alors!*" he growled, and threw his cigarette aggressively on the road. Waving his arms about in the air like he was conducting an orchestra, he mumbled loudly to himself about how he couldn't work because *un etranger* had taken his place.

"*Ah, merde,* I'll go and find him, *merde!*" he shouted and stormed off in the direction of the market. "But you will have to move," he said to me sternly, looking over his shoulder. He pointed his fingers at me, like a pistol. His eyes squinted as he pulled his meanest face.

I probably could have moved a metre or two, but I had done the French thing and said it wasn't my problem. Anyway, this idiot had been a pompous prick from the start.

People stared at him as he disappeared into the market square, swearing and cursing as he went. The market was coming alive and more and more people were flowing past my stall.

I saw Roger walking towards me with the Parisian, who was flapping his arms as he spoke. I could see by Roger's expression that he had already had more than an earful of Parisian pleasantries.

"I'm terribly sorry," Roger said politely, with a wry smile. "I forgot he was coming." He rolled his eyes. "Would you mind moving up a little bit, please?"

"OK, no problem," I said, "but can you help me move the table?"

"As you can see, there's not a lot of room, two metres," Roger said to the Parisian.

"*C'est bon, enfin!*" he said.

"I'll grab this end," Roger said. "Pull it up as far as you can. Leave a passage between you and the fruit and vegetable stand."

The elderly couple next to my stall had a collective age of one hundred and forty-five. Their 1970s Peugeot van with sliding doors had been to more markets than I'd eaten hot dinners.

Roger and I pulled the stall over as far as we could.

"*Merci*," Roger said. "I'll catch you later. I have to get back over there." He pointed in the direction of the main market and walked away, filtering into the throng of wandering customers.

The Parisian went over to his parked car and moved it

forward to unload his cardboard boxes. His car was still blocking the traffic, and the long line of cars had to wait for a gap in the oncoming traffic before they could pass. He started to empty the contents of his stuffed VW Golf, piling the cardboard boxes up against the metal railings of the wrought iron fence.

He picked up a large cardboard box and turned around. As he did so, the bottom of the box flew open and gravity did its job. Crockery smashed to the floor. Porcelain ashtrays, saucers, plates, salt and pepper pots, bowls – all were obliterated into hundreds of pieces on the pavement.

"*Ahhhhhhhhhh, merde!*" he screamed. Deep down, I was happy. *That will teach him to be so obnoxious and arrogant,* I thought.

He salvaged as much as he could and kicked the box against the fence.

My stall was decorated with two hanging baskets that I'd made the week before while giving myself a crash course on basket making. I wanted to make a good first impression to attract customers. The bright, vibrant colours of the flowers were magnified by the glorious sunshine. People stopped and asked me questions, touching them with their hands. *That was a good sign,* I thought. Hanging baskets were practically non-existent in France. The selection at the garden centres was limited and their plastic holders were renowned for splitting and cracking in the sun.

I carried on filling the demonstration model I was making up on the table. Passers-by stopped to look at what I was doing. I poured rich potting soil into the coconut fibre lining, then picked up the plants in the punnets and planted the flowers in the soil.

The hanging baskets came in three sizes and the walls brackets came in three colours – British-racing green, black, and white. They started to sell. People gave me money and told me to hold on to their purchases and they would come back to collect them at the end of their tour of the market.

"*Ahhhhh, merde!*" the moustached man next to me yelled again.

The small, white 1960s picnic table, with hollow folding legs, was ideal for camping and eating with four people. It could probably take four plates, four glasses, a jug of water, a bottle or two of wine and a plate of food placed in the middle, but not what he had heaped on it.

It was piled up with boxes full of heavy twelve-inch eating plates, bowls, and other table ornaments. He had not kicked the leg of the table out properly, to lock it into position. The table was giving way under the weight, slowly tipping towards Armageddon.

I saw the table starting to move out of the corner of my eye and my automatic reflex was to spring into action. I lunged over and grabbed the table to stop it slamming to the ground. I pushed my elbows out to hold the porcelain on the table. It was heavy and I held it with all my strength. Everything rocked and chinked together. Some plates and a tea pot smashed into pieces on the ground. The man plunged his leg under the table like he was making a football tackle and the leg of the table clicked into position.

"*Putain table de merde, c'est de la merde!*" he shouted as people walking past looked at him in alarm, the children laughing and pointing. I steadied the table and made sure the various cups and saucers, coffee pot and other pieces stayed in place. He grabbed some of the plates and boxes and put them on the ground.

"I'll buy you a drink afterwards at the PMU. Thanks for your help," he said, smiling, and he held out his hand. "I'm sorry for earlier. I'm not good at the moment, sorry again." I shook his hand.

He was just having a bad day.

"OK, no problem, with pleasure," I replied and smiled back at him.

The market wound down at mid-day and I started to dismantle the stand. I had sold all four of the finished baskets, the two I had made for decorating the stall, and the two demonstration models. It was a really good first day. I had a pocket full of cash and preorders, with money down, for finished baskets to be picked up the following week. The most important contact I made that day was with the little old lady who bought the two finished baskets, and two hanging brackets. She told me her son was going to drive her home and put the brackets up on the terrace wall of her apartment in Amiens. She was going to invite all her girlfriends to the apartment to see the baskets. She informed me that they would all want them for their terraces. It was the beginning of a beautiful friendship.

"I'm going to leave everything like this," said the Parisian.

I looked at the large pile of cardboard boxes, smashed crockery, and other rubbish he had emptied from his car onto the pavement behind his stand.

"*Oui, oui*, it's OK, come to the PMU," he said.

"OK, I'll see you there," I said. "I still have to rope this up. I'll see you there."

I parked my car on the lot opposite the bar. Sunday lunchtime was the busiest day in the village and the car park was almost full. The place was full of day-tripper tourists and people from outside the area, who worked in Paris or Amiens, visiting family for the weekend.

I got out and checked the ropes of the roof rack on which I had tied my stepladder and the large, handmade wooden box I used to carry the stand. It was all secure.

I stood on the side of the road and was just about to cross, when I heard a screech of tyres as a car turned the corner by the boat chandlers. A vehicle roared towards me at great speed. It was Dominique, the local hairdresser and Johnny Hallyday's number one fan.

He was crumpled up behind the wheel of his blue Renault Twenty-One wearing a loud Hawaiian shirt with a cigarette clenched between his teeth. He raced past me towards the railway track, changing up gears, waving his arm in my direction and beeping the horn all at the same. He had no hands on the wheel. The small incline in front of the railway tracks helped launch the car – it took flight before bouncing down on the other side.

The car powered past the *Gendarmerie* on the right-hand side. He changed gear again as the car roared round the bend and disappeared behind the hedgerow in the distance. I could hear it racing up the hill that led to the supermarket.

I crossed over the road, shaking my head in disbelief. Dominique drove way too fast around the village. His son was the same as him, but on a moped with a broken muffler to make it louder.

I climbed the steps in front of Le Sulky. The name of the bar always made me laugh. When I visited the village for the first time, I stopped there to buy cigarettes and have a drink with my father. He commented on the name of the bar, which was run by a grumpy, sulking, miserable old woman.

"This place must have been named after her, or she's got the trots," my dad said.

In French, a *sulky* is what the driver sits on while being pulled by a horse in trotting races. If the horse breaks into a gallop, they are disqualified. The bar was also the village PMU (betting shop) and had a constant flow of punters placing bets, checking their bets, and drinking. The lucky ones picked up some money and stopped at the bar to down some of their winnings, the losers would lose more money on alcohol.

The café had recently changed hands.

A long queue was formed outside by customers who only wanted to buy cigarettes. I pushed past them and entered into the bar.

"*Salut chérie*, a packet of red, please," I said to Valery, a pretty blonde, who worked there at the weekend. "*Ça va?*" I enquired, smiling.

"*Ça va, merci... tiens*," she said handing me a packet of Marlboro rouge. She smiled back and dropped the exact change from the twenty Franc note into my hand. She promptly turned to serve the next customer.

"*Merci*," I said, and she smiled at me again.

I saw the Parisian's shiny bald head at the end of the bar. He thrust his arm in the air, as if he was greeting a long-lost friend.

The bar was packed and I squeezed my way through the small space between the bar and the tables and chairs along the wall. 'The knights of the long Formica counter top' were in their normal places. I shook hands with *Ch'pere* Roche, who lived in Paris but came back every weekend. He was drinking a glass of *vin blanc*, what else?

"*Ch'est du brun pour passer là-bas ti!* It's a nightmare to get up there," he said in a heavy Picard accent, with his *Gitanes maïs sans filtre* jammed in the corner of his mouth. The end of the cigarette was soaking wet, dampened by his saliva.

He owned many scrap metal yards around Paris. His company also handled all the towing for badly parked cars and the car accidents on the ring road around Paris. He had made a lot of money, but remained a down-to-earth, humble and friendly man who loved betting on horses. He was a regular at the PMU and very generous, buying rounds of drinks whether he won or not.

The small tables and chairs along the wall were where the wives sat. They talked amongst themselves, nursing Martinis and glasses of rosé as the men stood at the bar with their backs to them.

The punters who were returning to their glasses after placing their bets added to the difficulty of making it to the other end of the bar. I shook hands with the 'chevaliers' as I manoeuvred my way along the bar. The old boys sucked on their gums, then sucked up their glasses of different-coloured alcohol.

After manipulating my way through small gaps between large bellies and bottoms, I finally popped out at the other end of the bar.

"Hello again," I said.

"Hi, what do you want to drink? My name's Olivier, by the way." Again, he put out his hand and I shook it.

"Max, a beer please, Olivier," I said, unwrapping the plastic on my new packet of cigarettes.

"I'm really sorry about all that earlier," said Olivier. "I was late getting out of bed. I had a little bit too much to drink last night, too. Plus, I'm going through a bad time with my old lady, we have a kid together. You probably know her – Sylvia? She's opening the *crêperie* on the main high street, just opposite the florist's, on the corner."

"Yes, I saw it was being renovated," I said. "That wall is leaning over so much, if there's an earthquake it will come crashing down."

The *crêperie* was on the corner of a small street that was just large enough to get a car down. It joined the main one-way high street.

"I've been doing the renovations," he said, "and now that it's more or less ready to be open she's kicking me out. The house and everything is in her name. I'm just trying to get some extra cash together doing the markets."

"Dropping everything on the floor won't generate any cash," I said laughing.

"You know, that's just what I was thinking when I was adding up the cost of the stuff that got smashed. But what's done is done!" he said and we drank from our glasses.

"Anyway, next weekend it's the *Trans-baie* race," Olivier added. "All those idiots running through the mud, lots of people come to watch it. The village gets packed. It's one of the best markets of the year, you'll see."

"Well, I had a good first day. People are showing a lot of interest in my baskets," I said proudly.

"There's Dominique," Olivier said as a broad smile spread across his face.

Dominique stood in the queue to buy cigarettes. You couldn't miss him. He was at least six inches taller than anyone else, his loud shirt topped off with large, round, yellow sunglasses and a cigarette permanently stuck in the corner of his mouth.

Amongst his other talents, he was a hairdresser *extraordinaire*. His salon de coiffure was situated on the main high street, nestled between the Post Office and a café. He opened up at eight forty-five and by nine he needed to quench his thirst. He started the day with a *demie*, a small beer. After lunch, he'd move from a *demie* to a small glass of red wine called a *canon*. He'd fire off a constant barrage of *canons* throughout the afternoon. Cutting hair was thirsty work and his rhythm depended on his need to 'change up money' for waiting customers in his salon.

Dominique didn't hang around when he had a client sitting in the chair. His *canon* was placed on the counter the instant he walked through the door. He would greet his fellow *chevaliers* of the bar with the quickest of handshakes. Then, in one fluid move, he would flex his elbow and his forearm would catapult his hand up to his mouth, which opened at the same time. The wine would be launched into the back of his throat, instantaneously sending a message to his brain to close his mouth. After releasing the red liquid from its spherical receptor, his elbow would contract and bring his forearm down, placing the glass on the counter.

The instant the glass was released from the grip of his fingers, he would glide, swan-like, across the smooth tiles to the door, pull it back and pass through within a second, the door slamming shut as he ran back to his waiting client sitting in the chair.

Valery served him and he navigated his way towards us. He stopped along his voyage and shook hands with the natives perched on their different islands along the counter.

Behind me, I heard the voice of doom. It was Thierry. Everybody called him T-T, or is it Ti-Ti?

He proclaimed himself to be a *Garagiste, Pompiste, Mechanique*. He pumped petrol and diesel into cars – and Pastis, wine, and any other form of alcohol into his body. He was known as the drunk who had been fired from the family-run garage diagonally opposite the café. In a hazy state, he had told the fuel truck driver to put the petrol in the diesel reservoir. His stupidity had cost the garage a lot of money. Thierry totally totalled the Total garage!

He was argumentative and quarrelsome – constantly disagreeing with other clients in the café. I was the brunt of his anti-English racism. He was anti everything, even himself!

He had blamed or accused me of being part of every political and historical event that had happened between France and England over the years. It was me who had lit the match that burnt Joan of Arc, invented Margaret Thatcher, and given the world foot and mouth disease, along with the jelly and the butter mountain!

"Then you come over here, buy all our houses, pushing the prices sky high, then you steal all our women," he said to me loudly in front of the packed bar.

"Don't worry, I won't be stealing yours. There's absolutely no danger of that, I couldn't afford the food bill!" I said, and the whole bar roared with laughter, except T-T. He hated being the brunt of jokes, but you had to give it to him hard. That's just the way it was.

He was famous for shooting his television set dead. He'd been watching France in the football World Cup qualifying match against Bulgaria on the 17th of November 1993. It was the last chance for France to qualify for a place in the 1994 World Cup in the USA. France had either to draw or win, they needed just one point. *Les Bleus* had the home advantage, playing at the *Parc des Princes* in Paris. The match was drawn 1-1 until, in the dying seconds of the match, France mistakenly gave away possession of the ball to the Bulgarians. A poor pass by David Ginola led to a goal being scored by Bulgaria's Emil Kostadinov. France lost 2-1. Bulgaria got the points and qualified for the finals and France was eliminated from the competition.

T-T was so disgusted with the national team's performance, he took his twelve-bore shot gun from the cupboard, loaded both barrels and pulled the trigger. Boom! The television exploded into smithereens. He fired off the other barrel to make sure the TV was really dead. When the dust settled, there was no TV and a large hole in the wattle and daub wall behind where it used to be.

His wife's tantrums would cause him to lose his temper after too many tipples. She would peer through the glass windows of the café and, after a certain length of time, she'd open the door.

"*Entre à la maison maintenant salo!* Come home now, you bastard!" she'd screech through the door.

Everybody would laugh and Thierry would cringe. He would then try and teach her who was at the top of the totem pole. He would stand, if possible, puff out his little chest like a cock and hurl abuse at her. He would say the nastiest things, before telling her to get lost and shut the door on her way out.

Content with himself, he would go back to holding himself up at the bar. His wife would return regularly, in five-minute intervals. Sometimes, she just stood outside the café, staring at him through the window with her arms firmly folded across her gigantic chest. After a minute or so, she would stick her head through the door, stooping like a pelican, and growl in her high-pitched bark like a wild turkey. She never entered the bar, not even a foot came through the door. She was twice, if not three times, the size of Thierry and could easily kill him just by sitting on him. He would eventually give in to her commands and allow himself to be dragged home, just three doors down from the bar.

Thankfully, on this occasion, Thierry turned away and squeezed through the mass of bodies.

The betting office was situated at the end of the room. The loud machine continuously printed out the betting slips.

The bar was packed as usual, and there was always a great atmosphere in the place. Like every Sunday lunchtime, it seemed that the whole village and his dog was crammed into the café. Chatter about the football the day before, the *Tirece* results of yesterday's races, and the excitement about today's chances flowed like the beer and Pastis. Inside info and hot tips were shared, and hotheads discussed the main race of the day. The rumbling voices hummed around the bar.

"*Ace, quatre, dix, douze*, in that order," reverbed in my ear.

"*Non, le sept, et la huit, c'est sûr*, it's guaranteed."

"*Ace, douze, dix et quatre en ordre,*" in the other ear.

"*Non, le six et la cinq,* no, six and five, trust me," said Giles to my right. Everybody had the right combination and their money was on a dead cert.

The big news story in the press that week was about the Channel Tunnel, *Ze Chunnel.* The bonding of England to the European continent was going to be the commercial vein between Europe via France to England. The Romans had thought about doing it, Napoleon had plans drawn up to do it but had decided to invade Egypt instead.

It was now a reality.

The two opposing tunnels had been linked together. The continuing financial problems with the project had made bigger news than the actual construction, but the tunnel would become the transport jugular, pumping cash blood in both directions. England, after its thousands of years of being marooned in its damp isolation, would now be strapped to the rest of Europe.

Paris to London in only three hours, in the comfort of high-speed trains – amazing!

The café was now at bursting point with all the punters stuffed into the smoked-filled aquarium, the noise overwhelming. The patrons constantly shouted at André, the owner and barman, to recharge their drinks. He ran up and down the bar serving different-coloured liquids to his thirsty customers.

The French press was all over the story that Waterloo train station, named after a certain battle at which the French had suffered a resounding defeat, had been chosen as the temporary station to receive the Eurostar trains from Paris. In the original deal, it had been agreed that the trains would leave from the *Gare du Nord* and arrive at King's Cross. However, King's Cross station was having major renovations that would take longer than planned and wouldn't be ready until about 2010.

This really got under the skin of the French. I had already been targeted with questions about it. I knew I was going to have to answer for it again, and I wasn't wrong.

I received a tap in the middle of my back.

It was Coco. I greeted him with a handshake. I had missed him at first because he was very small. I don't think he was registered as vertically challenged, but he should have been. He couldn't even see over the counter to grab his beer. When the bar was less busy, he would climb up on a stool and sit with the big boys, but today he was in his own little maze of legs and bottoms.

Coco was a chef – a little chef! He had worked at two of the restaurants in the village, but was now retired. He rode his moped wearing a crash helmet that was way too big for his head. He would clip the strap under his chin, but the helmet would be pushed round by the wind. He had to turn his head to the left or the right, depending on the direction of the wind, to compensate. I'd seen him nearly looking over his shoulder as the helmet had spun round, almost completely blocking his view of the road.

Coco liked a drink on Sundays and would start early. You could find him at every bar around the market square with his wife in tow. He'd have a few jars in each café, then do his rounds of the market opposite and fill two wicker shopping baskets. He would send his wife home with the shopping and the moped, leaving him free to carry on visiting the bars.

He would always end up at the PMU, as he only bet on Sundays. He would place his bets, have a few quick drinks, then hustle a lift home to get him there at one o'clock sharp. Otherwise, he was in deep trouble. Coco was another husband in the village known for being dragged out of the café by a considerably larger wife.

"Why?" he proclaimed. "Why?" he asked again, his high-pitched voice screeching throughout the noisy bar. Coco grabbed my hand. I tried to pull it away, but he wouldn't release it. He put his second little hand around my hand and started to squeeze it harder and harder.

"Why? What?" I asked him. "Let go of my hand, you're not my type." I tried to humour him, but he looked at me with a stern face.

"Why?" he slurred. Coco's voice could be heard throughout the café. He had been on the juice and it showed in his little piercing glazed eyes. "Listen to me," he said. His voice was deeper now, as deep as it could be. It meant that what he was saying was serious.

"Why, is the train station in London, the one that's going to receive the trains from France, why are they going to stop at Waterloo? Don't you have any other stations with other names? They should change the name of the station! It's a disgrace! You're taking the piss out of us." He was angry and his voice had gone high-pitched again, making him sound like a young child wailing.

He looked up at me, while I looked down at his baby face, which was covered by its large, untrimmed moustache. He was gritting what was left of his brown, tobacco-stained teeth. His little hands still firmly gripped mine. He tugged and dragged me in close to him. I towered over him.

His concern was genuine – he wanted an answer.

Who was I to reply to such a question? I hadn't decided which station would receive the trains!

"Because, Coco," I looked at him seriously and thought for a moment. The other clients around us waited for my response. The bar suddenly went quiet. They all waited for my answer. "Because, we don't have one called Agincourt or Crécy," I said, "and Trafalgar Square is only an underground station."

He looked up at me in disgust, released my hand from his twin-handed grip and scurried off, disappearing into a sea of bottoms.

JOHNNY FROGMAN

Johnny Hallyday is the biggest rock star you've never heard of in English-speaking countries. Johnny was made a *Chevalier de la Légion d'honneur* for his contribution to music and sold millions of records in France, Belgium, Quebec, and French-speaking countries.

Johnny was Dominique's hero and personal Superman. Dominique, *plongeur, chanteur*, Jacques Cousteau, Johnny Hallyday and Vidal Sassoon all rolled into one chain-smoking, chain-drinking, superstar *coiffure*.

Dominique was on show 24/7. Never sober, he was the most extravagant and eccentric *'vedette'* in the small fishing village, and always dressed like the 'French Elvis', who he only ever referred to as 'Johnny'. Dominique had once actually made it into a studio and recorded a record. He gave me a copy of his 45 rpm, 7" inch single entitled *'Faites Plus La Guerre'*, the song title written in a red Rocky Horror Picture Show font and had dripping blood coming off the bottom of the words. The literal translation is 'Make More War', but it actually means 'Stop the War'. The cover photo shows Dominique singing, the microphone up to his mouth, as he fans out three fingers in a double 'V' sign, or is it a W? On the A side are the words 'In homage to the old veterans and the resistance', while the B side is etched with two tracks, *'C'est serieux'* 'It's serious' and *'Belle Maman Chérie'*, meaning 'Beautiful Mummy Dear'.

Frank's restaurant, Le Globe, is situated on the main high street, *rue de la Ferté*. At the back of the narrow building, a large window offers its patrons a magnificent view of the Bay of the Somme. The hundred and eighty-degree panorama stretches from the point, with its constant flashing red light, right across the large bay with the duck-hunters' huts, and out to the open sea of the English Channel in the distance.

It was gig night at Le Globe and 'the band' was in town. The blues-rock trio would be playing on the small stage, next to the toilet. The pool table was pushed into a corner to make maximum space in front of the stage. Dominique burst into the café as the musicians were setting up their gear, and walked directly over to the lead singer and whispered into his ear. He didn't stop for a drink, which was very unusual for him. Normally, he couldn't walk past a bar without going in for a quick one. He had other pressing engagements, but made hand gestures indicating that he would be back later.

Dominique returned to Le Globe as the band was in the middle of its second set. The café was rammed full. He was dressed in his stage attire of black shirt, black trousers, and a tan leather jacket with the collars turned up.

He was on a mission!

The band finished their forlorn version of 'Hotel California'. The singer's pronunciation of the lyrics was incomprehensible and he sung out of tune. They had completely ruined the song, but the singer proudly smiled like he was Glenn Fry of The Eagles. It was probably the worst version of the song I had ever heard, but I was in a small village on a cold winter's night. At least there was live music, bad as it was. There was a great atmosphere, and people laughed and joked. All the tables in the dining area were taken and it was standing room only at the cramped bar.

The band members should have spent their money on music lessons instead of their clothing. The rocker-style T-shirts, featuring American trucks, flying eagles or wolves, stretched over their pot bellies. They all had large chains attached to their wallets dangling down from their belts.

The rotund lead singer had seen Dominique walk back into the café, and gave him the thumbs up as the band fumbled to the end of the song.

"*Merci, merci*," the singer said, wiping the sweat from his forehead with his forearm.

The crowd clapped enthusiastically and Frank wolf whistled so loud it pierced my ear drums. People tapped on the tables with their glasses and stomped their feet on the wooden floor so that the whole thing bounced. The old building wasn't built to hold so many people.

"*Merci beaucoup*," said the singer again as he ran a towel over his sweaty red face.

Frank handed three cold Heineken beers to people standing directly in front of the bar and they passed them over to the band. Taking a long swig of a beer, the singer spoke into the microphone.

"That's better, *merci* Frank," he said, giving Frank the thumbs up. "OK, you know that Saint-Valery-sur-Somme is home to the legendary singer, Picardy's Elvis!" His voice lifted as he spoke.

The audience applauded loudly and stamped their feet with overzealous enthusiasm. Loud whistles and cries called out

Dominique's name. He waved to the people, his fans, who turned their heads in his direction. The band started to play their next song, 'The House of the Rising Sun' by The Animals. Johnny Hallyday's version was called '*Les Portes du Pénitencier*', the doors of the penitentiary. It made it into the French Top Ten in November 1964.

"*OK, ce soir, pour vous,*" said the singer into the microphone, combing his greasy hair with his hand. "For you, tonight, he's here, he's in the house and he's going to sing for you, his loyal fans. Ladies and gentleman, the voice that Johnny lost, a legend in his own mind, make some noise for the one and only, Dom-in-ique." He drew out the name for ten seconds or more and pointed his arm in the direction of Dominique, who was leaning against the pool table next to the entrance. He slowly made his way towards the stage through the packed crowd, absorbing every second. He jumped up onto the stage and slid in front of the microphone stand, grabbing it with both of his shaking hands. He launched into the tale of a life gone wrong in New Orleans.

"Zer iz ur oose in Noorleenz, zey cull ze rizing surn..." Dominique was singing the English version, not Johnny's French adaptation. He smiled and tilted his head to the side, winding the long microphone cable around his hand. "An iz been ze wooin of mini pure bouy, un Gode I noow him un."

The band played on. Dominique almost swallowed the microphone as he plunged his head forward for the second verse, his mouth open and his eyes closed.

"Me muzzur was a tayor, sued my nu blue gin." Dominique pushed the microphone away from his body and posed in a Robert Plant-like stance. He flipped his head up to the ceiling, leaning backwards, nodding his head to the music.

"Me fazzer wus a gablibmun..." Dominique looked out at his

fans. He pointed to Freddy and gave him the thumbs up. He tipped his head and winked at him. "Zer iz ur oose in Noorleenz, zey cull ze rizing surn." Dominique didn't know the other lyrics and mumbled through the rest of the song. The band leader turned around to the drummer and nodded to the bass player.

They were bored of playing the song and Dominique was murdering it!

"One last time," Dominique shouted into the microphone, swinging an arm around in a circle, like a windmill. He moved forward and snuggled up to the mic stand.

"Zer iz ur oose in Noorleenz, zey cull ze rizing surn."

He kept the last words drawn out as the drummer crashed the cymbals for the grand finale. The crowd broke into a loud raw, exaggerated hand clapping, deafening cheers and wolf whistles, while glasses banged on the tables. The band started the song again, as the crowd kept clapping and cheering. Dominique smiled and lifted his right arm, clenching his fist.

"*Faites plus la guerre, merci,*" he said proudly.

Waving at the crowd, he moved away from the microphone and stepped down from the small stage. Hugging the wall like a cat, he quickly made his way to the front door without stopping to address his fans. He opened the door briskly, stepped outside and lit a cigarette.

Outside was Johnny's green room, his sanctuary. He couldn't face his fans straight away, he needed time to relax after the show. I could see him walking up and down in front of the restaurant through the glass front door and windows. After chain-smoking two cigarettes, he stepped back into the room and swaggered over to the bar.

"How was it, guys?" Dominique asked rapidly. "Good? Or was it just, OK?" He tilted his flat hand back and forth, to demonstrate the alternatives.

"*Fabuleux, Dominique, merci,*" said Frank, taking a glass off the shelf behind him and holding it up to the beer spout. "Here, have a beer on the house." He placed the pint of beer in front of Dominique. "It was really good, like always," Frank said seriously.

You couldn't tell Dominique how it really was, that would be too cruel. You had to let the dream live on, let him believe he was a star. Other people bought him drinks and the filled glasses were soon lined up along the bar.

The restaurant was officially meant to close at 1 am, but tonight was going to be a late one.

When the gig had finished, I helped Freddy carry out the band's cases and boxes to the van parked on the pavement. The drummer arranged his drums and carefully placed the guitar cases on top of the road cases. Frank pulled out a wad of notes from his pocket and paid the leader singer and we all said goodbye to them. Frank waved as the van drove away. He bolted the door to the café and pulled the heavy velvet curtains shut.

"OK, boys, I'm going to push the broom around and sweep up," Freddy said with authority.

I drank my beer as Freddy swept up the cigarette butts and broken glass. He filled the water container and grabbed the mop from the cupboard.

"She'll do the rest in the morning, I just have to move the table back to its place," Frank said, wiping down the floor quickly. "OK, let's have a drink while that dries out. It'll be easier with six of us. There were only four this afternoon. It weighs a ton." He charged everyone's glasses, and we chatted as we drank our drinks. Once the floor was dry, we moved the pool table back into place.

Frank was happy. It had been a full house, the booze had flowed and the cash register hadn't stopped pinging as the drawer opened and shut constantly. Tomorrow, he could have a lie in, with a pocket full of money, knowing that he could pay for the deliveries that were turning up on Monday morning. He had finished his whole stock of beer. His wife would be happy with him for a week or so, before she got back to nagging him every day. I had spent many evenings sitting in the cellar, drinking cases of 1664 and playing cards with Frank when she had thrown him out.

Dominique had a late-night pass – his wife was away visiting her mother with his younger daughter. His teenage son, Stevey, was doing his own thing as ever, driving around the village at full speed on his moped without a silencer on the exhaust. He had been caught by the police breaking into cars and tagging graffiti on the school wall. He had been fined for not having a silencer on his moped, but he refused to fix it, 'Coz it sounded cool!'

Dominique told us how he hadn't wasted any time warming up for the gig. He'd spent the first part of his evening doing a pub crawl around all the cafés in the village. Then he'd come to Frank's to do the gig, and now he was drunk.

He steered the conversation towards his diving skills and experience. Dominique had bored the whole village with his diving escapades – except me. I was a whole new audience.

"I live from day to day, for tomorrow, not for yesterday," Dominique said, slurring his words.

"You're a poet, too," Freddy said, and we laughed. I tried to work out what he meant and concluded that he was talking crap.

"When I was in Thai..." hiccupped Dominique, "when I was in Thailand, I went diving. I dived on the coral reefs, you know, I can dive! I've got my certificates." He looked at me over the top of his glasses. His glazed eyes showed that he had passed into the twilight zone.

"Really? You dive?" I said. "My uncle was a diver. He was a saturation diver. Heard about that, dude?"

"I can dive, I can dive," Dominique insisted, grabbing my arm.

"I believe you, man, keep cool!" I looked down at his hand and he released his grip. "I've dived, too. Look, like I said, my uncle was a professional diver, trained at Siebe Gorman diving school in the UK. My father passed the course, too. I think I know a thing or two about diving. Have you done any welding under water – blindfolded, can you do that?" I asked.

"What do you have in your tanks on your back?" Freddy asked. "One with wine and one with beer? Forget air – it takes up too much room!" He laughed and the rest of the bar joined in.

Didier slapped Dominique on the back with his huge hand. Dominique's head rocked forward violently, and his glasses shot off the end of his nose. They crashed onto the bar and slid across it. Frank tried to stop them, but missed and knocked over Dominique's glass, projecting beer over Dominique's trousers and shirt. His glasses fell onto the empty glass carafes in an inox counter under the bar.

Dominique looked at Frank, then turned his head to Didier.

"*Putain*, fuck!" he growled, swaying on his stool. "Why did you do that? *Merde*, I'm all wet," he slurred and hiccupped again. He wiped the wet patch of beer on his shirt with his hand.

"Sorry." Frank made the Indian peace greeting signal. "I tried to stop them sliding on to the floor." He picked up the spectacles, cleaned them with a towel, and passed them back to Dominique.

"I'm soaked," Dominique exaggerated, putting on his glasses. He pushed back his shoulders and sat up straight on his stool.

Frank started to imitate Nicolas Hulot, the well-known French explorer and TV host, who would speak under water using an adapted mask on his show. Dominique took this as an insult to his diving prowess.

"I can show you how good I am," Dominique assured the bar. "I am a diver. I told you!" He was agitated. "I have my certificates. I can show you!"

"Yeah, yeah, Dominique, you've already shown them to me," Frank said.

"Man, I wouldn't go diving with you, sorry," Freddy added. "Do you have a mask that allows you to smoke while you're diving?"

We all burst into laughter.

"Jacques Cousteau is alive and well in Saint-Valery-sur-Somme!" I declared.

"You can just imagine him down there, swimming about, a little puff on his cigarette. It would have to be housed in a box taped to the end of his hand. That way, he doesn't get his fingers wet and dampen the end of his cigarette," Phil added and we all laughed again.

"In his outfit, he must look like one of the seals in the bay," Didier said.

"*Ah, mais Dominique n'est pas pédé comme un phoque!* He showed me pictures with those, what he called 'girls' when he was in Thailand." Freddy turned and looked at Dominique. "But seriously, the two girls in the photos you showed me had oversized Adam's apples!" He drew a semi-circle under his chin with his finger. "They're bigger than mine!"

"Lady Boys!" exclaimed Phil, and everyone except Dominique laughed.

"I'm serious!" Dominique said angrily. "I have had enough. I'll go and get them." He swayed and wobbled as he shuffled to his feet, holding on to the pool table to regain his balance. He trudged slowly towards the front door and pulled the heavy red velvet curtain to the side.

"Hold on," said Frank, "it's locked. Where are you going? We're going to have a little drink for an hour or so while I clean up the bar, and then that's it. Stay!" he insisted, grabbing Dominique's arm to stop him pulling down the bolt on the door.

"No, let me go. I want to get my certificates and show Max I'm a diver." Dominique rocked from side to side as he spoke. "Let me out! I'll be back, you know where I live. I'll get them and come back. I'll be two minutes."

Frank took the keys from his pocket and unlocked the door. He slid the bolts open and let Dominique out. Closing the door behind him, he drew the curtain shut and returned to his place behind the bar. Picking up the tea towel, he carried on drying glasses and placing them on the wooden shelves behind the bar. Freddy wiped down the tables and brought over more dirty glasses and placed them at the end of the bar. Frank bent over and pulled the tray out of the little dish-washer and a cloud of steam bellowed from the open door. He closed it with his foot. While Frank and Freddy worked, Didier, Phil and I drank and watched them busily running around.

Twenty minutes went by.

"Where's that crazy fool?" Frank said, looking at his watch.

"He's probably fallen asleep on the sofa," Freddy said. "He was really drunk, it's better if he doesn't come back. He can sleep it off. He was a rock star tonight! Don't forget he did his show."

"Rock and roll attitude," said Phil laughing.

"He doesn't know the words," I said. "It's really bad, I'm sorry. Zer iz un ooose in New Oleeenz, and that's all he knows. It's so bad, it's funny!"

"Of course, it's bad!" said Freddy. "What did you expect?

215

He's always pissed, every day! He can't even remember his phone number, let alone lyrics in English."

Freddy paid for a round of drinks and my glass was refreshed. We were holding our glasses in the air, in a toast, when there was a loud knock on the door.

Frank turned the quiet background music off.

"*Merde, c'est les flics*! Shit, it's the police! What do they want? The music stopped at midnight. Maybe some of the people leaving made a noise in the street," Frank said as he pulled back the curtain. He saw who it was and unlocked the door.

"*Entrez*, come in," he said. It was Stevey, Dominique's teenage son.

He stepped into the café and Frank closed the door. They spoke together for a while, then Frank turned to us.

"He's gone off on Stevey's moped," Frank announced.

"Where can he go? Everywhere is closed," said Freddy. "He was supposed to come back here and show Max his diving certificates and those photos of him with the Thai ladies, the ones with balls and tits."

"Stevey was in his bedroom playing video games," said Frank. "He heard him crashing about downstairs. Then the front door shut and he heard his moped start up. He went to the window and saw Dominique driving down the road. By the time Stevey put his shoes on and ran downstairs, he had disappeared. He thinks he saw Dominique going towards the sailing club. He saw the lights of a moped, but he can't be sure it was him. It was too far down the road." Frank returned to his place behind the bar. Stevey stood at the front door looking at us.

"I think he had his diving suit on," Stevey said sheepishly.

"What, are you sure?" asked Didier.

"It was dark and he was already going past the florists. From my bedroom window, it was hard to see exactly, but he was dressed in black. It shone with the lights. It's now starting to rain," said Stevey. He was genuinely concerned. He knew what his dad was like after a few.

"I'm not driving anywhere tonight," said Phil.

"My car's broken, anyway," added Freddy.

"Nobody is driving anywhere!" Frank said, taking control of the situation. "OK, go back home," he said to Stevey. "If he turns up there, call the bar, or come back here if we're still open. Don't worry, he'll come back, he just wanted to go for a drive," Frank added, trying to reassure Stevey, who turned around and slammed the door behind him.

"Bizarre," said Freddy, "where's he going at this time of night? Normally, he falls asleep on the sofa when he's like that."

"Thank God it wasn't the police snooping around," Phil said.

"Where has he gone?" pondered Frank, as he walked to the large bay window at the end of the restaurant. Three pairs of binoculars for the customers to use to observe the different birds and seals in the bay were placed on the shelf below the window. Frank picked up a pair and searched the darkness.

Suddenly, the door of the restaurant flew open. It was Stevey. He was panting, and spoke in quick bursts:

"I've seen him. I saw the headlight, I know my moped engine. He's on the point. He's heading towards the light at the end. He's on the other side of the port."

Stevey slammed the glass door shut so vigorously I thought the thin windows were going to shatter. He ran off up the street in the direction of his house.

"What did he say?" said Frank from the other end of the narrow restaurant.

"He's heading for the light on the point," said Freddy.

"He's there," said Frank, looking through the binoculars.

Didier and Phil picked up the other pairs and they all focused on the light heading towards the point.

"He's wearing a mask, and he's got a snorkel in his mouth," said Didier.

"He's even wearing flippers," Phil said.

"No, it's not possible," Frank said with concern. "We have to go and stop him."

"But he's on the other side. It will take ages to walk over there. Are you crazy?" Didier said, shaking his head.

"He's the one who is crazy," I said, looking through the binoculars Phil had just passed to me.

I could see that Dominique had stopped the moped at the square cement base of the tall light at the mouth of the port. The bright red light reflected off the swelling waters.

The light from the street lamps that ran along the quay opposite, plus the light generated by the nearly full moon, lit up the point enough to see Dominique's movements clearly. He flipped a flipper over the petrol tank of the moped and placed his feet firmly on the ground. He let the moped fall against the wall and started to waddle towards the end of the grass bank. Water lapped at the steps.

Everybody in the bar knew in their minds that it wasn't the right thing to watch a mad alcoholic hairdresser and failed rock star throw himself into freezing cold water, but we all kept watching, mesmerised.

"I'm going to go down to the quay to shout over to him to stop," Frank said. "He's going to kill himself, the fool. *Ch'gros*, come with me, quick!" he ordered Didier. "Don't drink the entire bar while I'm gone," he said, grabbing his jacket from the hook on the back of the cellar door. Didier swigged his beer in one large gulp and they ran out of the front door.

The scene was set for some spectacular entertainment. Dominique was performing his after show as his second personality, 'Jacques', was taking over from 'Johnny'. We went back to the large window at the end of the restaurant and looked out at the bay through the binoculars. We could see Frank and Didier trotting towards the point.

"He really is a frog," I said to them. "That's what we call a diver in English – a frogman! So he's a frog dressed as a frogman, the first one I have encountered." Nobody understood what I was going on about.

Dominique continued climbing down the slippery steps, slowly descending towards the lapping waterline. The water was agitated and waves crashed against the stone wall with force. We watched as Dominique slipped on the wet surface, but he gained his balance by opening his arms out like a bat. He suddenly stopped, grabbed his mask, and threw himself off the second step. His body made an almighty splash when he hit the water.

"He's going to drown," said Phil, taking a large sip of beer.

We could see Dominique splashing around in the choppy water. The waves were coming over his head. He waved his arms in the air.

"He's waving in this direction," said Freddy. "He's got to get out of that water, he's going to die!"

"I can see Frank and Didier on the quay. They're shouting at him or something," I said as I looked through the binoculars.

"Listen," said Freddy. "The siren... it's the fire brigade. Someone must have called them."

"I can hear them," I said.

A couple of minutes later, a van raced down the empty high street, its blue lights flashing. A second van, pulling a trailer with an inflatable dingy, passed in front of the restaurant, followed by a long, wheel-based Land Rover.

Frank and Didier walked back into the café.

"It's too cold out there," Frank said, rubbing his hands

together. "A load of people have turned up and there's no bar down there."

"He's a fool. We told him to get out," Didier said, picking up his glass. "He wouldn't listen or couldn't hear us. The tide is still coming in, so hopefully the fire brigade will pick him up in the port."

I kept looking through the binoculars and followed the van's flashing blue light as it moved along the road, heading towards the harbour light at the end of the point. The fire brigade have a dual purpose, serving as the local coast guard as well as the fire service. The powerful searchlight on the small dingy lit up the water and the grassy bank.

"The boat's there," Freddy said.

A police car raced towards the point with its siren blaring. The flashing blue lights lit up the sky. Dominique swam, or the incoming tide pushed him, towards the grassy bank inside the protected port, and he crawled through the pampas grass by the water's edge. The small boat flew past him, turned around and came back to where he was starting to climb up the grass bank. Dominique stood up, still wearing his flippers, and took off his mask. He turned around and waved his arm in the direction of the boat. The police car skidded to a stop and a cloud of dust rose from the loose, gravel surface. Two policemen looked on as Dominique arrived at the top of the small incline.

"He's shaking hands with them," Phil said.

I could see Dominique explaining everything to the policemen, waving his arms about. He was giving his account of what had happened, or what he was doing. Two firemen came over from their parked van and placed a blanket round his shoulders.

"They are going to arrest him and put him in the cells for the night," Phil said. Freddy was still watching the action through the binoculars.

"He's taken off his flippers," said Freddy. "He's walking over to the moped. No, they're letting him go. He's started the moped and heading down the track. The fire brigade are following behind with their lights flashing. He's getting escorted back." We returned to the bar.

"I need a drink," said Frank.

"*Vive* Dominique, *bonne viver, raconteur, voyageur,* and frogman *extraordinaire!*" I said, raising my glass in the air.

"But definitely not a *chanteur,*" said Didier.

EPILOGUE

"We shall not cease from exploration, and the end of all our exploring will be to arrive where we started and know the place for the first time."

T.S. Eliot.
(From 'Little Giddings' the last of The Four Quartets)

The rain started to fall harder, tears from heaven. The dark grey autumn skies stretched out in front of me as the rental car drove along the narrow country road. I still knew all the back cuts – rat runs to keep off the main roads. The local radio station was finishing its show about tourism in the Somme Bay area. It had been a good year. More hotel bookings, the campsites had reported higher numbers, and the restaurants had served more clients. The host rounded up the programme and thanked his guests.

"And now, a little bit of music before the mid-day news. Odyssey and 'Going Back to My Roots'."

The iconic disco track's hypnotising electric guitar intro burst out from the car speakers. I turned up the music, then I changed down a gear and slightly touched on the brakes as I approached the last corner before the village. The road gleamed brightly with the freshly fallen rain. The windscreen wipers flipped back and forth in rhythmic harmony with the music.

I started to sing along.

"Zippin' up my boots, goin' back to my roots, yeah…"

The car rounded the corner and there it was. I passed the sign indicating the name of the village, Villers-Sur-Authie. I was back, eventually. I had not been back in ten years. Through the misty rain, I could immediately see that the skyline had changed. The field on the exterior boundary of the village was now full of new, indiscreet, nondescript breeze-block houses instead of mud-splattered Friesian cows grazing.

I drove down the main street, rue de Montreuil, that runs through the middle of the village and slowed down in front of the *charcuterie* (butcher's shop). The logo for the shop, a huge pig running at full speed, smiling, was painted in vibrant colours on the wall of the outhouse that lined the road. You couldn't miss it. Gérard, the butcher, was a gentle giant, tall with a huge round belly. His wife was equally round. They obviously enjoyed the dishes they made. Their incredible pâté de campagne was the best I had ever tasted. The pork chops, boudin blanc and numerous delicacies made from any part of the pig were equally delicious.

I opened the gate and scurried across the small courtyard to hide under the eaves of the roof. I tried the door, it was locked. I pulled on the thick metal chain that clanged a large bell. After a short wait, the light came on in the shop and I heard the locks turning.

Madame, I had never known her name, stood at the door. She recognised me instantly.

"Come in, get out of the rain," she said eagerly. I climbed the two steps and entered the shop. Impeccably clean, the knives and cleavers of all sizes hung on the wall. The glass-fronted cold plates lay empty. "I'll call Gérard and tell him you're here." She shuffled off to the back of the shop and shouted out to her husband.

A couple of minutes later, Gérard came into the shop. He wasn't wearing his white bloodstained overall. We shook hands and exchanged pleasantries.

"As you can see, we have now closed," said Gérard. "I have

now retired and hung up my knives and sold the van. Everybody now shops in the new supermarkets they've built in Rue. There's now a Lidl, Carrefour, and an Auchan. My daughter got married to a desktop publisher and moved to Paris. She had no interest in running this place. I'd always hoped she would settle down with a local boy, who would pick up the business and slaughter and sell pigs, but alas." I could hear the sadness in his voice.

"The café, épicerie, opposite your old house, has closed too," he continued. "Ginette, who lived next door to you, died and her family sold the house to a couple of Belgium psychiatrists. The château has been bought and renovated by 'the Parisians.' The moat is now clean and the toads don't croak like they used to. The lawn is neatly mowed and the wooden windows have been replaced with shiny new white double-glazed ones."

I asked him about the characters that had been my French professors, teaching me the Picard dialect while we guzzled aperitifs at mid-day and again from five to eight o'clock every evening.

"Jean-Claude?"

"He died."

"Chou-chou, Lou-lou, Dédé, G-G, Jacky, Phi-phi?" I asked.

"They've all gone to the bistrot in the sky," Gérard said solemnly. "They're sitting around a table drinking the eternal aperitif, probably talking about the weather."

Gérard went into the cold cellar and returned with a large slice of his pâté de campagne and handed it to me.

"I still make my pâtés and other dishes, but it's only for us, or family and friends that come to dinner."

I bid them goodbye and returned to the car.

I drove slowly along the road. The high poplar trees that lined the avenue leading to the château no longer stretched to the sky. Large tree stumps were all that were left. They had caught a disease and had to be chopped down.

They'd given the statue of Jesus a coat of paint and the plinth had been retouched in fire-red paint. He was now silver, hanging from the freshly stained wood. It now looked like he'd donned a skin-tight spacesuit and forgotten to put on his boots and a helmet. I stopped the car in front of the café. The old Vega Pils beer sign still hung above the door to the bar, but the shutters were tightly shut and a curtain drawn across the door. The shop front and glass door were whitewashed out. It was sad not to see a collection of cars, bicycles and mobylettes parked outside. I had timed my arrival for the mid-day session, but it was not to be.

I turned and walked across the road to the house where I had written my notes and stories, many years before. The blue shutters were shut and there was no activity. I had sold it to a couple from Lille, who used it as a second home and came down regularly at weekends. The courtyard appeared well looked after and they had given the house walls a fresh coat of white paint. Everything looked more or less as I'd left it.

I drove through the town of Rue. L'Escale café, where I had many happy memories, was now part of the pharmacy, two doors up. The big window displayed wheelchairs, Zimmer frames and other accessories needed in a nursing home. The nursing home was handily situated next door to the pharmacy.

The rain eased off as I drove around the Somme Bay. I entered Saint Valery-sur-Somme, the town from where William the Conqueror had set sail in 1066 and where, nearly three hundred years later, Joan of Arc had been imprisoned on her way to Rouen to be burnt at the stake. Exactly six hundred and sixty-six years later, I returned. Parking in the car park, the magnificent bay didn't disappoint. It never did. Its forever changing form and colours are always postcard perfect.

The various cafés and restaurants mentioned in my stories have now changed their names and been renovated into gastro-chic characterless food stuffers.

I met my friend, Hervé, who had kindly kept my car in his barn. We pulled the heavy dust sheet off the car; the battery was obviously flat. He suggested that we try to jumpstart it with the tractor that was parked next to the car. I opened the boot of the Lancia Monte Carlo, where the battery was housed. An old box file was lying between a bottle of home-made calvados and a bottle of Bisquit Cognac that were given to me as a leaving present. I knew instantly what was in the box. I'd spent the last ten years looking for it. I opened it and saw my handwritten manuscripts. The different inks of various colours had faded and smudged with the damp and time.

I read through the stories and managed to decipher my handwriting. I typed them up while sipping on more than a glass and a half of the beautifully aged cognac and calvados.

Printed in Great Britain
by Amazon